KINGDOM

Russ Litten

Kingdom

Russ Litten

ISBN 9781903110324

First published in this edition 2015 by Wrecking Ball Press.

Copyright Russ Litten

Cover design by humandesign.co.uk

the
James Reckitt
library trust

Supported using public funding by
ARTS COUNCIL
LOTTERY FUNDED ENGLAND

Supported by
Hull UK City of
Culture 2017

And he said to them, "Why are you troubled, and why do doubts arise in your hearts? See my hands and my feet, that it is I myself; touch me and see, for a spirit does not have flesh and bones ..."

Luke 24:38

HER MAJESTY'S PRISON
LIBRARY
8.40 AM.

The librarian is the first to notice him. To suspect that something is amiss. He looks out of place, somehow, in a way that she cannot immediately identify. Not his face. An ordinary enough face; dark chin length hair, sun-starved pallor, five-day growth of beard. A face you'd find in any prison or public institution. His clothes, perhaps; plain and anonymous enough on the outside, but incongruous here; black overcoat and dark trousers, worn and shabby looking, but an expensive cut. Not the usual jeans or logoed-up tracksuit of the enhanced or the standard grey sweatshirt/green polyester trouser combo issued on induction. And shoes, proper shoes, not trainers. Staff, she thinks at first, a recently arrived tutor she hasn't been introduced to yet, or a visiting civilian perhaps. But something about him is vaguely troubling. His bearing. Not for him the sullen head down subservience of the newly arrived, or the slumped blank eyed stare of the hardened. He sits bolt upright in the corner near the computers, set apart from the rest of the men, surveys their babble with a tightly wound unease, a contempt bordering on fury, almost. Tight knuckled fists gripping the arms of the chair. Heels hammering the carpet beneath the table.

A voice raised in complaint at the desk, some angry squabble over an unreturned DVD. The librarian turns her attention away from the man in the corner and deals with the complaint, sends the aggrieved offender away with a list of available titles and his local paper. She returns to her desk behind the panels of glass and wood that serve as her office, but no sooner has she sat down then another offender is at the door, bugging her to chase up a certificate from a previous prison, his fifth identical query in the last two days. Another offender wants to know about Story Book Dads, is his CD ready yet Miss, the Gruffalo at Christmas, Miss, and if not why not? The first of the day's minor dramas.

The day's major drama starts with a phone call; Control asking for a headcount. The librarian reads him the number from her tally and replaces the receiver, returns to her typing.

Ten minutes later the phone rings again. The request is repeated and this time she stands and counts the bodies through the glass; relays the information, pauses, listens, nods.

Yes, she says, yes, that includes Orderlies.

Five minutes later the phone rings again and the request is repeated and then again, two minutes later, with an added instruction. She puts down the phone and signals to the assistant.

Stand-fast, she tells her. Don't let anyone out.

A group of men at the door holding gym bags and beakers overhear, raise an immediate chorus of complaint.

Aw, what, for fucks sake ...

Again? What's up Miss, can't they count?

Useless bastards!

Beyond a fucking joke, this ...

Gonna miss me fucking session ...

The head librarian looks at her assistant.

One extra, apparently ...

Jangle of keys from the other side of the door and the men are forced to jostle back and stand aside to admit the two officers. They lock the door behind them and advance into the centre of the room. The younger officer carries a clipboard with a list and mouths one, two, three, four, as his eyes scan the men sat around the tables or stood at the bookcases. Radios in his count and looks at the librarian.

What wing are these?

B, she tells him.

All of them?

Yes.

He scrutinizes his list, frowns, looks around the room again. Moves among the milling group of men, glancing from the names to each face.

Keep still please lads.

Fucks sake, guv ... I'm missing Cash In The Attic ...

Stay still ...

The officer spots the man sat at the corner table near the computers. Walks across, looks at his list.

Name and number please mate ...

Kingdom.

Number?

The man glowers up at him.

Not got one, he says.

The officer keeps his eyes on his list, pen tap-tap-tapping.

Don't be clever, he says, I'm not in the mood. Number.

I'm a man, not a number.

Sigh from above. Pen slotted into top pocket.

Stand up, says the officer.

Say please.

Titters from around the room. The men have stopped moving and fallen quiet. All eyes clamped on the corner.

The older officer takes a step forward.

The younger officer tucks the clipboard under his arm.

On your feet, he says. Now.

The man's eyes widen. A thin, mirthless smile.

Make me, he says.

In prison, it is often said that time seems to stand still. This is such an occasion. Minute but perceptible shift in the atmosphere, a slight tensing and murmur, bodies braced. The man issues his challenge and time stands still.

The younger officer has been in the job for three months. The older officer is six months away from retirement. The librarian has being doing this for twenty years. She has already made her way over to the wall, to the green panic button. She hears the words from the corner of the room.

I said make me. You deaf as well as fucking stupid?

Five seconds later the morning explodes in clamouring bells, a stampede of boots and a riot of raised voices.

PART ONE

SEPARATION AND CARE UNIT
CELL 1/005
10.02 PM.

You're the listener, yeah?

Sit yourself down bud. Thanks for coming.

As you'll no doubt be aware, I've had the world and his wife down here. Psychiatrists, social workers, police officers. SPO's, PPO's, healthcare workers. The Independent Monitoring Board, they popped in as well. All the various players in the British penal system. I can't recall their individual functions, but rest assured that all techniques have been deployed; everything from straight-talking tough guys spelling out my statutory rights to earnest college-type chaps in corduroy offering coffee and a sympathetic ear, and every man Jack and Jill in between. An endless parade of concerned professionals. And the foot soldiers of course, the dim-witted key janglers, giving me the beady eye every ten minutes. They're far from happy, that bunch; mainly on account of me giving one of their brethren a bit of a slap in the library back there. I'm sure you've heard all about it. It was nothing personal. Only way I could guarantee my stay. I must admit, I was expecting a proper kicking when they got me down here, but it wasn't to be. Disappointing, in a way. I suppose me being an unknown civilian confused them. Not so much as a raised hand. Very professional. But I'm not on the Officer's Association Christmas card list, they've made that much clear. Slamming that bloody hatch open and shut all evening. Making sure I don't sleep, I would imagine. Standard technique: disorientate the captive. I know the drill, bud, and I'm under no illusion about their level of concern.

One or two of them have popped in for a chat. Very civil. I didn't even give them the grace of eye contact. Monosyllabic morons, for the most part. You'll know all about that, though, won't you bud? No sense of personal space either, some of them. Noticed that? Like you're not there? One borderline psychopath, he thought he could crack my code of dignified silence by pushing his ugly mug right into mine and breathing his dinner all over me. Know who I mean? Him with the nervous tic and the poor dental hygiene? Jesus, he could strip a wall with that breath. Or maybe it's just my newly heightened senses. Delicate soul, me, you know. But yeah, he was a proper treat, him. The odd one or two have been OK though, it has to be said. The occasional glimmer of compassion. But anyone wearing a uniform can fuck off, basically. The Separation and Care Unit? Yeah, right. I don't need their version of care. And I'm not taking orders off them either. None of them. Not me, bud. Wouldn't even grace them with a glance.

Some of the other visitors have been pleasant enough, though. Spokespersons from all the popular religious faiths. The Imam, he was OK. And the Chaplin, he was a decent chap too. Concern etched all over his face. Quite touching, really. And there was another sweet faced little woman who popped in around meal time, left me some interesting leaflets about Her Lord Jesus Christ. Ever heard of him? It's his birthday soon. He loves me, apparently. That's nice, isn't it? He loves me, despite everything I've done. Who else? Oh yeah, the Number One Governor. He finally graced me with his presence. Yapped on for a bit, gave me the official line about rights and responsibilities and all the rest of it. Tried to appeal to my basic sense of citizenship. And when that didn't work he tried the softer, more personal approach. Touchy-feely stuff. The hey-I'm-just-a-guy-like-you tactic. Asking me about my family and wouldn't they be worried about me at this time of year and all that heart-rending bullshit. Playing the Christmas card. Believe that? Then he sort of run out of hands to play and we both sat in grim-faced silence before he finally shook his head, sighed, looked at his two grand watch and took his merry leave. Off to his fireside festivities and his glass of mulled wine, no doubt. Can't say I blame him, really. I'd do exactly the same if I had a fireside to flee to.

And that's been my day, Mr. Listener. The varying faces of officialdom, all asking essentially the same questions: who am I, where did I come from and why am I here? And I've told each and every one of them the very same: nothing, naught, nada. Radio silence maintained.

But your job is just to listen, yeah? Your job is not to press or probe or form opinions, am I correct? Impartial bystander, that's you, bud, yeah? An open pair of ears? None of this yak-yak-yak business? See no evil, speak no evil? That you, is it? The caring face of the prison population?

Alright, then. I'll talk you through the process. But remember; this is told in the strictest confidence. This is not for general consumption by any other body, be they professional, medical, clerical or the general Joe Soap public, incarcerated or free. Tell not a soul, Mr. Listener. And listen carefully, yeah? Because this is it; the one and only rendition, and then I'm out of here. After I'm gone, you can tell who you damn well like. If you think they'll believe you. Best of British with that one.

My name is Alistair Kingdom and I was born a ghost. A *real* ghost, I'm talking about here. Not dealing in metaphors. Don't mean that I was a shadow of my former self, or a lost soul drifting aimlessly through an empty life or any of that vague symbolic nonsense. I've studied all that stuff, bud, believe me. Got all that nonsense out of the way as soon as I learnt to read. But this is not one of those stories. This is not the tale of a man who lost his way and became invisible to all those around him. This is the other way round. This is the testimony of a misplaced soul who wandered in from the fog and made himself flesh and bone through sheer force of will. Through total non-stop application. I mean, yes, to begin with I was feeling lost and empty and anonymous and all that poetic bullshit, but not in the same way that you normal three dimensional earth dwellers do, with your self imposed states of exile and your immobilizing self pity. I wasn't just an outcast skulking on the margins. No, I'm talking about a proper ghost here, my friend. A *spirit*. You get my drift? An invisible presence floating around in the land of the living. That's the first thing you've got to get your head around, if you want to know what happened and why I'm here. That there is a world you cannot see and it's occurring all around you, as you live, eat, sleep and breathe. You may well smile, bud. I know what you're thinking. Ghosts don't exist. And you're right, they don't. They don't exist at all. But they're very real. They're as real as the bars on that window.

So anyway, yeah, I was a ghost and I moved among the general population doing the spectral thing. I hung around parks and streets and offices and homes, peering over the shoulders of the living. I was the shadow on the staircase, the fleeting shape of a figure on the landing, that half-imagined glimpse of another face hanging at your shoulder in the bathroom mirror. I was that horrible unspeakable dread that clutched your stomach at three in the morning when you woke up thinking - no, *knowing* - that someone else was in the room. I haunted places, bud. And people. Well, haunting isn't the correct term. I suppose, if I'm being exact, the correct word is terrorism. I terrorized the living. Yeah, I was the vendor of dread. To certain individuals, at least. I'm not proud of it, but there you go. Had to be done bud. Hey, listen; being born a ghost can do things to a man. It can make him bitter, for one thing. And there's nothing worse than a bitter man. Or woman. Either of the species can become infected. Turns a good soul spiteful. Anyway, as I've said, it was only certain people I targeted with terror. Those that were worthy of my attention. Deserving causes, I liked to think of them as. Beneficiaries of my hard won wisdom.

It was born more of frustration than malice, to begin with, though, the haunting. With Martin, at least. I didn't mean any of that to happen. I was just blundering around in the dark. But little by little things became clearer, and I started haunting with a purpose. With a newly focused malice. I understand that now. Spite and malice, bud. Malevolence. I know where those things come from. Didn't at first. Didn't really understand any of your bizarre human emotions, to be honest. But when you learn them all again, one by one, when they start to seep into you and tug at your guts, stuff like love and longing and fear and wonder, when you encounter them afresh and learn their names and their nature and see their effects unleashed right in front of you - wow. Yeah. Then you understand the depths of human emotions. Appreciate their raw explosive power. And it all started with frustration. The ferocious need to know. Because I was born a ghost, bud, and I didn't have a clue who I was. So I took it out on the living. Caused mayhem among them. Then I found out who I was and what had happened to me, and all the aching frustration fell away like a cast off coat and along came shame and self-pity and disgust and everything else that comes with being a real person.

And now here I am.

So let's be clear about this from the very beginning, yeah? My name is

Alistair Kingdom and I was born a ghost but now I'm a man, a real man with a real human heart that pumps rich red blood and a reflection in the mirror and a hand that can reach out and touch. And I'm here because I deserve to be here. OK? I deserve every second of this. I have earned my stripes, bud. You'll just have to take my word on that one. So I'll talk you through the process, the basic training and any further questions can be asked at the end. Yeah? You happy with that?

Alright. Here's the drill. I was born in a derelict house down a side street just off a main road at the edge of the city centre. This is about ... what? Ten, eleven months ago? A year, nearly, I think. Still trying to get to grips with this time business, to be honest. I'm not one for sleep, so day and night haven't been much of a divider for me. My personal passage has been marked largely by the regaining of my senses, all five of them, such as they are, and the events that sparked them back into life. But I think it was around ten months ago, all this, thinking about it now. Maybe eleven. It was just after Christmas, as I recall, when I was born. Not sure how long after, but there were still decorations hung up here and there. In the streets and some of the shops and houses. Short days at first. I did notice that, yeah. Short days and nights. Then the sun and the snowdrops and the school holidays. The lighter nights. Then the days of seemingly endless light. Then the light drawing in again. Retreating. And it's dark now again, isn't it? Dark all day and all night, nearly. So almost a year, I would say. Within a year, certainly. It's hard to make a positive estimate when it comes to time. Slippery concept when you're not tied to the hands of the clock. Anyway, the important thing is I can remember the sequence of events, the names and faces and places that set it all off. I can pluck it all back into the here and now. Put things into the right order

This is one of the benefits of being alive.

But the first thing, the very first thing I remember, is a quick blast of pure white light. Like an old fashioned camera; whoosh, that sudden white flare. A small magnesium explosion in some Victorian sitting room. No noise, you understand, no actual boom or bang, just that one quick flash and everything suddenly lit up white, then gradually dimming to a kind of sickly pale yellow. The brightness fading at the edges at first, and then this dull throbbing yellow swimming in and out of focus.

I'm not moving at this point, you understand. Totally immobile. I can't hear anything either. Deaf at birth, I was, more or less. I was aware of a faint noise, but it wasn't external, more like a subdued humming somewhere behind the eyes. Or where my emerging consciousness registered that my eyes should be, rather. An industrial generator at the edge of the embryonic brain, let's call it that, yeah? A radio kind of silence. White noise. Subdued static signals. Stay still, they seemed to say, stay still. Whirrs and squiggles and squelches. Gradually it all subsides and the yellow slowly stops moving and fixes itself into something solid.

It's a wall. I arrive at the realization that I am lying on my side in a place, a room, facing a wall. I grasp this purely from the perspective of vision, yeah? Understand this, bud: I have no physical sense of my own self at this point; nothing, not my head or my body or the floor beneath it. All I can do is see. I'm a camera switched on and laid on its side. Lop-sided point of view, but it's all crystal clear now and I start to pick out everything in front of me in micro-fine detail; scuffed black marks on the skirting board, damp crumbling patches where the woodchips peeled away, the cracks in the plaster behind branching off in tiny hairline fractures. I'm combing everything in close-up. I start to put it all together. There's a disconnected pipe jutting up from the floor and then a rectangular patch of grubby mustard yellow where a gas fire used to be. I register all of this, but I'm just grasping round the edges at this point. I don't know the exact words gas and fire yet. I tilt my vision upwards and the yellow darkens as it spreads further up the wall, upwards and outwards, turns to brown and then black; scorch marks fingering the ceiling and then a patterned border at the top, a narrow strip of green. A snake with white and yellow diamonds studded down it's back. And it's moving fast, it flies around the top of the walls. I watch this snake race around the ceiling for what feels like ages. Round and round and round it goes.

Snake, I think. Snake.

The word slots into my head, click, like the first piece of a jigsaw puzzle. It seems to make a kind of sense. I've got no experience to draw on here, you understand. No reference points. I had to accept what was happening in front of my eyes. I didn't know if it was a real snake, but the word seemed to fit, seemed to make sense and I knew that I was awake and this was happening above me and that I was somewhere real. Somewhere in the physical world with its walls and corners and hard edges and patches of shimmering colour.

Then I find myself stood bolt upright.

You'll have to excuse me, Mr Listener; all of that first day or so is like a series of snapshots on fast-forward. Fragmented pictures laid side by side. The actual mechanics of the thing are all a bit vague. Like, one minute I'm laid out like a frozen corpse, staring up at this green and yellow snake racing round and round above me, the next I'm a fine upstanding citizen. Stood to attention like a soldier. You tell me how it works, bud. These are just the facts as I recall them.

So, OK, I try to move. Nothing happening. No way can I move. I can't feel anything, inside or out. I can feel only the absence of myself. That was problem number one. Nothing was responding, like I was swathed in some kind of viscid jelly. So then I stop trying to move and try to focus, to concentrate, but my mind is just mush. I'm struggling to link my thoughts together; yellow, wall, snake, house. Cant. Fucking. Move. The words come to me, popping on and off like random light bulbs, then fading away before I can grasp the full shape of their meaning or string them all together into any kind of lucid order. Queasy, bud. Everything was shifting and pitching. Not a nice feeling. I was like one of those little plastic souvenir snowstorms you get from a sea-side novelty shop, like I'd been picked up and shaken by some ham-fisted tourist. There was all kind of debris whirling around inside that brand new brain of mine; words and pictures, flashes of unfamiliar scenes, faces briefly looming. Snatches of noise too; muted shrieks and catcalls and distant rumblings, fragments of disembodied voices calling from the other end of endless tunnels. Echoes in the attic.

And all the time that permanent low throb of static that seemed to hum inside of me. I'm sure it's not like that for real new-borns. Real living babies, I mean. I hope not anyway. It was like being spat out of a ghost train into the dazzling white lights. All I could do was wait for the pieces to slowly drift down and settle into some semblance of order.

Eventually I understand that it's the daytime and I'm in what seems to be a derelict house, but outside of that I don't have much to go on. The place is completely gutted, there's nothing; no sofa, no chairs, no tables, no furniture, nothing at all. The windows at the front are steel shuttered up, all the light in the room coming through two big back windows, both of them smashed. Just a filthy net curtain hanging down in shreds and a lake of broken glass on the carpet beneath the sill. There's stuff scrawled everywhere, graffiti all over the walls; name tags, initials, illegible symbols and squiggles. Loops and lines and jagged signals. I couldn't work any of it out. More scorch marks on the opposite side of the room, the carpet in the corner burnt to a black and stiffened scrub. A burned out house, that's where I was born, bud. Not the most salubrious of starting points, it has to be said.

Funny the things that stick in your mind though. I remember looking at that burnt black carpet and thinking "cavemen". Click, another piece of the jigsaw, right there. I know I didn't fully understand the word itself, but I remember thinking it loud and clear: "cavemen". It seemed to have some weight. These things that lodge in the mind. Oh, I can join the dots up now, with the benefit of hindsight, but at the time I was reeling. Helpless. Like I was the sole surviving victim of some momentous car crash and I'd struggled to my feet at the roadside, swaying, incredulous.

It took me a good few minutes before I could get myself anywhere near composed. It was like waking up after an operation. Like when you have surgery. I don't know if you've ever undergone a serious operation, but you come round from the knock-out blow, the anaesthetic, and you wake up in a strange bed in a strange room dressed in a paper robe and everything seems slow and ridiculous and refracted and you can't co-ordinate yourself. You're all sluggish and useless, as weak as a sickly child. No, not weak. Not child. But you can't pull yourself together. You can't get a fix on things. Drifting under anaesthetic. That's how it was for me when I was newly born. Exactly the same. Exactly the same, bud. Like waking up from the operation and everything floating away from me, bits broken away and drifting off in tiny bits. The vital part of me had set sail into inner space and there was nothing, no centre to hold onto.

I don't know how long I stood there staring at the scenery but it eventually occurred to me that if I could stand upright then I could surely move and so I tried once more to get moving, to leave the room, but it just seemed like an impossible task. The slightest movement took everything I could muster. It was like trying to wade upstream through a churning river of mud. A heroic effort was clearly required here, and that was beyond me at that precise point. I couldn't do a thing. Useless.

But then the next thing I know I'm in the back way. The kitchen had been gutted as well, ransacked of all remnants of the living; no fridge, no cooker, no washing machine. No home comforts. Everything stripped out. It was a skeleton of a house. No cupboards on the walls or cupboard doors or worktops even, just the bare bones of the units holding up a metal sink full of what looked like dried up blue paint and a million tiny gems of shattered glass. All the piping had been ripped out from beneath the sink, just the bare red brickwork. The place had been properly scavenged long ago, picked clean and left to rot. Scarred red brickwork. I'm starting to focus now. The view is sharpening. Getting clearer. And I've moved. I'm not sure how, but I've stirred myself.

The back door's wide open. I want to look outside. The compulsion to look outside is very strong. Human curiosity, right there bud. Pandora's Box. But I still can't seem to move, no matter how hard I try. So I stop trying. And as soon as I stop trying, hey presto, I start to move. To glide, I mean. Fast forward into physical space. It doesn't register at first, the gliding thing. I just look to where I want to go and move towards it. A camera zooming in. So I'm starting to suss that moving my body is not an option and I have to move my mind. Free your mind and your arse will follow; literally in my case. That was how it worked, bud. Mind over matter. I wanted to go outside, and there I was, on the back doorstep, looking out onto the garden.

It looked astonishing, like everything was freshly painted; rich and bright and madly intense. Forty thousand shades of everything. I could see it all in fine and infinite detail; every square of faded red brick, each brown and blue-grey tile on the rooftops and every bare black branch of every tree, each and every last blade of grass in that scruffy little patch of a garden. Frost clung sparkling to fence posts and guttering and laid across the tops of bushes like discarded veils. That dirty white solid mass of cloud hung heavy in the sky. Stunning. Full-on visual rush. I didn't know where to look next. Everything laid out brand new before me, everything pulsating with detail.

The garden, to be fair, was an emaciated tip but it just looked so beautiful on that first day, a small scrub of green bejewelled with all manner of intricate decoration. There was a burnt out bonfire near a sodden heap of burst open bin bags and I could see every scrap of rubbish spilling out of them; each serrated edge of tin can that caught the light and sent it spinning back and sparkling, every single faded orange baked bean on the weather-worn labels, the newspapers and magazines mushed grey and damp, the whorls and knots in every lump of wood, the smashed up bottles and the shiny melted puddles of pitch black plastic; all these fragments of junk ablaze with infinite detail. It almost hurt my eyes to let them rest anywhere. Everything just shimmered with the brazen miracle of it's own existence.

It annoys me, you know, thinking about it now. Knowing that I'll never get that back. That beauty. Innocence, I'm talking about here. Once you lose your innocence you're soiled forever. There's no beauty in the mundane anymore. A tin of beans is just a tin of fucking beans to me now.

But there were further complexities. Like a door slung across the ashes of the fire. It looks like an interior door that's been dragged outside. It catches my attention. It looks odd to me, absurd, almost. I go over to take a closer look. I'm focusing on a dark blue wooden frame with a frosted inlay. Big diagonal crack across the glass. Crystal doorknob, ugly, the size of a fist. Just a ruined old door, but here's the thing; I couldn't remember what it was called. I mean, I was soaking in every last detail before me, but my brain could only fumble at the outer edges of the concept of the thing. The name, the word, eluded me. I'm scrutinizing this knackered old slab of wood and glass, the sense of bewilderment inflating. I knew the essence of the object beneath me, what it was a door actually did, it's plain and basic function, you understand. I just couldn't remember what you were supposed to call the damn thing. I think it was the incongruous nature of it all, this indoor object laid horizontal across a patch of burnt garden instead of being where it was supposed to be, stood upright in a solid wall between two rooms. It was like it had had been robbed of its true purpose and therefore robbed of its name. A door that led to nowhere.

Door. I could not remember it. I groped about for it. Door, door, door. The word wouldn't come. It bothered me. Other words had come, like wall and snake and sky and grass and roof. Why not door? Why the gap?

I can't work it out and I can feel the frustration building inside and that starts the snowstorm again, the crackle and the static and the buzzing, and that just culminates in panic, so after a time I give up, I abandon the mental quest and I'm wandering around the garden, restless, trying to distract myself, trying to fasten onto anything familiar. But other things look impossibly strange as well. There's a washing machine on its back, the porthole flipped open like an escape hatch leading down to somewhere. I can't understand it. Dials and numbers and switches. Does not compute. I move around the edges of the garden, near the fence, look at the ground. I zoom in on a patch of flowers, this cluster of tiny purple stars. Stars, I'm thinking, more words; stars, purple, flowers. The sound of the words inside of me gave a strange and warming comfort but no true insight. It was all surplus to requirements, almost. I knew it all meant something but what? I couldn't fathom it. They were just words. I'd dropped out of the sky into an incomprehensible paradise. I was a perfect idiot. The sky had given birth to a dolt. That's what it felt like. And this anaesthetic hangover. Stupor, that's the word for it. I was in a stupor, Mr Listener. A state of numb dormancy. Young, numb and feeling dumb. Glide and gawp, that was me. All I could do was stare at things I didn't understand.

That back garden. I stood there for God knows how long, just scoping stuff. Everything in front of my feet. An empty crisp packet being chased around the edges of the burnt out bonfire by some invisible pursuer, tumbling over and over like a pale green moth swatted down to earth. Every little detail. Things in the distance made vivid, like the shapes the chimney stacks cut into the sky. Triangles and squares and the skeletal shadows of arials and telephone masts. Disconnected lines. Then a swift pull back and focus on whatever was beneath my nose. Dark green moss growing on the lip of a drainpipe. A sink grate crusted black with filth. The camera zooming in and out. Every minute thing that entered my field of vision.

Then I looked back at the house I'd just emerged from. An abandoned two-up two-down in the middle of a terrace of identical design. Uniform blocks of brick beaten dull by the elements. The houses either side looked unoccupied as well, overgrown gardens dumped upon and left to die, the remnants of impromptu fires, piled up rubbish, abandoned rusting bikes, windows sealed with steel. A bombed out parade of former human dwellings. No idea where I was. It could have been anywhere, I suppose, any row of condemned houses in any city in England. A place that was beaten, out on it's feet and waiting to die, former homes propped up against each other, crumbling and exhausted, waiting for the men in hard hats to come and put them out of their misery. To start afresh and liberate the land.

I thought I could see shapes moving in some of the houses, some of the upstairs that had un-boarded windows. I thought I could see things. It was hard to tell though. It could have been a mistake, or it could have been memories turning somersaults through my head.

Houses, though. The word made sense, I was surrounded by houses and that led me slowly to the word city. You've got to understand bud, it was a tortuously ponderous thought process on that first day. Like someone dropping stones down a well and waiting to hear them hit the bottom. I was in a city, I'd grasped that much. I remembered cities. Or understood the concept, at least. People lived in cities. Civilisation. I didn't know whether that included me though. Me? *Me?!* Sweet Lord, the mere thought made my brain start to swirl. The novelty shop snowstorm starting up again.

So I did my best to put my mind into neutral and I got myself moving. I lowered my outlook and my expectations and I set off into the great unknown. It seemed to be the best option.

There was a no fence or gate at the end of that garden, it was all opened up. I came to a small path that led to an alleyway that emptied me out onto the front way, onto the street. It was quiet and still, around midday I think. I could see a main road in the distance, small specks of movement, people and cars. No sign of life around me though. No human beings. Most of the houses on each side of the road were shuttered up or burnt out, plastered with warnings of imminent destruction, both official and informal. Messages painted or sprayed by former resident's hands or fixed up there by way of council notice:

GAS OFF

DO NOT ENTER - DANGER OF DEATH.

KITTEN LOST, BLACK AND WHITE CALL 07968043568

JASON = NONCE.

BIRCHY OV OPE

FAGGOT AND BRINGHAM - SHIT ROOF BUYERS.

Those particular words would become familiar to me in time, comforting almost. But on that first day they didn't compute. Meant less than nothing. Just more shapes, like the names tagged on the walls in the house.

But I'm moving now, bud. I move along the street. I move slowly. It seems to go on and on. I have no idea where I'm going. I'm just looking ahead, fixing on the road. And, like I say, I had even less idea about how I was getting there. That I was actually floating, I mean. Or gliding. Call it what you will. I couldn't feel my feet on the ground, that was the point. But I didn't think about that. Never occurred to me. My feet were only a small section of the body that I couldn't detect anyway. I couldn't feel a thing and I couldn't hear a damn thing apart from the faint hum of distant machinery inside of me. Anaesthetized, still. No sense of my legs beneath or the air that I moved through. Couldn't feel the cold or the struggling sunlight or whether the wind was stroking my face. Couldn't hear the distant traffic from the main road at the end of the street. Vision was the only thing really working for me. All I could do was see. I was a camera being pushed slowly along a track. One long tracking shot. It was OK, actually, once I got used to it. And anyway, I knew I had to keep moving. As long as I maintained constant movement and didn't question my destination or manner of getting there, the swirling sickness abated and I could start to feel some kind of inner resolve, some kind of purpose.

And the view was a constant distraction. Not much to see in that desolated corridor of brick and steel squares, but I soaked it all up in dazzling high definition. The clouds were rolling away above me and the day was sharp and bright now, patches of shining black on the roads and pavements from recently fallen rain. I got the sense that everything was beginning to dry out. It felt like something had passed.

There were occupied houses further down, cars parked at the kerbside, some indication of life and order. I passed more and more un-shuttered windows and began to see shapes and figures moving behind glass. Paper chains and unlit fairy lights hanging behind net curtains. The first murmurings and snatched glances of life. Bear in mind, bud, I'd not seen one of your number before. Not man, woman or child.

So OK, here we go, here's my first human encounter. Here it is. A van comes down the street, pulls up a few feet in front of me, opposite side, and a fella gets out. Crosses over and walks right in front of me. The sight of him stops me dead in my tracks. My very first human being, in full and startling close up. Small, wiry, sandy haired fella in paint-spattered overalls and boots. I'm about three feet away from him. He's stood fiddling with a key at a front door. I'm close enough to see the grubby white patches of paint on the back of his hands and the ragged edges of his bitten down fingernails, see the hairs on the folds of his ears and the pale red broken threads running riot around the side of his nose.

And then, for a single split second, this man switches, like he's some kind of shape shifter, like his face is melting, like he's falling to bits, the flesh sloughing off and hitting the pavement like heavy handfuls of melted wax. The sudden red flush of his cheeks; I can almost see the blood pounding beneath the skin. The veins in the neck throbbing. He's a bag of meat, that's what he looks like. Just pipes and veins and flesh wrapped around bone. Then, snap, he's back to normal again, just a small middle aged man with thinning sandy hair trying to get his key into a door. I felt something then; some sudden tug at a hidden part of myself. Stab of recognition, must have been. Empathy. I'd like to think so. A subconscious acknowledgement of my own previous mortality. That's what Claire would have said. I'll tell you about Claire and all the rest of them soon. All the other humans.

So anyway, this particular human man, this first encounter, I'm thinking I should maybe stay still, wait to see what happens next. But nothing happens next, or even after that. The man doesn't notice me, not so much as a glance in my direction. Just twists the key, opens the door and slips inside the house.

I move on. I kept drifting. The red dot moving on the radar. I don't encounter another person down that street, apart from the occasional shape of a body in a front room, and the two or three cars that pass. I stop and gawp as each face slides by, hanging pink balloons in slow trundling boxes of steel. No more terrifying close-ups, though, just passing, there and then gone. I fix my vision ahead and keep moving.

Eventually I come to the main road at the top of the street. I turn right and slam to a dead halt in the middle of it all. Woah! Everything too much here, bud. Like the film has suddenly been sped up. That easy going rose-tinted wander from my house to the real world? Gone. This was a madness. There were too many cars for a start and fast, way too fast, an endless stream of glass and metal pouring from each direction, whipping past me at impossible speeds. And the people on the pavement, too many, too many; they swarmed and swam, dipping in and out of each other's path, all vying for some small advantage in their own personal race to wherever. A mad current of flesh striding and shuffling and rushing and pushing past me and through me; yes, they went straight through me from both directions. I don't realize this small but vital detail at this point, too confused in the general whirl of movement, but I'm petrified, bud, a butterfly caught in a hurricane. A truck could have thundered through me and it wouldn't have registered. Which makes some sort of sense, looking back.

I escape to the edge of the road and hover in an empty bus shelter, try to keep some distance on this unholy riot of motion that was exploding all around me. The fear was mounting within me. The cars, they scared the holy shit out of me, so I concentrated on the pedestrians. The human race. I couldn't work them out. I stood and stared at the people and they filled me with a deep unease. They looked all wrong. The shape of their bodies and their faces looked wrong; and they kept moving. Kept changing, I mean. Like that first man I had seen, the fella in the overalls with the face like a melting lump of meat. It was happening everywhere I looked. Each human form that passed me seemed to shift its shape for one brief snapshot second, and the seconds stacked up, one on top of another, thick and fast. Like the gang of kids riding slowly past on their bikes were suddenly a murder of black-clad crows; yellow beaks replacing the peaks of caps, feet turning in the air, elbows stuck out like oily wings. One of them stands up straight on his pedals and for one mad moment it's like they'll all follow suit, all raise themselves up and take flight into the sky. But then a passing car obscures them and they all emerge on the other side as young boys on bicycles again.

It was everywhere. I was grasping for something to fasten onto, but the snowstorm was spinning with a sick fury and nothing seemed to stick. And the longer I stood still and watched the passing parade, the faster the flakes seemed to whirl.

Madness, bud. Madness at every turn.

The double fronted glass door to a shop across the road swings open and a woman in high heels totters out, laden down with parcels and bags full of shopping. Tall and slender, fragile looking, like she might get swept away in a strong gust of wind. The word *giraffe* comes to me, and then that's exactly what she is, a knock-kneed quadruped with an elongated patchwork neck and doll's eyelashes, skittering away up the street. This other guy stood in the open doorway of a betting shop, he turns into a ladle, a human length ladle propped up on its side, like some chef of the gods has been stirring hot soup and then put down his utensil, leaned it in the bookies doorway to rest, still steaming. Cartoon world. It was happening everywhere I turned my gaze. An OAP coasting along on a mobility scooter becomes a small purple and silver submarine chugging its way through the depths of the deep blue sea, the shoals of dark grey people-fish swimming around her, then, woah, what's this, she's followed by a huge iridescent crab which one eye-wink later is two teenage girls, their heads huddled together in giggling conspiracy over something in their hands, some device, a mobile phone or something. A young guy hangs out of a window above a shop across the road, his arms two full sleeves of tattoos. He's lifting a cigarette to his mouth. I get a close up on the rising coil of smoke and then boom, the guy's on fire, his head just bursts into a ball of flame, zip, like a sweetly struck match. He takes a pull on his cigarette and bellows smoke and leaping fire out into the street, flames dancing above the heads of the people.

All this Loony Tune chaos unfolding around me; like the young girl on rollerblades with the green helmet and pink and yellow armbands, she's a multi-coloured parrot swooping straight past the bus shelter. There's a group of council workmen leaning against a wall further up the road on the other side, eating bacon sandwiches; their bright yellow vests a pack of playing cards splayed out; jacks, queens, kings, aces. Alice in Wonderland stuff. I look further down the road and see large buildings in the distance turning into dinosaurs. Big lumbering behemoths craning their necks and stamping their feet, darkening the horizon. Oncoming cars are sleds pulled by teams of barking mad blue-eyed Huskies. It was all going insane, everywhere, the more I stared. And I stared and stared. An umbrella unfurled in front of me, sprouted legs and wings and veered off into the sky, a giant bluebottle as big as a bi-plane. It was like having the pages of a children's encyclopaedia flicked in front of my eyes at a million miles a second. Imagine it; you're freshly born and all this info's pouring in. My eyes, bud. My poor bewildered eyes.

I was warming up, that's what it was. The anaesthetic was starting to wear off. Words swelled from somewhere inside me and burst like popcorn into my rapidly forming brain, the names of things coming thick and fast now, crowding in and elbowing each other aside: giraffes, dinosaurs, paper clips, fire engines, mannequins, newspapers, prams, parrots, windows, shops, apples, bicycles, hats, flags, cigarettes and doors, yes, doors at last, and on and on and on. And some of were starting to stick to the correct targets. Nouns. Proper nouns I'm talking about here, you understand; the names of things my mind could actually get hold of, if not my hands. All the other slippery ethereal business like happiness, sadness, desire, jealousy and joy, that wasn't on the menu. Not at this point, anyway. It was strictly stuff you could reach out and touch in the physical world. Reach out and touch somebody's hand. That particular joke was lost on me at the time though, you understand. I was too knocked out by this riot in front of my eyes.

Gradually, though, the hard and fast bombardment subsides and I start to get a fix on things. The physical world slowed down enough for me to see it, that's what I reckon. The world as it really was. Is, I mean. Is. I started to see the reality. I realized that the buildings in the distance were not going to uproot themselves and come stamping over the horizon towards me, were not going to grow an enormous scaly tail and thrash the surrounding landscape to rubble. A car was not a submarine. An umbrella was not a bluebottle. I still wasn't sure what it was, but I knew it wasn't a bluebottle. Things gradually settled into their own correct form, and some of the right words began to cement themselves into my understanding. Which came as something of a relief, as you can no doubt appreciate. I mean, I'm as visually stimulated as the next man, but this was taking the piss.

So I'm starting to get a bit curious now. I'm waking up. I'm waking up, bud. The cobwebs are sliding off me. I move out of neutral, engage first gear. A tentative trundle forward.

There's a petrol station and shop at the top of the road. I find myself gawping into open fridges, the stark bluish light and the yellow and orange blocks of cheese and the gold wrapped butter and the puffed up bags of greenery. All the tubs of white and yellow and the packets of pink fluorescent meat. I wander up and down the aisles and examine everything in minute detail; toilet rolls and cans of polish, loaves of bread, bottles of wine and cartons of milk, sandwiches and cards and bags of coal and bags of crisps and bars of chocolate and everything, bud. Everything. Some of the words I knew, but not all of them. It was all too much gathered in one place; like a surreal art display laid out for an uncomprehending audience of one.

It was around this point that I started to get my head into something like proper focus. Started stringing the words together in my head. And once I started to form coherent thoughts, I was forced to concede that something was seriously amiss. And that's when I really started to panic.

Kate Middleton, it was all her fault. She triggered the wave of fresh unease. My snake in the Garden of Eden. Because I was looking at the front page of this newspaper and there was a photo of her, that Kate Middleton. You know the woman, yeah? You know who I'm talking about? The royal princess? Course you do. There's not a person in the country who doesn't know who she is. Kate Middleton, the mother of the future king of England, stood smiling and waving at me from a black and white picture. I knew who she was. I recognized her. The very first face I recognized, really. And for the life of me I could not remember her name.

I try to reach out, to lift the paper from the stand. But I can't do it. I am as weak as water, still, my arms are two dead weights of nothing at my side. Helpless. And I'm staring at this picture of this dark haired girl with the warm smile and I'm trying to remember who the hell she is. I knew she was supposed to be someone, but her actual name was slipping around the edges of my brain. Queen and country. That's all I could think. I knew her face but I couldn't remember her fucking name, and it was slowly inflating me with dread. Because she was a real person and she should have a real name, like door or shop or umbrella. People have names, don't they bud?

It was slowly dawning on me that I didn't know who I was. And that's when I felt that first proper jolt of pure and sickening fear. I don't mean the mild panic of seeing something freaky. I mean the gut churning knowledge that you are totally lost and alone and you don't know what to do. That's when the full uncomprehending weight of my situation started to press down from above. I knew a few words, and I could grasp the basic rudiments of the world as I saw it, but I didn't know where I was or who I was or what anything in this brand new existence meant.

I got the notion that if I could remember who the dark haired girl in the photograph was I could remember who I was as well. So I'm looking at all these other magazines and papers, trying to put names to people, staring at these heads and going through a kind of vague and desperate classification process: blond pop star - well known businessman - politician guy - TV presenter; just thinking to myself: who the hell are these people? I knew they were meant to be somebody. I knew I was meant to be somebody. But I didn't know who anybody was. Nothing was matching up.

After a while I gave up and went back outside onto the main road. I had not got one clue about my location. Didn't have the slightest idea. I mean, this was a place that I had never seen before. All I needed was the name of a street or a familiar face. But nothing I clapped eyes on seemed to make any sense. After a while I thought the best thing I could do was go back in the petrol station and ask somebody where I was. I sort of grasped that they wouldn't necessarily know *who* I was, you understand, but if I could put a pin in the map it would be a decent enough start.

There were two women behind the tills; an older lady, heavy set, and a young bleached blonde girl. The girl was stood with her arms folded, chewing gum and looking out of the window at the cars on the forecourt. I could see the make-up thick on her skin, the fine dusting of beige powder on her forehead and jawline as she worked the gum around her mouth, the fragments of black mascara caught in her eyelashes. She looked bizarre, ridiculous, like a gaudy clown. The older one looked like her face had collapsed; the jowls hung in loose baggy folds, like a slumbering lizard. She was fiddling with a display of air fresheners on the counter, those things you hang off your rear view mirror, all these tiny dangling Christmas trees; green and blue and red and yellow and lilac. Some of them had been knocked and scattered onto the counter and the woman was putting them all back up onto their hooks.

I tried to speak to her. Excuse me, what street is this? But it was impossible. I could hardly form the sentence in my head, let alone open my mouth to speak. This woman didn't look up, didn't acknowledge me in any way whatsoever, just kept hanging all these cardboard trees back onto their hooks. She was saying something to the younger girl. I could see her mouth moving, but I couldn't make out the words. It didn't sound like proper words, just a faint noise, wah-wah-wah-wah-wah. Like the teacher out of Charlie Brown. Remember that? That droning voice from above? Or like when you pull yourself out of a swimming pool and there's a hard bubble of water trapped in your inner ear, everything muffled. Listening to a world behind glass. That was me. I'm in this emporium of glaring light and stomach churning colour, strings of Christmas lights and tinsel hung around the tills and I'm a deaf mute who doesn't know where the hell he is, and this woman with a landslide for a face is ignoring me.

Someone walks up behind me, this young lad twirling his car keys on his finger like helicopter blades and the older woman straightens herself up and smiles. The lad says something to her and she taps at the till and he slides his card into the machine and she tears him off a receipt. Her smile vanishes the minute he turns his back and she's back yapping to her pal and tending to her miniature multi-coloured tree display.

I've got this primitive thing that I can barely comprehend welling up inside me now, beyond fear even, just this overwhelming need to make contact, to engage. Except I haven't got the energy to get this woman's attention. All I can do is stand in front of her like a wilting plant in a dried up pot, desperately willing her to acknowledge me. But she simply doesn't see me, and neither do the other customers who come in and out of the shop, paying for their petrol and their milk and their scratch cards and their cigarettes and their bars of chocolate. All the things they stuff inside of themselves. I stand there and watch them come and go, but none of them even so much as blink at me. Not on the radar. In the end I give up and drift out of the garage, back out onto the street.

I stopped to look in the window of this Oxfam shop and tried once more to fasten definite names to definite things. A renewed stab at the naming process. Start with the world around me and work back towards myself. There are books and boxes and board games and mannequins dressed in second hand coats and hats and skirts. I can see the reflection of the street behind me, the people passing with their prams and shopping bags and dogs and beyond this shimmering procession I can see a café on the other side of the road with the people sat inside with coffee and newspapers and a red car parked just further along, and I'm standing there looking at this mirror image scene and then it suddenly strikes me that there's something missing.

Me.

I was missing.

I look round and there's the café and the people with their coffee cups and newspapers and there's the red car, bright tomato red and sat in the sun on it's four black and silver wheels and its fringes of rust around the driver's door and its sticker in the rear side window. We are Premier League, it says. I turn back to the shop window and there it all is again, café and people and low-slung red car, but there's no me in front of it all.

Now it doesn't take a genius to realize there's something amiss in a situation like that, does it, Mr Listener? I was still groggy from the birth so my mind was still a bit sluggish, synapses not yet fully firing, but I knew beyond doubt that this wasn't right. So I'm trying to piece it together. Main problem was I didn't know what I was supposed to be looking for. I didn't know what I looked like. Hadn't even entered my head. I was so knocked out at this bright new world in front of me that I didn't even consider myself as a part of it. Until I looked in that Oxfam window, that is. And there I wasn't: the invisible man with no memory for names and no reflection he could call his own.

I found a bus shelter and paused to reconsider. I'm not sure if the word *ghost* had popped into my mind by now. Maybe a word like it. Or the concept at least, with no word attached. Yeah, maybe that. Something like a ghost. I wasn't quite sure where it fitted, but it felt right. Felt like it might slot in. I mean, I started to allow myself to consider that possibility. It appeared at the edges, but I wasn't ready for it. An unwanted guest. The ghost at the feast, if you like.

But there's constant diversions out there, bud. You know that. No time to pause and ponder. Never a second to yourself on the streets. And now I'm aware that two people have set themselves down on the bench behind me; a scruffy young couple, in their early twenties I would say. They have a pram with them. I tried to see inside the pram but it was turned away from me. They were a tatty looking pair these two, begrimed and battered looking. The young girl had a corker of a black eye, a proper comic book shiner. It intrigued me, this wobbling purple egg on her eyebrow. Intrigued and repelled me. It looked like something that definitely should not be there. Her partner was a whippet thin young bucko with a deathly white pallor and a face full of rhubarb and custard. They were each clutching a can of beer, more cans in a carrier bag hanging off the handle of the pram. Daytime drinkers. They were arguing as they arrived. I could see their mouths set into sneers, spittle flying. From the look on their faces and the animated body language I could tell it was a heated exchange of words, probably ignited the minute they woke up, a steady burning resentment that was batted back and forth all day and night until a fist hit a head or a head hit the pillow. Simmering through sleep and then flaring up again at sunrise the next day. You could tell that it was an on-going twenty-four hour arrangement for these two, as natural as breathing. Their aggression unsettled me. I looked away so I couldn't make eye contact, but it didn't matter; they were both far too interested in tearing lumps out of each other, and, of course, they couldn't see me anyway.

... stoopidbitchgimmethafuggincardtellinyernowsharleensweardown-allfuggin ...

... garriyerdooinmefuggineadinfukoffwiwyer ...

... gisthatfuggincardsharleenamnotfugginjokinall ...

That's what it sounded like, all vague and muffled, the words coming from underwater again. Then the girl stands up and slings a loop of beer.

It slaps the lad on the shoulder, soaks him down one side. He shoots up and grabs her wrist, tries to wrestle the can out of her hand, and they start throwing each other around, beer flying everywhere. They spill out of the bus shelter and onto the path. People are stopping in their tracks and walking around them, trying to avoid getting bumped or drenched. Then this big fella sticks his head out of one of the shop doorways and starts yelling. I can see his knitted brow and the anger in his eyes. They don't take any notice though, the gruesome twosome, just carry on grappling. There's a few other people getting involved now; this younger bloke comes out of the shop and a woman stops to look in the pram and then she's remonstrating with the lad and the girl, looks like she's giving them a proper telling off. The big fella from the shop has stepped out now and gets hold of the lad by the shoulders, he's turning him away and trying to march him backwards up the street, away from his shop, but the lad keeps trying to slip out of his grip and get back at the girl. She's following them both, making a flapping mouth shape with her hand, like yeah, yeah, yeah, keep talking kinda thing. Like she's taunting him. The lads attempting to climb round this big fella who keeps grabbing handfuls of his jacket, trying to get a proper grip. Then the lad pulls back and sticks the head on him, bang, nuts him one full on the nose and there's a sudden spray of scarlet.

Proper pandemonium ensues. The other younger fella from the shop steams in and the pair of them are trying to wrestle this lad to the ground and the girl takes off one of her shoes and starts leathering the big fella on his back. There's blood on the pavement and the older shop bloke has a dark splash of claret all down the front of his shirt. The woman drops her shopping and pulls the pram out of the way of all these flying bodies and the contents of her carrier bags are spilling out and kicked about, carrots and cans of soup and eggs splattered. Instant and utter madness in the space of a few seconds.

My first taste of violence in the brand new life. Action. Animation. It shocked me, bud, like the air had been suddenly charged with electricity. Seemed to jolt me into some sort of action as well, because next thing I know I'm moving away down the road, leaving all this chaos in my wake. I didn't stop to look back, I just kept going.

Fight or flight. The sympathetic nervous system colluding with the adrenal cortical to activate the hormones necessary for the preservation of life. Now, seeing as how I didn't have nerve pathways or a bloodstream, I can only assume my reaction was one of disinterest. Or disgusted withdrawal. I didn't fear for my life, because I didn't have a life to lose. Maybe I feared for my soul? Maybe that was it. Because violence is not the answer, is it bud? We both know that. Violence solves nothing. We've had centuries of the stuff and look where it's got us.

Next place I remember is the Internet café. I looked through a window and saw people, two rows of people, all sat facing away from each other and staring at a row of screens. I think I must have reckoned it was some sort of education centre, a seat of public learning perhaps. Citizens receiving instructions. Christ knows. In my fresh and glistening dumb-head state I thought they might be hooking themselves up to portals of information. I thought that's what it must be. They were all so rapt. It looked promising, anyway. Looked like an option.

I find myself inside. I scrutinise every screen. I move down each row of seats, looking over every shoulder. Most people were checking or composing emails, which made little or no sense to me. They may as well have been bashing out complex equations in ancient hieroglyphics. Like the graffiti back in my bombed out house or the signs on the street outside. Couldn't read a word. But the more I examined the shapes on the screens the more came back. Like those 3D posters, remember them? The very first forays into visual trickery. Looked like a blur of dots at first, but you'd stare hard and concentrate and the dinosaurs would slowly emerge. Shapes arising. I kept staring, and the full picture started to appear. More words, but linked to images this time. I spotted a young man looking at a football web site, a video clip of a goal. Football; the shape of a ball and the word and the game on the screen, the tiny men in red kicking and running and hugging each other. It all started to marry up. It was just a case of prompting the old memory box. I looked at houses and cars and holiday scenes and Facebook pages and news and views and bits of plain old nonsense. Video clips of babies laughing and kittens falling off sofas. And I quickly discovered that my memory had not been wiped completely clean as I first feared, just stuck in deep freeze. That Internet café was my fast track college course in dragging back bits of knowledge. Plus, like I said, that woozy post-op feeling was wearing off. The more I fed my head, the sharper I felt. Warming up, bud. Waking up at last.

I stayed there all afternoon drinking in the info. It was like switching a broken machine back on, the various components sparking into life and firing connections. Countries, animals, pop stars, planets. The pictures became coupled to their proper names and slid into context like the tiles on a huge mosaic. Kate Middleton, there she was again, smiling and waving, the same photograph, almost. The shape of her name underneath. I stayed there drinking it all in, until the last screen had been switched off and everyone had packed up their things and gone.

The last person to leave was a Chinese lad. He'd left this diagram up on the screen. It was something to do with engineering, a blueprint of some kind. It intrigued me no end. All the lines and numbers and exactitude. I couldn't relate it to anything else. It didn't help that the text was in Chinese. Mind you, it wouldn't have helped much more if it had been in English either, despite my slowly emerging vocabulary.

I stood there pondering the thing until the guy who had been sat behind the counter all afternoon came and switched the machine off. Then he walked away. I was rooted to the spot, heavy with the weight of all the info I'd took on. That snowstorm in my head was beginning to abate and the flakes were finally settling.

I was so absorbed in this new fusing together of the world that I failed to notice the shutters descending outside until it was too late. The manager must have locked the door whilst I was lost in my musing and made his exit out the back. This was him on the other side of the frontage now, lowering steel and banishing the daylight. It crept away from me across the floor, an ever-decreasing slice of light, like a fading smile. And there I was, trapped in a shop with only a row of winking red lights for company.

I stood in the gloom and considered my options. I could stay there until the morning, when presumably the place would open up again. Or I could try and get out. I went over to the door. For the second time that day I found myself bewildered by a bloody door.

Then, the next thing I know, I'm back out on the street.

That threw me, I must admit. Previous to that I liked to think I had maintained a state of reasonably Zen-like calm about my situation. I mean, taking into account being virtually deaf and unable to feel my legs, and the fact that I was seemingly invisible to myself and all around me, I like to think I coped it with all of that quite well on that first day; the street full of hallucinations, the dinosaurs and submarines and people bursting into flame. Lesser men would have run screaming to the edges of insanity. But the walking through walls sketch, that was a definite first. Did put the fear in me, I must admit. One minute I'm trapped in a shop, the next I'm stood outside among the rest of the High Street crowd. People walking towards me and through me. At first I hadn't noticed the lack of physical contact; now I couldn't avoid it. I remember turning around and seeing these teenage kids, a gang of them strung out across the pavement and looming right up onto me, the girls arm in arm and one kid swinging his bag and I tried to move, to get out of their way but then they were past me, behind me, *through me*, and I was left standing there thinking what the actual fuck?

I can't remember if the word ghost had finally lodged itself into my head by then. I was still a little bit spangled at that point. Walking through walls seemed no more unusual than anything else that had happened so far. I mean, why not, yeah? I'd seen the world bent out of shape in front of my eyes. Monsters and mayhem. Walking through walls wasn't too big a leap for me at that point.

So I set off again.

After a while I realized I didn't have the first notion where I was going. Just drifting with no cause or purpose. So I decided to go back to the derelict house. The place where I had started. I remember thinking I might get an idea there as to what I should do next. Something left behind, maybe. I was still clutching for physical clues. I tried not to worry about the way the people went though me and I fell in step with the flow, started back down the road. Studied the faces around me as we moved together. They look tired and blank for the most part, irate, some of them, set in proper sour grimace, like they were ready to spit. Then I notice the bodies seem to have quickened their pace; putting up umbrellas and flipping collars, darting into doorways, shoulders hunched and ducking under bus shelters. Windscreen wipers were moving on the vehicles. Sudden spots of something spiralling in front of me and laying themselves on the pavement. The light was fading fast and the snow was starting to come down. I had a vague notion of night and day then, a first inkling. Car headlights popping on, shop windows extinguished and streetlamps starting to ignite. And bear in mind I'm receiving all this with the sound set to mute. I'm going purely by the visuals at this point. But I could see it; a tightening of the atmosphere. A drawing in. I looked upwards. That big blank sky had started to shed it's white.

After a good while wandering and double-backing and half-recognizing various landmarks, I remember where the street is and eventually work out the way back home. I found the garage and the bus stop and the Oxfam shop on the main road. I stopped for another inspection, but I still wasn't there. Thought about going inside, but it was closed and dark. No people in there. So I headed back home.

As I turn down the street and head towards the house, the snow really starts to come down. It fascinated me; millions of white flecks falling directly in front of me, around me, through me. I felt glad somehow. The snowfall in my head made real, but everyone was getting wet apart from me. I was in the world but not of it. I was separate and untouched.

I think this is where the fullest sense of my power started to sink in.

Imagine it, though, bud; being able to walk with impunity anywhere. The possibilities are endless, right? Good weapon to have in your locker you've got to agree. The ability to move through all form of matter; walls, doors, crowds of people, oncoming ten-ton juggernauts. Access all areas. You can walk through flame. You can go underwater. You can stroll into a band saw whilst whistling a merry tune. Spend the night in a deep freeze. You can sit yourself down next to a rabid panther. It was a buzz at first. But like all forms of novelty, it wore off in the end. Obviously such a skill would be invaluable in your situation, locked up as you are, but all it did was prolong mine. And that became more like a curse as time rolled on. As the mission intensified and the pressure mounted. Believe me, there have been countless times I would have gladly stepped off a high building and dropped into the traffic below. In fact, I did, one afternoon, without thinking. Nothing happened.

I just wandered off and then I was on the street below. No sensation of falling, so I didn't even get the mild treat of exhilaration. So, yeah. Useless. I had access all areas, but ultimately everything was locked out to me. I may as well have been sat in here with you, staring at the bricks in the wall.

That screw with the bad breath and attitude. He won't be happy until we've had words. But fuck that bud, conflict is not my thing any more. It used to be. Arguments used to fascinate me. I think it was the shock of that couple in the bus shelter, the sheer energy with which they flung their venom straight into each other's faces. Compared to everyone else, it looked like proper interaction. This was something I noticed early on. Everyone ignores each other – even when they're in direct dialogue – or they treat the bodies around them with mild indifference. So a good blazing row would really enthral me. High octane involvement, I think is how I looked at it. Engagement. That was the appeal. And laughter. When two or more people are in proper helpless hysterics. I used to like that as well. Any form of extreme release. But arguing, I reckon that was the main fascination for me in those early weeks. I would go from house to house looking for domestic upheaval. Couples arguing. Kids arguing. They are the worst, actually, kids. Flashpoints over the most unpredictable nonsense. Kids are bullies. They find a weak spot and drill into it mercilessly, like little prospectors of hurt, pushing and poking and probing until they hit the jackpot and the victim erupts in a fountain of tears.

I used to hang around playgrounds. When I was looking for the kids. Listen, I know how that sounds now, now that I've lost all my innocence. I never thought about it at the time. But playgrounds bud, wow, seething cauldrons of energy. I'm talking primary school age here, Ryan's age, like six or seven years old. They're insane, human beings at that age. They live totally in the moment. Their ability to exist utterly in that instant, that little grubby pocket of space and time. Kids that age are constantly on the brink of explosion. They bounce about like pinballs in those playgrounds, they swing off bars and run around in mad screaming gangs, push and pull each other, jumping and chasing all over the place. And even before I could hear I could almost feel the air pulsating with the jabber and yells and shrieks around me, the dozens of little mouths flapping at each other. I use to watch the games. Trying to remember, I suppose. Remember myself when I was little, if I ever was such a thing. What did I like to do? Can't remember bud, still to this day.

I couldn't remember ever liking to do anything.

That was a strange feeling. I mean, I used to like watching the kids at Ryan's school playing basketball. They were really good for such little kids. They didn't all just swarm around the ball like the proverbial wasps round a jam pot, no, they adopted the proper positions and signalled moves. Worked as a team. That glorious whoop of exuberance that greeted a ball dropping clean through, the quick swell of the net with no bang of backboard or rattle of hoop and they'd all wheel away with their hands in the air. I used to watch those kids play basketball and it would make me swell with joy, but I couldn't conceive of ever doing that myself. I was looking for that tug of recognition. I'd felt it with Gemma, so I knew I was a real person with real feelings somewhere in the depths of my invisible chest.

Gemma. I thought at first that she might have been a former wife or partner, but I know that's not the case now. The tug wasn't a memory of the physical. It was an acknowledgement of kinship, a recognition of the species - you and me, we're part of the same existence. The human race, bud. I was getting static shocks of recognition from human behaviour. Kids playing in the playground, and the way Gemma stopped to fondle that dog's ears, I must have been that carefree once. I must have been. Maybe it triggered a memory, a very early one. A happy one, I hope. I must have been small once. Small and happy. I'd like to think so, bud. I'd really like to think so.

Anyway, this was all to come, Gemma and the kids and all the rest of it. At the end of that first day I just got spooked and ran back to the place where I was born. I didn't know what was happening, but I had my superman vision and my cloak of anonymity and when that snow came down I started to feel something like alive.

Which was more than could be said for the poor soul they were sliding into the back of the ambulance that was parked outside the house. For him, all options were closed, like the zip over his face.

I knew it was a body. There were police cars and police and paramedics and people stood out on the street and yellow and black tape across the front door. I started over to the ambulance as the bag went in. I had an idea I'd try to get inside and see who it was. But the doors were slammed shut before I got within spitting distance and then the paramedics jumped into the front and the ambulance moved off. There was no blue light so I assumed there was no siren. The police didn't hang around either. They got back into their cars and followed the ambulance up the street. The people standing around went back into their houses.

So then there's just me and this uniformed copper stood in the street, in the snow. He's standing at the end of the alleyway, guarding the entrance to the back of the houses. Young fella, looked like he'd hardly started shaving. I walk right up to him, nose to nose, position myself directly in front of him, so close I can see the veins in his eyeballs and the dots of white settling on the peak of his cap. I stood as close up to him as I could possibly get and he didn't blink once.

So anyway, that was me at one day old. Like I said, I remember it now like a series of photographs laid out next to each other. The yellow wall, the garden strewn with rubbish, the streets erupting with words, the garage, Kate Middleton, the young couple fighting, the Internet café and the lights popping on. The ambulance and the copper. It's all emblazoned on my mind's eye still. It's different now, I can tell my eyesight isn't so good. By "isn't so good" I mean, I suppose, its what you would call normal. I used to be able to see in the dark. Can't do that anymore. Shame. Could have some fun with that now, now that most of my new-born innocence has evaporated.

But the things I've seen, bud. The things I've seen.

I hung around the house all that first night and it dawned upon me when it dawned upon me, stood in that scruffy back garden watching the sky slowly brighten and the sun spread itself weakly in the sky over newly laid surfaces of pure white. The body in the back of the ambulance. The effortless movement through solid partitions. My lack of discernible presence in the eyes of the people or the shop windows of the street. After a thorough debriefing I was forced to accept the facts as I barely understood them; that I had died in that house and risen up again, somehow free from the shackles of flesh. I was a shadow of my former self. An indiscernible presence.

A ghost.

I knew the word. I grasped the concept, bud.

Those first few days were just aimless drifting, retracing my steps. But I made a few fresh discoveries about myself. For a start, I soon realised I didn't have to waste my time travelling. If I wanted to visit a place I just visualised it and bang, I was there. Once I knew a spot well I could whisk myself back in the bat of an eyelid. Instant recall through time and space. Which was handy. I spent a fair few hours in the Internet café, soaking up fresh information. I liked to see what people looked at. What they were interested in. Most of it was just random rubbish, but I devoured every scrap. Desperation, bud. The nose pressed up against the window. A frantic desire to understand, and the Internet café seemed the best place.

Apart from that, I stuck around the main road and city centre during the day and wandered further afield at night. I felt a bit more confident when there were less people around. I had no idea where I was going or what I was looking for. I just mooched aimlessly about from doorstep to dustbin. Started to get my bearings. There was the long main road at the bottom of the street that led to the city centre if you turned to the right and towards the outer suburbs if you did a left. There was a hill with a large park at the top just beyond the streets on the other side of the road and then a cluster of streets after that with terraced housing and more roads with pubs and shops. If I started to lose my way I'd head back to the house and start again. The place of my birth.

I spent a fair amount of time just hanging around the house. Hoping something or someone would visit, I suppose. A face from the past. Give me half a clue. But nobody did, apart from the occasional gang of truant kids playing round the back alleys, or the homeless souls seeking refuge from the rain and the hassle of the streets. The occasional junkie jacking up or smoking. I didn't like that. Unsettled me, that did. Leaving their bloody needles and burnt bits of foil all over the place. I remember this one lad used to sit in the back kitchen of one of the houses with his head in a carrier bag full of glue, sucking on this sticky plastic lung until he slumped unconscious into a dribbling heap. Sad, but it used to piss me off, to be honest. It was my house, and these bastards had no right to lounge about the place, treating it like a grubby hotel for the dispossessed. There were plenty of other houses to damage themselves in and I was always grateful when they took their leave and moved on to pastures new. I had my own problems to contend with without bearing witness to theirs.

The night times were OK. It snowed most of those first few nights. The snow was useful for me because it tended to clear away the people and I preferred cruising around the silent streets. I allowed myself into the houses, purely to catch a glimpse, a quick in and out to begin with. But I soon realized my initial suspicions were entirely correct. Nobody could see me. Not a single trace.

The proximity of real people freaked me out at first. Took me a while to get used to their indifference, but once it was established I became bold and I was soon sailing in and out of homes like a carefree Father Christmas. I watched the people live their lives. I stood to one side of the room and watched families laughing and arguing and eating together. I always felt more of an intruder in the homes of families. Felt a bit estranged and left out. I was more at home with the single dwellers; the solitary man sat eating his microwaved meal in front of the TV, the dole moles who surfaced after sundown, the old lady chuntering away to the dozing dog curled up on her lap.

Dogs and cats though, I avoided them for the most part. I realized pretty quickly that animals could see me. Or sense me, at any rate. Most of them weren't bothered by my presence, not on the streets at least, but they could be a tad territorial if you wandered onto their patch. Occasionally you'd get some poor pooch going postal when I drifted past by his hearthside or an irate cat arching it's back and hissing a warning to get the hell out of their house. I respected all of that. This world is for the living not the dead, animals included.

Little kids, bud, they could see me as well. I got the impression they could, anyway. Really little kids I'm talking about here. Toddlers. They used to wave at me from their pushchairs as their mothers trundled them past. But I used to flinch at any hint of recognition, in those early days at least. I didn't like it when kids could see me. Knowing little bastards. Like those two, Connor and Harrison.

They turned up in the back yard of the house one afternoon. Must have been a week or so after the ambulance had left. They were about 9, 10 years old. I didn't hear them, of course. I was upstairs inspecting the bedrooms. I only went back downstairs because I'd decided to go outside to check the pattern on the main bedroom wallpaper against the little purple star shaped flowers by the back fence. Looking for connections, however vague or fleeting. Hey, you can smile, bud, but this is how I used to spend my days and nights when I first landed. Staring at every available surface and item. Trying to link stuff up. Anyway, I ghosted down and out the back way, and came face to face with the biggest one, Connor. He was leading the way. Harrison was scared, I could tell by the way he hung behind. C'mon Connor, let's go, his body was saying. Connor was scared too, but trying not to show it. Or maybe he wasn't scared, I don't know. He was a hard-faced little bastard, him. Some kids are just plain ugly, don't you think? They look like twisted little adults before their limbs have stopped extending and their fleshy carriages have been made full. I don't like kids at the best of times, but he was a horrible little shit, that Connor. Not his fault, I suppose, in retrospect. Grown up too fast. Forced to. Anyway, he ventured in and made his way tentatively through the kitchen, eyes skittering this way and that. Walked straight through me. Not a hint of acknowledgement. Like I said, some kids, smaller kids, I often got the impression that they could detect my presence. But Connor, he was too big to be a kid. He'd stop believing in fairies a long time ago.

I swung round and followed him through to the front room. I didn't like people in the front room. It was my head office, my parlour, my humble birthing room. And he's rooted to the spot, staring at the floor in front of the yellow wall, at the precise place where I'd first raised my head. Transfixed, he was. I stood to the side of him and tried to read his expression. The set of his features. He looked angry, almost. And puzzled. Angry because he was puzzled, maybe. Puzzled because he was angry. Whatever he was, I didn't like the look of him. Unnerved me, he did. Staring right at the very spot where I'd started.

I knew right then. That little bastard. I knew right then that he knew something about me.

Then something broke the spell, probably Harrison shouting his name, because he span around and bolted out of the room, through the kitchen and away, the pair of them tearing off out of the back garden and down through the alleys. Too quick for me, the little bastards.

That's when I started hanging round the school playgrounds. I wanted to see him again, Connor, latch onto him and see where he led me. See what he did. Because he knew, yeah? It was obvious. He knew something about me. And I knew I had to find him again.

But I drew nothing but blanks until a week or so later when I saw him, Connor, out on the main road with another lad, a smaller lad, his brother, and this chubby young woman with short dark hair and a blonde stripe flicked across her fringe. This was Gemma. That was the first time I saw her. The very first time. She had hold of the little one's hand, leading them both through the slush and the afternoon shoppers. I spotted them from across the street and headed after them, but they got onto a bus that trundled away before I could get to them. I remembered the number on the back of the bus and hung around for the next few days, but no, nothing doing. I stuck with it, though. I patrolled that main road through rain, snow hail and weak sunshine for the next few days. And it paid off, eventually, because I saw her again.

What it was, I was drifting along as usual with a head full of befuddlement when I saw her getting off her bicycle and locking it up to some railings. I knew straight away it was her. Very distinctive looking, was Gemma; chubby, short dark hair with this streak of blond in her fringe. The kind of face that looks like it's always ready to start laughing. Pretty. I always thought so, anyway. She dismounted her bike and pulled out her earphones, took a rolled up towel from the back pannier and trotted up this flight of stone steps that led to the entrance of a big glass fronted building.

I think it was then that it started, my obsession with Gemma. At that precise moment. I mean, I'd built her up in my head ever since I'd seen her that day with the boys, knew I had to latch onto her again, but it was more than just that. It was the way she moved, I think. That's what made me zoom in on her. She was a big solid lump of a girl – fat, even, like a baby hippo - but she moved with such an effortless grace. And when I say hippo I don't mean she turned into a cartoon animal or some other vaguely related object. She stayed very much a human being. Very much a solid mass of person. She couldn't be anything other than herself. And I think that's what drew me to her. Self-confidence is what I'm talking about here, bud. It belted off her in waves. I couldn't stop looking at her. She was stunning, bud, an absolute stunner. To me, anyway. Her face ... I mean, her face was just a joy. That smile, that was never far from her lips. She was happy in her own skin, that was what it was, and that made her beautiful. She skipped up the steps and then stopped and petted this small dog that was tied to the rail at the top. This little brown and white terrier with a panting pink tongue, she reached down, ruffled its ears. Scratched under his chin. That was it for me. Right there, when she ticked that little dog under his chops.

See, what I've come to notice is this; people walk around with all of their senses denied. I mean, they block themselves off; whether it's a pair of sunglasses the size of dinner plates or the little buds of noise they plug into their ears or the way they shrink away from each other on the buses and the underground trains. Clammed up tight and folded away into their private pockets of space. They keep their mouths tightly shut or their gazes locked onto newspapers or some imagined horizon out of the window. Or else their phones, Christ, yes, those ever-present phones, either glued to the sides of their heads or thumbs tapping on those little glass squares of magic; tapping, sliding, flicking, tap, tap, tap, like a séance, like they're trying to make contact with the living. So when that girl bent down to ruffle the ears of that dog it was like a rope thrown out to me. If I was a piece of flotsam bobbing about on an ocean of indifference, this girl was a life raft. I knew as soon as I fastened my eyes on her that I had to be close to her. Feed off her, yeah? Feed off her energy.

I think that, right there, was the first time I had felt any strong positive human emotion. Something other than sudden bewilderment or rising fear. First time I'd been affected by a human interaction that wasn't fuelled by ignorance or aggression or indifference. She bent down and ruffled that dog's ears and the dog got up on two back legs and pedalled its paws, delighted. Happy, that's what it was, this dog. Yeah. She made the dog feel happy and she made me feel happy as well. This solid stack of joy stepping into my vision and setting off these ripples of delight. She disappeared into the building, carrying this rolled-up dark green towel and I had a quick-flash mental image of all that green wrapped around her, swaddling the thickness of her flesh, wrapping her up safe and warm.

That was it, yeah? The first primeval tug, right there. It faded as quickly as it flared, but it was there, bud, it was there. It must have been. Must have been. And I don't mean physical attraction, either. I had no notion of the more basic animal needs. Not at first, anyway. Not for a long time, in fact. Didn't get tired or hungry or thirsty or need a shit. I didn't even think about any of those things. All of that stuff is coming back, yeah, but slowly. Very slowly. Still a few pieces of the puzzle missing, I reckon. I didn't have my first drink of water until today. And it was wonderful. A whole new world. But there was no hint of physical need back then. This was brought home to me by what happened next, because without thinking, I'm following her, this girl, I'm right behind her, through the door, stood at her shoulder as she passes money to a woman behind a Perspex screen and then I'm following her down a corridor and through another door and I suddenly realize I'm in a ladies changing room.

You'd have thought that would have been one the perks of being of being a ghost, right? If you're a heterosexual male of the species, I mean. Imagine that, Mr Listener; surrounded by naked women and none of them can see you staring. And surrounded I most certainly was. There was unfettered female flesh at every turn; hips, tits, arse, pussy, thighs and buttocks in a full assortment of shapes, sizes and colour. There was a row of showers at the far end where three middle-aged dears were lathering themselves up in jets of steamy water, bits and pieces wobbling everywhere. Soapy bushes. Glistening arse cracks. Nipples stiff as docker's rivets. I was in a cathedral of naked womanhood. And you know what? None of it did the remotest thing for me. All those pink and brown private parts, all that curved and glistening skin; it may as well have been a butchers shop window in the rain. Not the slightest tug of sexual instinct. What a kick in the non-existent dick, eh? The proverbial spare prick at a wedding. An impotent presence. Water, water, everywhere, and not a drop to drink.

I spotted my chubby stripe-haired target getting changed. I stood right next to her, watched her slide a finger around each arse cheek to tuck herself into her costume, scoop her huge breasts into shiny black polyester.

Again, there was no physical pull. I was just besotted with her effortless self-confidence, the way she threw off her outside clothes and snapped on this second skin. I followed her through to the pool and watched her lower herself in. She began to swim, to pull herself through the water, the bulk of her gliding effortlessly through the shimmering blue. I stood by the side and watched her swim up and down, up and down, her arms rolling and rising and dipping, her legs kicking out behind her.

I don't know how long I stayed there, but the next thing I know, I'm back outside the building watching her unlock her bike and ride away into the traffic. I couldn't follow her. I didn't know how to keep up. All I could do, it seemed, was wander slowly along the street and watch her get smaller in the distance. Frustration, bud. Real frustration, I'm talking about here. But at least I knew I had felt something real then, something positive taking root as I watched her disappear amongst the traffic.

Anyway, after my stripe-haired girl had cycled away I resumed the street patrol. I floated with a newfound purpose, it seemed. I felt a little more energized. Things were starting to click into place for me. Not just words and facts either, but feelings. Proper stirrings of emotion. That heavy post-natal blur, that zombie feeling, it was a distant memory by now. That girl had lit a tiny flame beneath me. I was thawing out.

I went back to that pool every day, like a simpleton, but she never came back and I had no clue as to where to search, and that left me with an ache, bud, an ache where no ache could possibly be. An *absence* of an ache, that's what I had. I don't know if it was just pure desperation or actual love. Real love I'm talking about here, you understand. I'm not talking about simple physical desire. That's part of it, yes, for you, ordinary civilians like you, but I'd been robbed of that. I'm talking about the primeval pull of human recognition, yeah? The perception of a genuine form of beauty and the overwhelming need to be touched by that beauty. That yearning. Beauty of the spirit, let's call it. When you wander into the orbit of someone you find utterly bewitchingly beautiful and every part of you aches to get close. To be acknowledged. To be touched by their power. Look at me, you think. Notice me. Recognize me like I recognize you. Forget the physical. The flesh is a real and powerful thing, yeah, without doubt, not denying that; but the pull of the physical alone is never a recipe for success. It's not the sole ingredient for true love. I know that now.

But this is a recent discovery for me. I didn't know about any of this in my previous life. There was no time for me to find this type of stuff out before I was a ghost, in the short time I was previously afforded. I had no love, bud - no love that I can recall, anyway.

I thought she might have been my wife, at first, Gemma. And that they were my kids. That was my first impulse. I thought that was why Connor was staring at my deathbed and why I felt such a deep and instant connection with Gemma. None of that turned out to be true though. I'll tell you now, from the off, I have no wife and I have no children. And it's just as well. Because when it all unravelled and I discovered the true nature of myself and the circumstances of my previous time on this pale blue dot spinning in space I was fucking glad, bud. I was glad there's nobody left behind to grieve for me. Because the plain fact of the matter is I'm not worth grieving over. What I did was unforgivable. Whatever they've locked you up in here for, rest assured bud, my crimes are tenfold anything you could ever dream up. Because what I did to those children was unforgiveable. I robbed them of everything. And I knew full well what I was doing at the time. No excuses.

But I was made that way. You've got to understand that, bud. People like me aren't born, they're made. Do you understand that?

No, course you don't. And you never could. But your job is to listen, yes? You're not here to judge, you're here to listen. You've had your training; don't judge, don't offer opinion. But I can see it in your eyes, though, bud. Don't think I can't. However much you try to hide it. It's shining out of you and I can see it. In my previous life I knew a lad who overdosed on heroin. I remember him telling me he got into heroin because he liked the way it shrunk his pupils. Said he'd read somewhere that the eyes were the windows to the soul and he didn't want anybody looking into his soul. It was too fucking dark in there, he said. The heroin helped to black out the portals. Well it's the same with me bud, except I didn't take heroin. I could have done though. I used to be surrounded by the stuff. Acres of it.

Oh Jesus Christ ... you people.

You have no idea.

... FRAGMENTS RETURNING ...

... shock of white light in dark sky ... not stars ... not the many stars studded up there ... light that has no natural place ... sudden light put there ... purple edged mountains briefly electrified, vast and distant and then strangely close with this sudden light ... climbing light, colours now, climbing red tailed lights ... red lights that flare into flower ... black clock hands crawling around the orange disc of sun ... night-time ... night-time framed at the edges ... greenish outlines ... fuzzed shapes etched on grainy grey ... shapes loom closer like this ... fading darkness singed by rising orange then sudden blue sky banking this way and that ... seasick with the sudden lurching ... dull yellow spattered with scarlet and then blue again ... yellow and blue, yellow and blue, yellowblueyellowblueyellow and then black again ... flashes of yellow against rolling clouds of white ... flashes of yellow and spitting black against rolling clouds of white ... gold scattered on caked hard yellow ... black cracked into hard caked yellow ... whiteness hanging over hard baked yellow as far as ... the shimmering light allows ... black spat from the side, leaping away, falling like tiny teardrops ... crouched in yellow clouds, caked on grey and green ... black snouts pointing upwards into brightest blue ... radial exploding in discs of white light again ... hands dipped and fumbling into yellow, shaking, spilling, the entire picture shaking and the heat rising and white rolling clouds kicked up, swirling ... this constant cloak of heat haze swimming ... red dot in a black circle ... flower of dust ... black plumes ... bright green disc ... orange and red ball ... red white and blue fluttering against pale blue ... halos of light ... beams of light sweeping .... blue ink on fingers and necks ... orange through a disc .... pale amber eyes ... fields of nodding pink ... pitch black sky pinpricked by white dots ... the same dots that follow red tailed shooting trails ... deep purple velvet ... line of grey squares ... a line of slow moving grey squares in the distance framed in shimmering heat haze small at first, then growing larger, these grey squares ... blank amber eyes ... white teeth smiling ... then not smiling ... huddled together and the stars are dead ... all the stars have died by the time the light hits your eyes ... by the time the light hits the back of your eyes, all the stars are dead ...

PART TWO

SEPARATION AND CARE UNIT
CELL 1/005
12.11 A.M.

There was snow for a long time. It seemed to go on for weeks. Seemed like weeks, looking back. Could have been days, I suppose. But there were periods when it was just relentless. Snowed and snowed and snowed. It blurred everything. I didn't mind. It made the streets quiet on a night. Quiet as in nobody around, I mean. It made the streets emptier, is what I should have said. Emptier. Yeah. The sound of emptiness. That was my soundtrack to those early snowbound days and weeks. The minutes and the hours and the days and nights of banked up blank white. The everlasting seconds. I just wandered around outside, in the semi-dark, the streets all deadened. The houses were glowing black-orange coals embedded in the white. Lights of the living, burning in frosted windows. I dipped in and out, but I couldn't stand it bud. Everywhere I stopped to look, it was just an unending horror show. Theatre of the macabre. People in armchairs snoring with their mouths wide open. Sat scraping food off their laps in front of the television. Gawping at computer screens and phones. Reading newspapers with nothing in them. Brushing their filthy teeth. Sat shitting on toilets. Staring into space. Picking at their feet. Scratching themselves like monkeys. I just felt utterly dislocated. Marginalized. Even amongst the occasional bursts of drama, I just felt helplessly on the edges.

Bizarre things, I've seen, bud. Mute plays enacted before me. A man coming in from the pub drunk and snatching handfuls of clothes from his wardrobe, pulling them off the coat hangers and out of the drawers and then carrying them all downstairs and setting them alight in the back garden. A woman getting down on all fours to talk to her dog in her back kitchen at three in the afternoon. Not a crazy woman or a street dweller either, a seemingly normal well dressed middle-aged middle class woman pretending to be a dog. Madness. A man conducting an orchestra in his bath, sat there splashing away, pointing his finger at imaginary musicians. Swinging his arms about in the bath, he was, flinging up water to the invisible music.

I positioned myself in his line of vision and went through the entire orchestra, acted it all out in my mind's eye. The frantic sawing of the elbow at hip and chin for the string section. Fingers buttoning the air in front of my mouth for the brass. I knew what he was doing even though I couldn't hear the music. I'd seen how it worked on the television. I knew what an orchestra was, and I was a one-man orchestra in my head. Banging those big kettledrums. Splashing the cymbals. Imagined I was each of them in turn, I did, without moving a muscle. I still couldn't conceive of having any limbs. I looked down at nothing as I looked around at everything. I was an absence. But I must have remembered music, looking back. I must have. I knew all the actions.

In a way, it was easier having no physical presence. No limbs, I mean. I saw a picture on an Internet page once, a man who was just a head. The Caterpillar Man, I think he was called. Mr Caterpillar. He had a bald head and moustache and he looked reasonably relaxed about things. I think he was smoking a cigarette. A cigarette that someone had jammed in his mouth, I assume, just before the camera clicked. Compared to him, my existence was a gift from the gods. Imagine the day-to-day frustration of being that guy. Squirming about from pillar to post, waiting for someone to light your smoke or feed you a scrap of food. But at least he had his name in a book, or on a computer screen or whatever you want to call it, Mr Caterpillar Man, with his moustache and cigarette and his little half formed tubular trunk of a body. He was only fifty percent there, but at least he had an entry logged. Was seen to exist. Me, I was everywhere and nowhere, bud. I could bear witness to anything and anyone. But without a scrap of recognition, what's the point?

Humans held little to enthral me, to be honest. Once you've seen them fuck and fight and feed and scream and claw at their bits and hammer on their keyboards and stumble about their days crashing into each other like dodgem cars navigated by pissed up chimpanzees, once I got used to their strange habits and formations, there was no real appeal. I suppose I was rather a sulky, uncommunicative child, if truth be told. No good at making friends. Having no audio didn't help, to be fair. A constant silent movie with no subtitles. I'm not much of a people watcher, if the truth be known. Body language only gets you so far. I could read a mood on a face, see the switches of emotion and intent, could anticipate a sudden smile or darkening mood, but it was ultimately frustrating. I didn't know what any of it meant. How was I supposed to behave or what I was supposed to believe? How could I know the way to live, having no prior knowledge or instruction manual and operating on limited functions? It was like watching a play through a theatre window, banging on the glass and the actors aren't hearing you. I couldn't even bang on the fucking glass. What I would have given for subtitles. The man in the bath with the invisible orchestra, he was a rare treat in an otherwise dumb and baffling display.

Windows. I spent a fair amount of time gazing into windows. They changed the Oxfam display on the High Street every couple of weeks or so. A different dress on the dummy, a new stack of second hand paperbacks. New ways to tempt people inside. In stark contrast, I remained the same – conspicuous by my absence. Absolutely no change there. I'd position myself in front of the glass and kid myself that I could see some faint trace, an outline, maybe, the suggestion of a shadow. I tried to imagine the space I would fill. Imagined the faces of passers by who had appealed to me for whatever reason, whose features I had filed away for future reference. Small details that loomed large. I was grasping for significance. I started to convince myself at one point, later, that I had been attracted to Gemma because of the stripe in her hair. I was into signals to begin with, you see. Signs and signals. Mainly because I was learning to read, I suppose. Signifiers. But passers by, what made them stand out to me, I think, were the qualities that I wished for myself. Physical qualities, I mean. I had no way of imagining myself so I must have been looking for things I found attractive. Mutual recognition. Like in here, all the grafters and all the lifers and all the bag heads hang around together, yes? All the scousers and the mancs and the north London firms and south London firms and the postcodes and all the rest of it. Am I right? It's the same everywhere, isn't it? Plumage, bud. Birds of a feather.

I must say, I imagined myself taller than I turned out to be. Fancied myself as a big strapping chap, I did. Towering. Heroic. I'll fill this window one day, this charity shop window, that's what I thought. What I used to think. I'll block everything out behind me and cast a shadow the width of the street. Put everything in the shade. Cause a total eclipse of the city. That's what I used to think. What I hoped for, anyway.

The city, yes. There was a city centre, but I soon tired of that. Well, it looked like a city centre. Looked like the hub of things. Big wide chunks of glass and steel and concrete that towered above me and everyone else. I spent a fair few nights in the city centre. You get a different kind of tedium there. Not so much domestic as commercial, I suppose. Places where people went to work, to make money. Keeping the ball rolling. I used to spend a lot of time at social functions. People eating and drinking, Christ yes, the amount of time people spend throwing stuff down their necks. People in suits and ties and expensive dresses and coats. The shiny ones, I used to call them. Important people doing important things in big, important buildings. Not like the people at the edges. Movers and shakers, I suppose. I found them to be either extremely attractive or extremely ugly. This is just going off looks, you understand, physical appearance. Or maybe it was more than looks. I don't know. It's all I had to go on at the time. Beautiful people, some of them were, the most attractive I'd ever seen. Hair and clothes and jewellery. They seemed to radiate some kind of golden aura. Money, bud, and the confidence it brings.

I remember seeing a huge pile of money on someone's kitchen table once. I wandered through a back extension of a house somewhere beyond the park and there were half a dozen blokes sat round a room with a big rectangular slab of notes on a kitchen table. They were counting it all out and stacking it up into tight blocks of purple and brown and red. Maybe Beaumont was among them. I don't remember seeing him. I think he was still in prison at that point. Anyway, I didn't know where it was from or what it meant, but I would hazard a guess that it wasn't a local Bob a Job collection. Tell you bud, if the police could mobilize a ghost division, they'd crack crime within a fortnight. Nationwide swoops in the dead of night. No need for a battering ram.

But the city, yeah. Non stop. In certain places there was always light. I suppose that's what I craved, really. Like a moth to a flame. I wandered through the full-length glass of offices and shops and private parties and headed towards the lights. The works parties, the functions, the clubs, the late night drinking dens. The nightclubs. The lights throbbing behind the bars and bouncing off the mirrors. Ultra violet toilets and corridors. The nocturnal scene. All those people you'd meet in the shadows of late night licensed premises. I put my stint it. I watched the young and the old do their thing, all over the city.

So, yeah. Getting my bearings. The city was in one direction and I moved around there for a while. Night times, mainly. I went to the top of the tallest building I could find and watched everything go on and on. Rooftops and buildings and streets and roads with cars and lights and non-stop movement. It was a big city I'd landed in. I understood that. And I knew the answer would be somewhere down there, down among the buildings and people. But I didn't have the energy at first. Or any idea of where to start. I just latched onto people and followed them. I used to follow the night time people around. The drunks and the speed freaks and the homeless and the prostitutes. Criminals. People like you, bud. I mean, no offence, I don't know what you're in for, but I'd wager you didn't ply your trade during daylight hours. Am I right? Perfect cover for those not wanting to be seen. I watched a team of young lads burgle a big office once. Watched them disable the alarm system and spray foam over the CCTV and unpick a window and then they were in, like a swarm of ants all over this office block. Electrical stuff, mainly, computers and laptops and telephones. It was quite amusing. They all had dark clothing and balaclavas and gloves, ducking out of the way of the windows and the passing lights. At one point a police car crawled past and they all threw themselves on the floor, crouched behind desks and drawers, frozen still like shadows. And me just stood there among them all, watching, the useless witness.

Prostitutes as well. I wandered into a brothel one night. That was an eye opener. A room full of women sat in their underwear, smoking and watching TV. I didn't realise what was occurring at first. Then the men started appearing and sloping off into the various rooms. Christ, bud, the things I saw in there. The things people pay for. Geezers tied up, whipped, trampled on, things stuck up their jacksies. Seriously bud, if I ever come back again I want to be a woman. They hold all the aces, I'm telling you. Men, they either want to destroy everything in sight or debase themselves for money. I had two or three nights in there and that was enough for me. I didn't understand it. Even if my sexual parts would have been working at that point, I could see there was nothing in the way of joy to be found in that sorry set up. I remember one morning after a night of sordid mayhem when the last of these jokers took their leave and all the girls were fast asleep in the living room, the TV still burning away in the corner. The sun came up and slanted into the room and they were all huddled up together on the sofa and it made me feel so sad and helpless seeing them there like that, with their bare legs and arms sticking out from under the blankets like they were, what, like some kid's broken and discarded dolls.

That was it for me and the city. I sacked it off. Went back home and set off again the other way. The route that led to the countryside. You're only a short scoot from the edges of the greenery if you go the other way from my street. If you follow the bank of the river. Watch the city dwindle till there are no more houses, just garages and lock-ups and warehouses and industrial estates and then fields and scrubland and the occasional building. There was an airbase, out there in the countryside. If I set off early and kept going I could be there before the sun got high. I liked it there, that old airbase. Abandoned, it was. Disused. I found it one morning on one of my first rural missions. I followed the river all the way out of the city and some way into the fields. That's how I discovered it. I saw it on the horizon. It looked like a small village from a distance, dark low rectangles clustered together. I could see masts on the buildings. I was surprised and actually somewhat relieved when I got there and realised it wasn't a village and there were no people, just what looked like roads overgrown with grass and empty concrete buildings. The city had been hanging heavy on me, bud, believe. All those bags of flesh bumping into each other. But the airbase. Things had soared there, once upon a time. The roads weren't actual roads, they were runways. I spent a fair few days and nights around that airbase when the snow was at it's heaviest. It was great there. My private kingdom. The light and the space and the wide sky around me. No cars or people. Just the occasional bird passing overhead.

I wish I could have taken off, Mr Listener. Flown away from the roaring fucking silence in my head. That airbase was perfect. The place had been abandoned years ago, it would seem. I liked it around there. It looked silent, so I didn't feel so handicapped. There was nothing to listen to. I could see that. So that's where I did most of my thinking, stood looking out into a blank swirl across fields of white.

I used to suffer terribly from daydreams. Usually when I stayed still for too long. This was the problem. Thing is, I never got tired so I never slept. Ghosts don't sleep. And that's not good for you. Your brain needs to turn your eyes off occasionally or too much floods in. Too much information. If the sign of a Shakespearean thinker is the ability to hold two opposing ideas in the mind at the same time, then I was the entire cast of Hamlet, Romeo and Juliet and As You Fucking Like It Or Lump It, bud. There was no respite, is what I'm trying to say. All I had was my headlamps and a broken Sat Nav machine that wanted to go everywhere at once. That's why I liked it out in the fields. Fewer options. Blank canvases of white and then grey and then green and then back to white again with each fresh snowfall.

I had to absorb a lot in a short space of time. No rest. So I used to fall into daydreams. I'd find myself paused somewhere, away from people, away from criminals and nightclubs and prostitutes and the wandering souls of the city at night and I'd drift off. The world in front of me would disappear and I'd find myself gazing into an imaginary distance. Like a radio slipping off the dial and the snow of static obscuring every living trace. Floating off into the white. Slow forming pictures. Just images at first, but when I got my hearing back and then everything else, it all started to congeal and fix itself in my mind. What brought me here. What I was. What I'd actually done. And then, once I had that knowledge, I couldn't fucking bear to be on my own, and that airbase was the last place I wanted to be. But I always found myself going back. And it was good while it lasted. There was peace out there.

Anyway, listen, right, before we get into all the self-confession drama, let's have some cold hard facts, shall we? For a start, around ten percent of the prison population are just like me. Share my condition, if you like.

A minority, granted, but right minded people would argue that it's ten percent too many. But the fact still stands. Eight thousand of us safely locked away from the unsuspecting public. And I'll tell you something else, bud – those numbers are only going to get higher. It's a sick world out there and it's producing more and more of my kind. It's a false idol factory and the production line will never stop. My brethren are increasing as we speak. Well, as I speak and you listen. Here's another fun fact for you: thirty percent of people in places like this can't read or write. Not me though. You can't include me in that statistic. Whatever else I may be, I'm no dimwit. I went to university. I've had training. English as a foreign language. Look, learn and listen, bud. All achieved simply by paying close attention. I've got June to thank for that. She was the one who set me on my way. She was the one who switched my antennae on. Tuned me in, so to speak.

You see, what I discovered was this: animals and tiny children aside, only a ghost can see another ghost. That's one of the rules. The average flesh and blood citizen might catch the occasional flash if they're lucky, the odd fleeting glimpse across the veil, but for full-on eyeball contact, you need both parties to be travelling on the same wavelength. Literally, I mean. You see, it's like this Mr Listener; the non-physical world vibrates at a faster rate. Much faster than you lead footed fools. Faster than the speed of light, the speed of sound, silence or the dark. No offence bud, but you fully fledged humans are weighed down by the unbearable tedium of your own existence. You've lapped up too much TV and stared at too many pointless messages. Your heads are stuffed with a million and one items of useless information and endless lists of pointless pre-occupation. Even in these non-stop fun palaces, where time moves like a funeral procession and a missing ping-pong ball is a major source of drama, there are still enough distractions to keep you blind to the other world around you. If you want to go ghost spotting my advice to you would be to stop in your pad and stare at the wall for a few years.

Because like attracts like, bud, in the afterlife as well as this one. And June was the first one I came across who properly engaged. Most ghosts are troubled souls, too wrapped up in their own problems to reach out to another fellow drifter. But June was different. She was at ease with herself and her place in this world. I was lucky to meet her. Very lucky indeed . And it came just at the right time for me as well, because I hadn't seen sight of Gemma or the boys since the swimming pool and I was starting to get a bit numb and helpless with it all. Days and nights spent floating about on the margins without a further clue or purpose. Got to be a bit too much, if I'm honest. The novelty was wearing off. There are only so many corners you can inhabit before you start to feel like a hapless dunce.

I'd become gradually aware of kindred spirits on my various manoeuvres through town. I'd realized the occasional pair of eyes were looking at me; not *through* me like most of the passing throng, but actually at me; the odd character drifting by in my peripheries, casting a keening glance in my direction. Recognition. Everyone craves a bit of that every now and again, eh? Don't you agree? The odd tingle that you are not alone, that brief spark of connection? Frankenstein's monster fizzing into life.

So, yeah, I started to notice the odd occasion when a glance would linger and eyes would lock, just for a brief moment or two. Occasionally I would work up the nerve to approach and engage, but they always drifted off before I could gather my wits and fully focus my energy. I mean, I didn't know they were ghosts at that point. I thought they were just normal people who could maybe somehow see me. Thought I was maybe coming into focus. Fact of the matter is, despite all the strong body of evidence I still wasn't totally convinced by the ghost theory. There was still a small part of me clinging on to the idea of a normal existence. That I was just a marginal character in all of this mad dance, some sort of wallflower who was getting the cold shoulder purely on account of my shy and retiring manner. What I mean is, I suppose wasn't entirely ready to accept that I was dead. Or had been dead. Much like yourself, I suppose. You must be sat there thinking this guy's insane. I don't blame you, bud. I don't blame you at all.

Listen, you'd be astonished at how many ghosts there are just floating around the streets of a day and night. There's dozens of dead people jamming up the pavements, and I'd just been flying straight past them, oblivious. Most of them are lost in their own private little worlds, just like I was at first. But they're there, bud, trust me. The fella nursing his drink at the end of the bar in a half-empty pub at lunchtime. The woman sat on her lonesome in the supermarket café. I'd built up enough confidence to try to make myself known. I'd spy a fellow kindred spirit and float up to them and will them to look at me, recognize me. Apart from the desperate or the disturbed, all I ever usually got was a look of blank eyed indifference. Usually they wouldn't make eye contact or acknowledge me in any way at all. Not me, nor the living. In fact, I'm convinced most of them are completely unaware of any kind of world around them at all, real or otherwise.

But they're there. Oh they are there bud. You'll find them in most public places, unnoticed, tucked away in a corner usually. Hovering on the margins. And that's just the streets. Pass through an average row of dwelling places and there are ghosts at every turn; in the bedrooms and bathrooms, hanging about on the landings or the stairways. Some of them actively engage. Some of them can even get a bit moody if you float into their personal space. I saw more and more of them after I met June. I wandered through this back kitchen one day on my way to somewhere and this old geezer was stood behind this woman as she stood stirring a saucepan on the hob. He had his arms wrapped around her waist, his head on her shoulder. I'd obviously interrupted an intimate moment, because as soon as he saw me he flipped his lid. "This is my house!" he shouted. Loud and clear, he was: "Get out of my fucking house!" And he removed himself from around this woman, his wife, I presume, and he came flying after me, shooing me out of the kitchen and the yard, out into the back alleyway. Some people can be very territorial, even more so after they've popped off, in some cases. Others were a bit friendlier, but they were usually the needy ones, those who came with tear stained faces seeking salvation or explanation. And I could offer neither.

There was one young lad who used to hang about one of the other bombed out houses down my street; junkie he was, he'd OD'd one night and couldn't work out what was going on, the poor bastard. Not the brightest of lads, unfortunately. He used to follow me down the street asking me if I knew where his Mum was. I could hear him wailing away and wanted to offer some consolation, some form of moral support, I suppose, but I still couldn't speak at this point. I tried to let him into my thoughts but he either couldn't hear me or he chose not to listen. I spent a couple of nights round his house, just being near him as he sobbed and moaned and carried on, but it all got a bit much. Depressing. I had my own state of confusion to deal with and I had no answers for him, only questions of my own. I had to blank him in the end. June had given me a lift, and this guy was in danger of wrecking my vibe.

I didn't feel too clever about this, but I ended up blanking most of the other ghosts I came across as well, to be fair. It's not the tight knit community you might imagine. No social nights down the ethereal boozer, I'm afraid to report. Most of the spirits still drifting about are a bit vacant and distant. June was the only one I met who seemed to have some semblance of common sense or capacity to communicate in a meaningful way. The rest were all too wrapped up in their own little dramas. Their own self-sufficient illusions. But meeting Grandma June was good, because I started to see the neighbourhood in terms of the living and the spectral, even if none of the buggers could provide any help or answers to my own good self.

But this one evening I was stood beside the bench at the top of the hill in the park and the sky was just beginning to turn purple at the edges and the lights in the houses at the bottom of the hill were snapping on one by one and the headlights on the dual carriage in the far distance were popping up like electric yellow flowers. The natural light fading and replaced by the false. I was stood there musing on this and that, considering the events of the last few days, the indifferent turning of the universe and life and death in general, when I became aware of a woman stood beside me. Her lips were moving and I could detect that familiar muffled vibration in the air between us, that subdued droning that indicated human speech. At first I thought she was just muttering away to herself, like so many others do when they think no-one's listening. People talk to themselves all the time, more than you'd think, so I wasn't really paying that much attention. But I gradually realized from the frequent sidelong glances that she was actually addressing me. Speaking to me.

She was a pleasant looking woman; I'd say early to late fifties, short neat greying hair and glasses, nicely dressed. Homely looking. I could imagine her stood on a school stage leading an assembly full of primary school children in a rousing hymn. She looked a long way from dead; in fact she looked very well preserved and healthy. Only the creases around her mouth and the loose folds of skin on the back of her hands gave away her age. She had a twinkle about her though. A genuine warmth. She was like a favourite aunty who would come around at Christmas time with an armful of presents and a delicious sense of naughty fun. The type who'd pinch your cheeks and ruffle your hair before slipping you a quid or two. And she was looking directly at me. Beaming in. Making contact. I could feel her eyes lock onto me. I suddenly realized she could see me, and she smiled, amused at my startled acknowledgement.

You're not on your own, you know, despite what you might think.

There they were, the first clear and fully formed human words I'd heard since I was born. Only I didn't *hear* them so much as *know* them. They echoed somewhere inside of me like they were my own thoughts, but not my own thoughts, no, gifted to me from someone else. Thoughts that arrived without the effort of thinking. Message received, loud and clear. I felt that tug again, that sudden wrench at the centre of somewhere. A sudden hole opening up where an ache should be. She was smiling at me, these pale blue eyes like magnified birds eggs behind the lens of her glasses.

Those words again: You're not alone, sweetheart. You can talk to me. I'm June. Like the month of the year. You've not been here long have you? What's your name?

I just looked at her, incredulous.

Do you know your own name yet? she asked. Or the name you used to have, I mean?

The voice was a soft burr and the words felt calm and gentle, like she was laying a baby to rest in a cot. I tried to speak, to answer her. I couldn't do it, couldn't form the words. I had never tried to speak since that first day in the garage. It took too much out of me and anyway, I didn't think I could do it. The only voice I had was the one buried deep within me, the one I couldn't yet find.

Do you know who you are? she asked.

I didn't, of course, and revealed as much inside. She seemed to be able to hear me because then she said: That's OK. Don't worry sweetheart. It's confusing, I know. But it will become clear, trust me. It will all come clear in time.

Her words swelled within me and it was as though everything she said was in anticipation of my half-formed thoughts, all of my doubts and fears and questions met halfway. It felt amazing, actually. I would have cried if I could, but new-borns don't cry. Not like you lot, shrieking your lungs out the minute you make an entrance.

You can see me, I thought.

Yes, I can see you, she said. And I can see that you're lost. You feel lost, don't you?

Yes, my thoughts agreed, I feel lost, utterly lost and completely alone.

Don't worry, she said, we all feel lost at first. But you'll soon get the hang of it. Just go with the flow. It's never like it was before, but you soon get used to it.

Before?

Yes. When you were alive.

She looked at me. Those pale blue eyes, steady as time. They held me and saw me and there was nothing in them but love. These were eyes that would not lie.

So I asked her the million dollar question: Am I right in thinking that I'm a ghost?

Well, yes, she said, that's the usual name for it.

So I'm dead?

Laughter, but gentle and kind, no hint of mockery.

No, sweetheart. You used to be dead. Now you're this.

What happens after this?

I don't know. Sleep, I would imagine. Rest. I used to get so tired when I was here last. I don't think I could keep up with that little monkey now. She's walking now, you know.

She pointed to the playground at the foot of the hill. A woman slowly turning a roundabout, a small child in a pink quilted bodysuit clinging to the bars.

Sydney, she's called. After her Granddad. I thought it was silly, giving her a boy's name. But I'm fond of it now. She's eighteen months last week. Should see her go now. No stopping her.

Does she know you're here?

Sydney? Yes I think she does sometimes. She never knew me. She's only ever seen me in photographs. I slipped away before she was born, bless her.

What about your daughter?

A sigh.

I don't know. Sometimes I think she does. I don't know whether that brings her any comfort. I try and keep my distance. I go and kiss Sydney night-night every bedtime but I usually leave after she's fallen asleep. I don't want to upset anybody. Not again.

I didn't know what she meant by that. I didn't ask her. I just watched this kid revolving on the roundabout. So small and fragile. Hands gripping the bars above her. She looked like a tiny pink jelly baby.

How did you find out? I asked her. Who you were, I mean?

Oh I knew from the off, she said. From the minute I was born. I fell asleep in my armchair and got up the next day. I was in my own home, you see.

Your own home. That sounds good.

June looked at me.

Oh, you poor dear. Have you not been home? Where you from, then?

I don't know. I woke up in a house. I just spent the first day wandering about in a daze. Like I'd been knocked out. I couldn't work out what had happened. When I came back they were taking the body away.

Who was, sweetheart?

The police. The ambulance, I mean.

From your house?

Not my house. It's just a house. Nobody lives there.

And you don't know this place? This house?

No, I said.

I thought about it.

But here's the thing, I told her: I didn't see a body when I woke up.

She shook her head.

That does seem odd, she said. I saw myself sat in the chair, she told me. My mouth had fallen open and my false teeth were hanging out. Terrible. So undignified. I kept waiting for one of the ambulance men to slot them back in, but they kept me lolling there like a pie-can until this young girl took pity on me and sorted me out.

She looked at me closely.

Do you really not know who you are?

No idea whatsoever.

When were you born?

Born? I didn't know what she meant.

When did you find yourself in this house?

Oh ... not long ago.

Days? Weeks?

I didn't know. I tried to think about it. I tried to count the days and nights. There had been a fair few. They all seemed to bleed into each other.

I don't know, I said. A few weeks, I think.

Well if I was you, she said, I'd go to the morgue and have a look.

I don't where the morgue is, I said.

Then something else occurred to me.

What do I look like?

She tilted her head, smiled. Well, you wouldn't win any beauty contests, put it that way. But you've got an open enough face. A decency about you. I could tell that from the off. I wouldn't have spoken to you otherwise.

Describe me?

Her eyes considered me, up and down. Well I'm useless at ages, but you're only a young chap. I'd put you at about late twenties. Maybe a touch older. You've got nice brown eyes, kind eyes, and dark brown hair hanging down to your chin. And you could do with a good wash and a shave, if you'll forgive me for saying so.

What am I wearing?

Just a normal black overcoat and a pair of trousers. Would have been a smart jacket at one time, that. But they'll have stripped you naked and laid you out on the slab by now.

She looked at me askance: Tell you who you have got he look of, though. That revolutionary chap. Him who the students used to have on their wall. What was his name? Yes, that's him: Che Guevara.

I considered this for a moment. The name sounded familiar but I wasn't entirely sure who she meant. Couldn't match a face.

Where's the morgue, I asked her.

Near St Cuthbert's, she said. Round the back.

She must have seen the look of confusion on my face.

The hospital, she said. On Alliance Road.

I don't know where that is, I said. I don't know where anything is. I'm not from round here, I don't think. I don't seem to know anywhere.

Sudden pity creased her eyes.

Oh, you poor boy, she said. Must be awful for you.

She gave me directions. Told me things to look out for. Landmarks and routes. Mapped it all out for me.

Go down there sweetheart, she said, see what you can find out.

So that's what I did. I said thank you in my mind and I floated off to find my dead body.

Ever been in a morgue? I wouldn't recommend it as a fun place to hang out. I would imagine they're not exactly vestibules of joy at the best of times, but the one round the back of St Cuthbert's makes Dracula's crypt look like the cocktail lounge in a five star Acapulco hotel. Dingy, bud. Depressing. Frozen faces under artificial light. Like the meat counter at Asda. It's all so bloody impersonal, that death business. That's the worst part about it. Zipped up in a bag. I didn't hang about in there for too long I can assure you. Miserable bleeding place it was. Who wants to knock about with a bunch of stiffs? I hung around for a couple of days and saw every body rolled in and out and prodded about and none of them answered the description offered by my new pal Grandma June. If her appraisal of my facial features was correct then I wasn't in any of those chilled compartments. No revolutionary icons on ice down there, bud. I tried following the full process, from the slab to the grave, following the bodies as they were shipped to the parlours, their relatives kissing their poor made up faces and then down to their final resting place. Stood with weeping families around open holes in the ground or grim faced rows before scarlet coloured curtains. Watched the dancing flames. Scoured the chiselled names on headstones for any hint of familiarity after everyone had gone to the pub or former family home. Nothing. Just names and numbers, none of which meant a thing to me. I stuck that out for a few days, going back and forth, but I sacked it off when they brought the body of a child in one day. Road accident, it looked like. A little girl. I didn't want to be anywhere near that.

I went back to the park every day, looking for June. As you can imagine, I had a million and one questions burning away inside of me. No joy though. After a while I gave up. But meeting her had been good for my personal progress. I raised myself out of the downcast groove I'd got myself stuck in and started paying more active attention to the wider world. No point in moping about. I had to seize the day, as it were. And the night. The endless meandering days and nights. So I lifted my head up out of my self-obsessed mire and tried to interact with the more immediate environment. Everything was whirling around me, and I knew I had to try and leap on, get a foothold somehow.

I had to get a routine together. A man without a routine is just a child's balloon drifting on the wind and bouncing among the treetops. I had to guard against drifting. I needed some gravity, some weight, something to tie me down to planet Earth. So most mornings found me in the Internet café waiting for the man to come and turn the machines on, waiting for the first customer to fire in their credit and get the screen burning. Student's mainly. That suited me just fine. I was a student myself. I stayed in the Internet café for the better part of the day, flitting from screen to screen, trying to soak as much info up as possible. Facebook, that cropped up a lot. Facebook and Twitter. People talking to themselves. What's happening? I like this. Do you like this? I am eating a sandwich. Today my socks are blue. Ha ha ha, here's a picture of a cat that looks like Hitler. Gripping stuff, eh? I don't know how long you've been in here, but believe me bud, you're not missing out on anything. Trivia, most of it. Well, it was to me, anyway. Bewildering. At first I thought it was people logging in to the state, registering for civic duty. A sort of legal requirement, if you will. It took me a while to realise they were just recording the mundane moment for everlasting posterity.

Then, when the numbers dwindled in the café I would wander outside and pick somebody at random and follow them. Shadow them back to their home or place of work. Mornings were theory, afternoons and evenings were practical. Hands-on experience in human behaviour. And when I got bored or horrified or frustrated or envious of what was on display, I took off, drifted far and city-wide. And when the city got too much I headed for the wide-open spaces. To the air base. Ground zero. Miles and miles of sweet neglected nothing.

That had been my daily routine.

June had raised my awareness in one other major way, too: my hearing was coming back. The mush of the everyday noise around me was starting to separate into distinct and separate parts. Slowly leaking into me. It happened gradually, but I started to definitely notice. I'd hear the occasional stab of sound through the fog, the odd blast of clarity from a passing car or gathered crowd. Startled me, it did. I'd pass people on the street, real people, their phones clamped to their ears, get their half of the conversation as I drifted by, just snatches really, unintelligible half the time, but definitely there, like a long wave radio tuning in and out. Garbled messages. It was frustrating. But the final breakthrough happened one morning. I remember it distinctly.

I'm standing in the back garden watching the sun come up and I gradually become aware of the birds in the trees above me. Become aware that I can hear them, I mean. The chirrups and trills and whistles, all the different calls, back and forth. Chattering away they were. And I could pick them all out as clear as day, each individual song. It went on and on and didn't fade away. It was there. It was constant. I stayed there for a happy eternity, listening to this cheerful cacophony in the branches above my head, the massed chorus swelling from the trees, each bird's call stepping forward like separate instruments from an orchestra. Then I become aware of all the other sounds of the daybreak. I can hear the wind moving through the grass and the branches. A dog barking from further down the street. A siren shrieking somewhere in the distance. It was like emerging from the bottom of a swimming pool, the eardrums finally popping.

I shot straight back through the house and out onto the street. There was a dustcart crawling along further down, the slow grinding rumble of the engine and the clatter of the bins as they were tipped up onto the hydraulic lift, the lads shouting and laughing to each other. Human voices. I could hear them! I could hear the actual words streaming from their lips. No more Charlie Brown teacher droning away from some vague place beyond me, no more mushy-mouthed murmur, no blurred static or radio interference, but actual human words, crystal clear, just like the ones June planted inside of me, but these words were on the outside, there they were, loud and clear.

I flew up the street to the main road and the world came flooding in. Traffic and footsteps and shop shutters rattling upwards. There was a radio on in the garage. Music! And do you know what, Mr Listener, I recognized the song straight away: Live Forever. You know that one? Yeah? You know which one I mean? Oasis? It was astonishing. It was only the second proper surge of elation I had felt since being born into this cold and unfamiliar world. I stood there in that garage and drank it in, that music, that yearning voice, that beautiful noise. Electric guitars and drums. Every single note flooded through me and lit up my very essence. You and I are gonna live forever. It built up and it built up and when it kicked into that chorus, I swear I could almost feel the tears streaming down my face.

Gave me a massive boost, getting my hearing back. And I could hear absolutely everything, bud. I could tune into all the stations of the human race. A sneeze in a bedroom two streets away. The rasp of a cat's tongue licking its paws on a rooftop. A raindrop plopping into a puddle. All in glorious three-dimensional stereophonic surround sound. It was all a bit much at first. Imagine it, living at the bottom of the deep blue sea for weeks on end and then all of a sudden, boom, your head breaks the waves and there's seagulls wheeling around your head, screaming into your face. The city, bud. Too much, sometimes, once the novelty wore off. I used to float up to the heath to get away from the cacophony of the city. Spent a few days and nights with the hooting of the owls and the wind in the treetops. The occasional jogger and their hissing, clicking iPods. I laid low in the greenery until the volume got adjusted and everything panned out to an acceptable level. It was like the dinosaurs and the flying umbrellas all over again, but the aural equivalent. Eventually it all calmed down. I mean, I could still hear a pin drop at a hundred paces but at least it didn't go off like a mortar shell.

So this was a big thing for me. The noise. One small step for man, but a major leap for Alistair Kingdom. Even though I still had no way of influencing my surroundings I was no longer limited to just my headlamps. I could hear the words the mouths were forming. Extra source of information. Vital, bud. Gathering intelligence. You're nothing without it. So I got back on the mission with renewed vigour. I hit the streets with my new antennae finely tuned. I was no longer a hapless bystander gawping at the human race. I had another weapon in the armoury. I became a dedicated eavesdropper.

First port of call for me and my new radar was the morgue. I knew my previous vehicle wasn't down there, but I was hoping some of the living might mention the handsome Che Guevara lookalike that had been scraped off the floor in the derelict house. But no, no such luck. Morose bunch of bastards down there. The main two operatives were this drippy young lad with a boy band haircut and an embittered old alkie complete with pockmarked face and trembling hands. They hardly used to say two words to each other unless it was work related: fetch me this, go and get that, have you filled that paperwork out yet? Social chitchat was confined to football or last night's telly. I stuck it out for a couple of days down there, waiting to get a clue but apart from learning the processes of corpse allocation and pre-parlour preparation, it was all Coronation Street and Eastenders and Queens Park Rangers' chances of avoiding the drop. I soon realized I was wasting my precious time. Plus, it was a bit dispiriting, hanging around in a chamber full of death. Especially when they got the hacksaws out and started all that autopsy business. Ever seen the inner workings of a corpse? Not the most pleasant of views, it must be said. I mean, I'm desensitized, I know, but even a seasoned campaigner like my good self gets tired of blood and guts and handfuls of human spaghetti. After a while I sacked it off as another blind alley.

I started hanging around late night bars and nightclubs. Anywhere where they played music and the people gathered. The people in their desperate milling masses, tipping drinks down their necks and leaning into each other to talk above the music. I hung at the shoulder of every solitary drunk at the bar and every flirting couple touching toes under the tables, skulked round the edges of every pissed up stag and hen night as they fell around the dance floors. All those rows of shiny bottles behind the bars. Happy hour. Three for two. Jugs of fancy named cocktails and slammed down shots. Jesus, all that drinking. Pint after pint after pint. The weekends were the worst. The states people get themselves into.

But it fascinated me as well, watching this mad carnival unfolding every night, gaining momentum as the volume increased towards the weekend. People getting louder and louder, more hysterical. Even the music seemed to get louder. There was one bar I liked in particular, one place just off the main drag to the city centre. It was an older crowd, less hectic, less confrontational. The music was better too, not as relentlessly pummelling. And not just the same three records played over and over again. There was one particular song at that time, played round all the bars and clubs, it used to drive me potty. Tell me that you waaaaant meee-yeah, tell me that you neeeed meee-yeah. Over and over again. Endless. Every bar you drifted in and out of. Used to drive me outside to stand with the smokers. That's another thing that fascinated me, you humans with your human needs. Eating and sleeping and shitting and fucking I could understand all of that, but drinking and smoking? I could see it was cold still, outside, could see the breath freezing into clouds under the streetlights. People in their shirtsleeves and short skirts, bare flesh nipped and puckered by the chilly night and still they stood outside and sucked smoke into their lungs. Started fires in their bloodstreams then went back inside to pour more liquid on the flames. Slow form of suicide, that's what I thought. And you could see it in the faces of the people who went to that bar, that older bar. The aftermath of years of this. The thread marks on their parched grey faces, the sagging necks and swollen bellies. People propel themselves towards the grave, don't they? Drink and smoke and fight and fuck themselves senseless. They think they're living it up, don't they Mr Listener? Living the dream.

Do you know what I think? I think life is wasted, bud. Wasted on people. Because life is short, far too short to get obsessed by the physical. You see, what I've noticed as an impartial observer of you humans is the amount of time that gets spunked away. Literally, I mean. Because blokes are the worst by a heady distance. No sooner has the missus popped out to the shops and the door's shut behind them then bang, the husband is straight upstairs, quick as a flash the laptop's fired up and the trousers are down. Like frantic monkeys tugging away. Shocked me, the first time I saw it, I must admit. It was totally by accident as well. I was hanging about in this block of flats when I saw this fella running up the stairs with a black sports bag. He looked like he was trying to vacate himself from the streets to get shut of something.

So I swoops up to his flat only to find it wasn't drugs or two million quid in used foreign currency. It was a chicken. A dead one I mean, plucked and packaged and ready for cooking. He stuck it into the fridge and switched the kettle on, got the mugs and milk out. I lost interest at this point. Blanked him and stood looking out of the window, regarding the city below and all it's infinite options, all the unseen corners I could infest. All the lives I could attach myself to. I was trying to think of where to go next. I was still looking for myself at this point, you understand.

Anyway, I stood there daydreaming for I don't know how long, when I noticed he'd disappeared out of the kitchen. I wandered through into the next room, and there he was, sat at a desk in front of a laptop. At first, because of the angle I was at behind him, I thought he was writing something or tapping on a keyboard. Then I looked at the screen. A heap of writhing pink flesh. I noticed the fella's bare legs and his jeans in a puddle around his ankles, his hand going ten to the dozen. Well, what would you do if you caught a stranger in an intimate moment of self-interest? If you're anything like me you would stay and watch him toss himself off to completion. Like I told you, I had no sex drive or carnal interest in the proceedings. The act of masturbation, to me, was not much different to the act of yawning or pissing or scratching your knee.

But I felt a strange and fresh emotion when I watched this man jerk off. I felt a deep blue sadness at the centre of me. Watching his back arch and buck, his ape-man grunts and then the sudden string of pearls shot skyward. The way it utterly spent him and the sag of himself into the chair. It was like I shared his post-wank guilt, that hollow feeling of uselessness that seemed to flood his body. It hung in the room like a bad smell. Don't tell me you haven't felt it, bud. I've seen it in people's eyes. That sad rag doll slump and the brain clouded over with a vague sense of loss. Then the muttered curses as he realized he'd not brought any toilet roll for the post operation wipe-up, followed by the awkward penguin waddle to the bathroom.

I stood and watched the porn while he ran taps and flushed chains. A threesome. Six legs, six arms, various other permutations, all wrapped around each other in a sweaty stack of meat. I didn't feel a thing. It all just seemed a bit soulless. And, like I said, an utter waste of time.

Not that I made a habit of watching blokes wanking, you understand. But you'd be amazed at how often it happens, and not just in the holy sanctuary of the homestead, oh Christ no; in the broom cupboard at work, department store changing rooms, the toilets of moving trains. What an enormous waste of energy, that's what struck me. All the things in the natural and man made world to look at, to listen to and to touch and feel and smell and taste and embrace. And all you sad bastards want to do is stupefy yourselves with self-abuse.

Anyway, after a while I got bored with the pubs and clubs. The night-time scene. I started haunting the places where people gathered together during the day; tea breaks in the staff room of factories, the queues at the supermarket checkouts, the pubs and cafes and street corners were people stopped to chat. I slipped in and out of people's homes still, of course, but the odds of hearing anything useful there were a bit more remote. Most families don't really talk to each other, I found. It's either minor conflict or petty complaint in a lot of households. Or stuff that's so wrapped up in the family's personal day to day dynamics that its largely incomprehensible to the average nosey-parker outsider. I spent many a wasted day and night straining to pick some scrap of a clue from the general blah blah blah. They spoke of holidays and family and work and telly and the people they knew, their tedious minor losses and triumphs. All manner of trivia. But none of them seemed to be acquainted with dead blokes in derelict houses.

And I still couldn't find those bloody kids anywhere. Not in any schoolyard or back alley or shopping centre. And I looked everywhere and I listened everywhere, believe me bud. Not a trace.

After a while I started to realize I was casting my net too far. There was never a familiar face two days or nights in a row. So I decided to cease all the far-flung wandering and avoid the city centre or beyond, just keep to the tight little hub around my place of birth; the main street and the park and the neighbourhood around there. Think global, act local, that was my mantra. It's a big city, bud, and I was just getting lost, drifting off without a paddle. So I stuck around the immediate vicinity and kept to tight little patrols, frequent, exhaustive, round and round the square mile, where the local people where.

It paid off. I finally got lucky. I was hanging around in this pub tucked away at the end of the main road one afternoon when bang, there she was: the hefty stripe-haired girl I'd seen with the boys. The girl from the swimming baths. My Gemma. Couldn't believe it. The room seemed to shrink to a tunnel point with her at the end of it. She was among a noisy group sat at a table by the window. They were laughing and drinking. Seemed to be having a fine afternoon of it. Gemma was in full flow, telling a story. I glided up behind her and listened in:

... so we're all sat there in a circle like a right set of mugs and this woman, this group leader bird, she gets up and she says, OK, hands up who likes chocolate?

... you are fucking kidding me ...

... that is what she said, swear to God: hands up who likes chocolate ...

... ha ha ha ha ha ha ha ha!!! ...

... she taking the piss?...

... so nobody puts their hand up, right, so then, right, she says: hands up who likes bread ...

... *bread?* ...

... aye, bread is a killer, full of carbs ...

... yeah, but you can't not eat fucking *bread* ...

... hold on, hold on ... so, listen, right, still no-one's putting their hand up, all just sat there gawping at her like she's completely mental ... so she's like, OK, who likes chips? Who likes a glass of wine on a night?

... well that's you fucked innit ...

... ha ha ha ha ha ha ha!!! ...

... bread and alcohol, ach, they're the bad boys ...

... and *still* no-one's getting their hand in the air, all embarrassed to fuck, yeah? Obviously nobody knows each other and it's bad enough as it is, a room full of fatties, right, all wishing the ground would open up and swallow them ...

... and this is the first night?...

... the first meeting, yeah, everyone sat there not saying a dickie bird and she's doing her best to get everyone to join in, put everyone at their ease, know what I mean, like an ice breaker innit ...

... how much does a polar bear weigh? ...

... so then ... what? A polar bear? ...

... yeah ... how much do they weigh? ...

... fuck you on about silly bollocks ...

... nah, come on, how much does a polar bear weigh? ...

... no idea ...

... neither have I, but it breaks the ice don't it ...

... ha ha ha ha ha ha ha!!! ...

... oh Christ ...

... that is fucking *awful* Eric ...

... listen, right, *listen* ... so I sticks me hand up don't I, can't take the bleeding suspense any longer, all these fat birds looking at this woman like she's fucking doolally ..."

... was she fat? ...

... was *who* fat? ...

... the woman in charge, the group leader ...

... what's that got to do with it? ...

... well I wouldn't want fucking lecturing on my eating habits by some skinny bitch ...

... aye, but some people are naturally skinny, ken ...

... wish I fucking was, I only have to look in Greggs window and I put ten fucking pounds on ...

... ya cannae help ya metabolism ...

... so anyway, right, I sticks my hand up, I says, yes love, I like chocolate and chips and a glass of a wine on a night and all the rest of it ...

... just a glass? ...

... so she's dead grateful that someone's piped up, yeah, so she starts asking me questions, like how often do I have a drink ...

... thought this was Weight Watchers? ...

... how often do I have bread with a meal ...

... Jesus ...

... and *then*, right, *then* she says to me, she says, what's the most you've ever weighed ...

... bit personal innit ...

… that's what they're like, these cults …

… ach, it isnae a cult, Eric …

… so I tells her, straight, I says fifteen stone ten pounds …

…. is that how much you weigh? …

… nah, not now, that's the *most* I've weighed …

… how much do you weigh now then? …

… dinnae be so fucking rude Cookie …

… what?! How is that being rude? …

… so anyway, then she turns round to me and she says: what's the *least* you've ever weighed? …

… the least? …

… how is that being rude? …

… yeah … what's the least you've ever weighed … so I told her: six pounds three ounces …

… ha ha ha ha ha ha ha ha ha !!! …

The table erupts with laughter. My insides were laughing too. I was so fucking elated. Couldn't believe my luck. My stripe-haired saviour. She was the most beautiful person I'd ever put my gaze on. Those laughing eyes. So alive. She didn't care about being a big fat person, didn't care that the joke was on her. She didn't care about anything. She was free, bud. Do you understand what I'm getting at here? She was properly alive.

I sat at her elbow all afternoon, in the company of her and her friends, drinking in the noise and the music and the banter. They were all having a good drink. I was trying to work out the dynamics of the group, who was linked to who. They all seemed to know each other well enough, judging by the good-natured jibes and easy laughter. There was Gemma, then a much quieter dark haired girl with a soft Scottish accent and specs called Claire; an older bloke, Eric, looked to be in his late thirties or early forties; scruffy looking lump with silver-flecked hair and a tatty five day growth. Big stupid grin plastered across his face.

Yeah, Eric. I never liked that bastard from the minute I laid eyes on him. Too quick to take the piss and quick to join in with the laughter, but the eyes were never in accordance with the shape of the mouth. Con artist. Always playing to the crowd. Never a genuine word escaped those lips in my opinion. Anyway, forget him, I'll deal with that bastard later. There were a couple of other women, looked to be a bit older than Gemma and Claire, more Eric's age. At the time I reckoned that Eric was hooked up with Stacey, the rough looking blonde with the crazy pencilled-on eyebrows. The woman with the car alarm laugh I guessed to be her sister. They had the same mannerisms and similar sharp-faced features. I was wrong about that though, as it turned out. Stacey was actually Gemma's sister. And she wasn't hooked up with Eric either. Stacey had her own bastard to deal with. Someone much more abhorrent than Eric.

There were two other males of the species there. The boy with the pony tail and the heavily tattooed forearms who they all called Brett or Brettski, he spent most of the afternoon in a kind of stupefied silence, just sat there grinning at everyone and everything around him. The occasional hushed confab with Claire. They were obviously close buddies and confidantes. Who else? Oh yeah, Cookie, a jovial young bucko in a blue tracksuit top and baseball cap. He was alright, was Cookie, just a daft young lad really. Other people joined and moved away from the table at various points of the afternoon, but these were the core of the social circle, it would seem. It was all good-natured banter for the most part. They ripped the piss out of each other in the way that only close friends can. There was comradeship in the air.

It was a busy afternoon in the pub. Gemma kept getting up and feeding the jukebox. I watched her dancing back and forth, through the bodies, through the blinking and bleeping of the fruit machines and the babble of voices, the roaring laughter from the table; the easy grace that belied her size, that same sway of confidence that had pulled me into the ladies changing rooms on that first day. She put her songs on the jukebox and everyone sang along.

Me too. I sang along inside.

They drank all afternoon and into the early evening, until it began to darken outside when they agreed to carry on the party "back at the house". I trailed after them, out of the pub and into the mini-mart across the road where they bought bottles of wine and beer and bags of crisps and cigarettes and rolling papers, then through the side streets that led off the main road until we arrived at a small terraced house on a back street near the edges of the park: 37 Buckingham Street.

It was an obvious student place inside; all mismatched furniture and barely contained chaos; piles of books and magazines and clothes and CD's, two pushbikes in the kitchen, a jumble of footwear in the hallway. Dishes piled high on the draining board in the kitchen. It was scruffy but it wasn't an unspeakable dirty pit like some of those student houses can be. There was a modicum of domestic order imposed. It was obviously a stoner's gaff though. There were a pair of DJ decks set up in the corner and a poster on the wall of Michelangelo's "Creation Of Adam", which someone had daubed with a marker pen, a burning spliff being passed between the fingertips of the deity and his first earthbound creation. There were two TV's in the front room, one small portable on top of the other large set. The portable was turned on with the sound muted and they settled themselves down with some tunes on the stereo and the room gradually turned blue with smoke as they started to roll joints and slosh the wine and beer about. I left them to it and slipped away to check the place out, see if I could scout the bedrooms for more of a clue about the interpersonal relationships. And I wanted to see if the kids were there, those two boys. I thought if Gemma lived there then maybe the boys were there too.

There were three bedrooms and a converted loft space. Two of the rooms had photographs that revealed them to be Claire's and Gemma's. The other room was obviously a lads room, either Cookie or Brett's, and the loft I took to be Eric's, given the unkempt air of tatty abandon. No sign of any kiddies though. No toys or clothes or anything. All the beds were built for full size grown-ups. I had a good nose around then joined them back in the front living room. Talking, drinking, laughing. I remember the music. The Clash, Lou Reed, Tamla Motown. The Best Of Burt Bacharach. A couple of pizzas arrived and an industrial amount of cannabis was smoked. They liked their puff, that little mob.

It wasn't hard to warm to them. There seemed to be genuine friendship there in that scruffy little house. A lot of noise and laughter. I stayed all night. I wanted to see who was sleeping with who. Gemma was the first to slope off upstairs, saying something about an early shift. Claire followed shortly after. Then Stacey and the other girl who's name I could never quite catch, they rang for a taxi that honked it's horn about one am. The three lads were the last to turn in, Brett the first to concede defeat at about 2am. Cookie was already crashed out on the sagging settee, smeared with ash and red wine stains. Eric finally staggered up to his crypt on the top level a short time after. They left the telly burning soundlessly in the corner and the needle stuck on the play-out groove of the last record turning on the deck, a Lee Scratch Perry album, the repeated clunk and bump drowned out by the steady snores of the comatose Cookie.

I stayed and listened for hours, entranced.

... click, bump ccrrrr, click, bump, ccrrrrr, click, bump, cccrrr ... click ...

I couldn't remember who I was. That was the misery, bud. I knew I must have been someone, a real person, like Cookie and Eric and Gemma and all the rest of them, but I could not for the life of me know that person. People had come alive for me through hearing their voices and the music they played and the words that babbled from their lips, and that made the world all the more heart-breaking. It was a world without me. My song had been sung, and now I was stuck in the ever-occurring present.

I couldn't put the needle back to the start of the record.

I left Cookie to his dreams and went upstairs to watch Gemma sleep.

I'd presumed up to that point that Gemma was the mother of those two boys. But it didn't look likely. I couldn't work it out, but I suppose at that point I didn't really care. I was just glad to have bumped into her again. They energised me, Gemma especially, but all them really. Even Eric. Not for the same reasons, as it turned out. Eric didn't flood me with waves of empathy. On the contrary, he was the first fully-grown human being to feed my disgust. I suppose someone had to have the honour.

Gemma, though, she was the one I really cared about in that house. I stayed in her room all that night. I stood watch over her until it slowly turned light outside again.

She was the first up. I listened to her singing Ella Fitzgerald in the shower and then followed her downstairs and watched her make toast and tea. She wore a uniform, a dark navy-blue smock and trousers affair. Health care orderly, I thought. It looked medical, but I still wasn't sure until I followed her out of the house and onto the bus and she hopped off at St Cuthbert's.

She was a cleaner, as it turned out. She pushed a trolley laden with plastic guns and cloths and bottles and bags around the corridors and the wards and the offices, spraying, wiping, cleaning, moving beds and bedside cabinets, sweeping in corners and emptying the bins. She worked quickly and thoroughly, on automatic pilot, tiny buds of plastic plugged into her ears. Loved her music, did Gemma. Soul, jazz, pop. Anything with a melody. I hung about her for a while, no more than two or three steps away as she went about her business.

After a while I went off for a bit of a wander. I'd not been around the actual hospital before; never occurred to me to visit the place on any of my previous manoeuvres, despite the morgue being just around the back. I knew they couldn't cure me.

Harsh white light in those places, even in the daytime. And quiet, too, a strange sort of stilted calm, broken only by the humming of various bits of machinery and the murmur of TV's turned down low out of respect for the sleeping. The occasional moan of some poor soul in sufferance behind a ring pull curtain. It was a big place. It depressed me. I floated around all the main wards, past the horizontal lumps of human meat tucked up beneath the covers, dozing in deep medicine sleep or else staring blankly at the screens that hung above their beds. The occasional family gathered with their magazines and bags of fruit and helpless small talk. I could sense the awkwardness hanging between them. What do you say to someone in hospital? How are feeling? What you been up to? Enjoying your stay?

The senior citizen's quarters were the worst. Imagine drawing your last few laboured breaths under the antiseptic smiles of strangers. I couldn't stand to hover around in there for more than a few minutes. Those skeletal frames propped up on pillows. Yellowing eyes and wheezing chests. Knotted knuckles clutching starched white bedclothes. Hanging on for dear life, some of them.

I floated out of the main entrance and found a smaller building behind the main block. Rows and rows of small plastic boxes containing tiny parcels of white. The new arrivals section. Maternity unit. I went from cot to cot, staring down at each small bundle. Except for the difference in physical dimensions it was startlingly similar to the old folk's section; walnut faces with eyes screwed shut, toothless murmuring mouths, tiny pink and brown fists gripping the sheets. Miniature human beings, all set to go.

I wanted to see a baby being born. I wanted to see life arrive on Planet Earth. I swooped in and out of the delivery rooms until I found a young couple, her all swollen and sweaty-faced, him holding her hand and trying not to look petrified. Various people drifted in and out of the room and checked her progress, taking her temperature, lifting her smock and slipping a hand between her legs, writing things down on clipboards. Every so often the girl would be helped to her feet and walked slowly around the room, doubled up, one hand on the small of her back, one hand on a belly that hung like a huge distended balloon. Deep breaths and more deep breaths, out of bed, back in bed. This seemed to go on for an eternity and the tension was killing me. She looked like she was ready to explode. I was about to leave when the room quickly filled with people pushing trolleys, snapping on gloves and arranging cruel looking implements on silver trays. They arranged themselves around the girl and held her legs up as she panted and pushed, wringing with sweat she was, sucking on a gas mask between protracted bouts of moaning.

Then the screaming. Oh God, the screaming. Put the fear of Christ into me, bud. Agonized fucking screaming, like a knife was being turned inside of her. Then everyone around her was talking at once, raising their voices above her noise. Baby's head is showing sweetheart, says one of the midwives. Do you want to feel your baby's head? Give me your hand, she says. She takes hold of the girl's hands and presses her fingers down between her legs. Can you feel that, she asks her?

I moved down to the business end to watch. Sure enough, there it was, a bulge of dark purple-pink and plastered wet hair and push, push, *push*, come on love, one last push, and out came the head and then you could see the face, Jesus, that tiny crumpled face between her legs, a person slowly being forced into the outside world and then with a sudden rush the rest of the body, a slick and bloodied jumble of arms and legs and then the first wailing from newly made lungs.

It was a boy. They held him up for his mother to see and then plopped him onto her chest. Everyone is crying now, the mother, the father, the little boy making his debut. There you go, baby, said the midwife. There you go baby. I wasn't sure who she was talking to, the child or the mother. She was crying now, and so was the boy. Not the new baby boy, the father, I mean. The father was crying. New-borns don't cry; not properly anyway. They screw their brand new faces up and make a fearful noise, but they don't produce actual tears. There's a fun fact for you. It's only when they get older that the waterworks come and they learn to cry properly.

It was a shock, seeing that for the first time. Knocked me out, if truth be told. I hung around the maternity unit for the rest of the day, watching new arrivals to the human race. Endlessly fascinating. Real life, right there in the raw. The sweat and the screaming and the blood. The miniature people, like soggy midgets emerging between thighs or from beneath serrated flaps of belly flesh, those first gasps of the outside world. The beginnings. I've seen sunrises that could stop your breath in its chest, but if you want to see a proper miracle, look no further than the delivery room of your local maternity unit. All life is precious, yeah? All life, bud.

All life.

Anyway, I went to work with Gemma for a few days, followed her around wherever she went, from work to the house to the shops or pub, but I didn't see those boys. So I started following each of the others in turn. Brett, Claire and Eric. I followed them together and alone, in al their permutations, got to know them all and their little habits and customs.

After a while I had it all mapped out. Gemma was the only one with an actual job. Brett and Claire were, as I suspected, students at the University. Claire seemed to be the more studious of the two. Philosophy. I sat in on a few of her lectures. Most of it went over my head, I have to say. Interesting, though. I'd hang on her shoulder and brush up on the finer points of utilitarianism, or ponder the harsh dichotic irony of the abstract idea of happiness in an age of manufactured absurdity, or some other giddy puzzle. I must admit, I could never work out what a degree in Philosophy was supposed to equip you for outside of University. I mean, what can you do in that game, except keep tunnelling? Because there are never any answers are there bud? It's just mathematics with words. Two plus two equals four, but then again so does three plus one. They're both right, just different routes to the same destination. But you can't have that in philosophy, can you? You can't just enjoy the view without arriving at some tightly defined endpoint. Well, you can, but then that begs another question. And then another and then another and then another. It's all why, why, why. She was a sweet-hearted girl with an interesting mind and an admirable thirst for answers, but hanging around Claire never offered me any clues or ideas about my own conundrum, I must admit. I was already baffled by the essential nature of my own being. Or non-being, should I say. Philosophy didn't help me.

She was obviously the brains of the outfit, though. Very focused young lady. I lingered around her room while she tapped out page after page of seemingly endless essays, breaking off only to look up some query in a book or on a website. Always more words, words upon words, and relevant words as well, no diversions. I've been privy to enough search histories to know how the human mind bunny-hops between various delights and distractions. A well intended attempt to fill a gap in knowledge or catch up on the news or surf the supermarket shelves usually ends up with a wander down some pointless cyber side-road, some nostalgic hit from all our golden yesterdays on YouTube, or a stupefied meander through banks of on-line fruit machines or pictures of famous people with their photo-shopped genitals exposed. Not our Claire, though, she was total tunnel vision. Every point was pursued to the bitter end. It was all how and when and what and why, why, why. But you can turn yourself inside out with all that stuff.

Brett, by way of contrast, was a bit of light relief. He'd just got back from Australia, I remember that. He'd been to Australia for Christmas. He told Gemma one night that it had been too hot to go outside. You should have stayed here, she told him. I never went outside either. Spent all Christmas sat on my arse eating. Could have saved yourself seven hundred quid, she said.

Brett was doing some kind of media degree. Film studies, I think. Spent half his days sat watching DVD's in the name of academic research, usually with a burning reefer in his paw. Gangster films, mainly. Blokes with guns swearing at each other. Quentin Tarantino, Al Pacino, all that mob. Wise-cracking motherfuckers spraying blood across the screen. The odd bit of subtitled Euro detective gloom as light relief. He was a nice lad, Brett, if a tad dull. No malice in him though. A man of simple pleasures. He didn't go to the University as often as Claire and when he did he usually ended up in the bar playing pool or sinking pints of cheap lager or crashed out in some fellow stoner's front room in one of the communal houses that fringed the campus.

That was a great place, the Uni. I liked it there. The leafy seat of learning. That's where I picked up the reading. Night classes for the non-English speaker. Eastern Europeans and Africans and Middle Eastern adults, every nation under the sun, all watching the sentences unfold on the white board, and me bent over their books with them, following their fingers on the page, mimicking the shapes their tongues made inside myself, soaking up the info. After the first few lessons it all came flooding back, thick and fast. They used to have different classes every night, from beginners to advanced, and I fast tracked my way through all of them. I went from Janet and John to phrasal verbs and past participles quicker than you could say "advanced learner". Look, listen, learn. Repeat to fade. I had nothing but time and I never got bored. I enjoyed it, bud. The mental computer whirring back into life. That's all it took, the first nudge, the first cat sat on the mat and I was away. After a couple of weeks I was devouring every available newsstand and notice in eyesight. And yes, I soon learnt Kate Middleton's name. I was left in no doubt about that one. And Mr. Cameron and Mr. Osborne and the rest of their shiny-faced crew. I read the front pages and watched the news in the garage, the twenty-four hour rolling news on the big flat screen TV set high up in the corner, the sound set to silent, the ticker tape scrolling at the bottom of the picture. Syria, Afghanistan, Iraq, Belfast. Crimes against humanity dispensed in sound-bite sized pieces. I saw the news from all around the world and the fragments started to fit together. Flashbacks, I suppose you'd call them.

Jesus Christ, though, I had to stop watching the TV after a while. Fantasy, most of it. Never the proper story is it, bud? Never the full picture. I think that's why I liked 37 Buckingham Street so much. They hardly ever watched the TV, apart from Brett and his foul-mouthed festivals of gore. If the box was ever on it was usually muted and ignored. Music was the thing at 37. Eric had a lot of vinyl.

Eric, right, yeah. Con artist Eric. Lazy idle thieving bastard Eric. He was a dole mole, spent most of the mornings in his bed and the afternoons horizontal in front of the box, or tinkering about with this clapped out van he had parked up on the street outside. His primary source of income came from petty drug dealing, fiddling the benefit system and the occasional bout of shoplifting. I followed him around the city centres on a couple of his lunchtime thieving sprees. Petty stuff really; packs of cheese and bacon and disposable razors, the odd item of clothing. He'd flog his wares in the boozers on the nearby estate. Hardly the crime of the century, granted, but he didn't draw the line at shops.

I saw him go through Gemma's room one afternoon when there was nobody else in the house. Rooted through all her drawers. His grubby fingers poking about in her underwear. Took stuff as well. Books, food, bits of pot. Scraped the odd handful of change off her dresser. That's scumbag behaviour, in my book. Lowest of the low. Whatever else I did in my wasted, wretched life, I never stole off my friends. I'm stone cold certain on that score.

I could never work out what he was doing in that house. The others were all a good twenty years younger than him. He didn't go to work or college. All he did was float about. A few odd jobs here and there. The only connection I could see was through Gemma's sister, Stacey. She used to come around every so often and if Gemma were out she'd sit and have a cup of tea with Eric. I'm not certain, but I think they used to be an item. They had that kind of familiarity. I'm kicking myself now, because if I'd have hung around them and tuned in more keenly I'd have probably found out who Stacey was a lot quicker than I did. As it was, I got distracted by my own personal dislike of Eric. He fucking annoyed me. And he frustrated me as well, reminded me of my physical impotence. Stealing off Gemma. Bastard. So I tended to wander out of the house if it was just him on his own or him holding court with Stacey or one of his other pals. He kept some very dodgy company, did that man. Anyway, despite provoking my disgust, I didn't go too hard on Eric. That honour went to that other piece of shit, that Beaumont bastard. He got both barrels, he did. Ruthless.

And he deserved it. By Christ he did. That cunt deserved every ounce of terror I visited upon him.

The worst thing about getting my hearing back was that I suddenly understood everything being played out in front of me. Because now I'd see people telling bare faced lies to each other. To friends. Ripping each other off for twenty, thirty, forty pieces of silver. An insight into the true essence of human nature, bud. The curtain wrenched back. I was God. All seeing. All knowing. And totally fucking helpless. An impotent omnipresence. Like, for instance, Brett standing with the fridge door open, outraged, shouting through to the others in the front room:

OI! WHO'S 'AD MY BLEEDIN' SAUSAGES!

No reply, so he stomps through. A gathering of bodies strewn around the two TV's, the air thick with smoke.

I said, who's 'ad my sausages?

What?

Sausages! Sainsbury's Taste The Fackin' Difference!

Not me.

No idea.

Dinnae look at me, I dinnae eat the fucking things ...

Facks sake! Full facking packet there last night!

And Eric sat there chuckling at the box and all the time I know Brett's Taste The Facking Difference Sausages are sat in his digestive tract, having scoffed them the very previous night after coming in from the pub with an attack of the munchies. Sneaky swivel-eyed bastard he was, in that respect. But I used to see it all in that house, all the sly subterfuge they weaved around themselves. None of them were the innocent party, but Eric was guiltier than most. I observed all of those contestants at close quarters, and he was by far the winner. He used to ooze casual falsehoods. I mean, Brett used to lie, but mainly out of confusion, I think, remembering half-heard snippets and recalling them as gospel, or claiming to have seen or heard things he could only have imagined. Mainly because he was generally too stoned to recall anything properly, I suppose. And Claire, she would never lie, it would be anathema to her analytical nature. She would see lies as self-defeating. Eric, on the other hand, definitely saw lies as his aiders and abettors. His slippery little soldiers of intent.

He'd lie about the most stupid things. How much did that watch cost you Eric? Oh, this? I got this for ten pounds. Car boot sale under the arches. No he didn't. He paid twenty and it wasn't from the boot sale, it was off someone in a pub further east. Trivial stuff, but it was telling. If Eric had told me it was raining, I would have looked outside first. The man was simply incapable of telling the truth. I use to stand and watched, astounded. Stand in wonder as the bullshit gushed forth from his mouth. Self-hypnosis, that's what was going on there. People convince themselves of a certain notion, or version of the truth, and they start to believe it. Act it out in real life. I've seen it, bud. Done it myself, in fact.

Eric was addicted to roulette machines. That was the root of the problem, really. That's what prompted all the money manoeuvres, the hustling, the thieving and the petty wheeling and dealing. Those red and black machines that stood in the betting shops like upright coffins. He'd stand there all afternoon, feeding in those gold nuggets. I got quiet absorbed, looking over his shoulder. I liked the noise. The click of the falling ball. Click. Click, click, click. Cliiiiiiiccckkkkkkkk-k-k-k-k-k. Like cocking and loading a weapon, and the noise getting longer and heavier as time slowed down and his eyes danced in the reflected glass and the imaginary ball fell into the imaginary slots of the imaginary wheel. Bang. Red number 19. Or whatever. Not the one he wanted, half of the time. But I got quite into it, the hypnotic lulling nature of the thing.

I sat and listened to him explain a system, once, a system for use on a real roulette wheel in the casino, not on those machines. It was the Bury System, so called because it was a guy from Bury who had supposedly invented it. What you do is, you observe at first. Just watch. You don't place any bets for around fifty throws of the ball. But during that time you note down the most common single and the most common quarter. You keep a tally, yes? So after fifty throws you've got a pattern. You look down on your card and you spot a pattern. It might be a vague pattern, but there will be a most common single and most common quarter. Alright. So what you do after that is put a chip on each of those locations for the next fifty throws. Never increase your stake, never change your bet. The logic is, a person throwing a ball is just like a person chopping wood or working a lathe or piping icing onto fairy cakes. After a while, they will repeat the same physical action time after time with similar results. So you watch. And you don't get impatient or doubt the system, the Holy Bury system, oh Christ, no. This guy from Bury, he was a butcher. He was relentless, apparently. Won so much money he bought a Porsche and wrapped it around a tree. That's how good his system was. A victim of his own success.

Anyway, Eric tried the Bury system. He went to the casino and got on a real table. And it worked for two or three nights. The pattern eventually emerged, and he walked out a winner to the tune of a hundred pounds or so. Which was a lifeline to Eric, at the time. But after a while, like all systems, the house found a way around it. Eric would observe for fifty throws and then start betting. And after ten throws the croupier would be replaced. The Holy Bury rules state you must withdraw at this point, because the equation is shot. Not our Eric, though; he gambled gamely on, against all best advice, and ended up losing his profits and more besides. Chasing the elusive dream. So after that he stuck to the upright coffins in Rossy Bros and William Hill and wherever else he ended up of an afternoon. I suppose he thought machines were less fallible than human beings.

Endless afternoons feeding those gold coins in, though. The bump of the numbers. Money that should have been helping to pay the gas bill or pay Gemma back that fifty quid she lent him. I could never work those two out. Why she put up with him. Because she was not stupid, Gemma. She was sharp as a tack. For all of Claire's intellectual philosophy and Brett's Zen Cigar Shop Indian Act, Gemma spoke the most common sense of anybody in that house. Kept the place together when everyone else was falling apart. Money, that was the general grief. Unpaid bills. Lack of drugs and food. At such times, the squabbling would escalate and a simmering resentment would infest the house until some small incident would break the ice and re-unite them again.

Like, Claire to Brett in the kitchen, late one night:

How can ya claim to be a pacifist when ya killed a wee defenceless spider?

I didn't mean to facking kill it did I, it was just a natural reaction.

A natural reaction? What, to stamp on the poor wee gadge's fuckin' heed!

It took me by surprise, innit. Facking ambushed me!

Ambushed ya?! Whit the fuck?! And you, what, six feet fucking tall?

Ambushed ya! Ha! Ya big fucking dolly mixture!

It was just instinct! Bastard thing ran over my facking foot!

And that's ya natural instinct, is it? Tae kill and destroy one of God's innocent creatures!?

You don't believe in God.

Dinnae avoid the fucking issue Brett. Fucking pacifist ma erse! Yer a killer is what ya are!

Aw, pack it in will ya Claire, I feel bad enough as it is...

Aye, I hope ya do. I hope ya dinnae sleep. I hope ya have fucking nightmares aboot big fucking spiders crawling all over ya heed an chewing ya heartless killer's eyes oot!

Aw, fer Gawd's sake, please ...

So are ya gunnae clean the poor wee bastard up then? Dispose of him properly?

What?

Gi' the poor wee bastard a proper burial, eh! Least ya can dae, ya cold blooded fucking murderer!

And then the slam of the front door, the clink of bottles in a plastic bag, Eric coming in from the pub, swaying into the kitchen:

What's up? What's all the drama?

It's her, she's accusing me of being a facking killer!

He stamped on its fucking *heed*!

What? Who's head?!

Facking spider...

A *spider?*

Aye, go on, you as fucking well. Try and dismiss a living creature just cos it disnae fit intae ya ain personal prejudiced idea of what is an isnae deserving ay a place on the fucking planet!

It's a spider! A creepy facking crawly!

Oh Brett, you haven't killed an innocent spider! Thought you were meant to be a, what is it, a Buddhist?

Don't you facking start!

Not very Zen though is it?

That's whit ah said!

The thump of feet on the stairs. Gemma in the doorway in her dressing gown:

JESUS! TURN IT IN WILL YA? HAVE SOME CONSIDERATION!

Don't blame me, it's these two.

What? How is it my fault?

He's just got the hump cos he hasnae had a smoke. He's getting all aggressive and taking it oot on innocent insects!

Yeah, and who's fault is that?

Eh? It wasnae me smoked the last of ya fucking shite!

No, it was him! That sly cunt!

Don't start on me!

WILL ALL YOU JUST, LIKE, KEEP IT DOWN YEAH? SOME OF US HAVE WORK IN MORNING!

It's these two! I've just come in!

Gemma rounding on Eric, finger jabbing in his chest:

AND *YOU!* WHERE'S MY *MONEY!* EH?

I've got it!

TWO MONTHS RENT ERIC! IT'S NOT ON!

I said I've got it, didn't I?

TWO BLEEDING MONTHS, AND MUGGINS HERE ... what?

Here you go, yer mad cow ...

And Eric clinking the bag full of bottles down on the table and reaching into his jacket pocket, pulling out a thick bundle of notes, peeling them off one by one, slapping them down before three pairs of incredulous eyes.

There you go. That's the lot, and next month's as well, yeah?

Yeah ... well, it's about time ...

Where did you get that facking lot?

Never you mind. And, for my next trick ...

He produces a big bag of sticky green weed and tosses it onto the table next to the carry out.

Aw, *what?!?* You facking *diamond!*

Eric, a smugly benign grin all over his slimy fucking kipper:

So lets stop all this undignified squabbling and give our poor deceased eight-legged friend a befitting send off. Claire, you wash some glasses, Brett, you skin up and Gemma you straighten your bleeding face out girl.

Eric takes an envelope from the pile of unpaid bills on the table and bends down, slides it underneath the squashed bug on the floor, carries it to the pedal bin and flips it inside.

There you go, he says. Goodnight God Bless Mr Spider. Now lets raise our glasses to the living!

Gemma, still scowling, but she plants herself down at the kitchen table and pulls a bottle of red from the carrier bag.

Yeah alright. Just the one, though ... I've got work in morning.

And then the tunes go on and the drinks are poured and the smokes are passed round and the laughter is soon bouncing off the dirty kitchen walls again.

At such moments I loved them all. At such moments I almost forgot I wasn't really a part of their lives.

I noticed that the days were stretching out, though, around this time. The light was lasting longer. And the flowers, I noticed them too. All that wet abundant greenery. I noticed it all sprouting up around the airbase. I went out there when it got too much in the house. I saw it all spring into life. The flowers opening up. The colours. Verdant greenery infesting the grey of the walls and the cracks and the rivulets that ran between the paving slabs of the runway. I liked the quiet up there. Listening to the silence. There were still large pockets of air that you could drift around in. Bear in mind, I was receiving input twenty-four seven. I was a mute witness at this point, a zombie spectator. It was a relief to tilt backwards and watch the owls swoop overhead. I don't think they saw ghosts. Wild animals, I mean. If they did they didn't let you know. Or they just didn't care, I suppose. This owl used to glide around at twilight up there, like an airborne yellow torch. Those eyes. And that silent swoop, I'd catch it in my peripherals, that long, low graceful flight over still paddocks and empty fields of scrubland. I never saw one soul in all the time I spent up there. I wandered in and out of the barren concrete shells that stood as reminders of rooms. Stood and listened. Skeletal memories of a previous life.

I never spent more that a couple of days and nights out at the airfield. 37 Buckingham Street was too intriguing to me. And obviously, it held out my best hope of a clue back to myself. Which was still the main objective. Sojourns back at Base Kingdom where all short lived; necessary, but essentially de-briefing sessions to stew over what I'd learnt.

See, bud, I used to have a system as well, like Eric's Bury System. Daytime, I'd pick one of the four of them to follow. If I wanted to get closer to the boys who had invaded my house I'd have to go with Gemma. This, it had to be said, was yielding very few positive results. So if I got bored with that and I wanted to put in an education shift, I'd follow Claire or Brett. Days of idle cynicism would gravitate me toward Feckless Eric.

See, it's a seemingly enviable position I held in that house: the outsider, the observer, the all-seeing eye. And there were no eyes on me, so I could watch with immunity. Diplomatic immunity. But that in turn meant that I shouldered the full weight of responsibility. I took too much upon myself, looking back. I should have just left them to it. But I watched that man's eyes, I watched where they went, what they lingered on, where they rested. I watched every tell tale twitch of his false grinning face. Life and soul Eric. Elder statesman Eric. The irascible big brother, the laid-back chuckling charmer. Heartbeat of the house. Yeah right. I saw through that bastard with X-ray vision. Body language, bud. It never lies. Even when you're a stranger in a strange land and you don't speak the lingo, you can read volumes from body language.

Anyway, despite my distaste for Eric and his phony behaviour, I decided to stay for a while. They were my first and only surrogate family, the boys and girls at 37 Buckingham Street. I just craved the company, I think. Needed somewhere I could at least pretend that I belonged. You can only hang around a bombed out house for so long before a kind of deep-rooted ennui sets in. So I hovered about for a few weeks, watching Eric tinkering under the bonnet of his van (and wishing I had the energy or the wherewithal to slam it down on his thieving hands and break every one of his thieving fingers), stopping up into the wee wee hours in the front room with Brettski, subjecting myself to endless hours of blood and profanity through a cloud of blue ganja smoke, or up in Claire's room, reading mind-bending prose over her shoulder. Gemma was my favourite though. I'd follow her around at work or down to the swimming pool and watch her pull herself through the water. Stand and watch her when she cooked. Guard over her while she slept. She didn't have a man, not as far as I could tell, anyway.

In my head, she belonged to me.

Ever been in love, bud? I mean, properly in love. That's the biggest baffler. There's no why why why there. None you can really put your finger on, anyway. But there were several reasons why I loved Gemma. For one thing, she never looked out of the window and worried about impending rain. Never dressed to the weather. Happily sail out beneath a sky full of grumbling clouds in her short blue jacket with the fake blue fur collar, no hood, no umbrella, unsuitable footwear. And she never cursed the weather when it punished her indifference. Just plugged into her music and pushed on. Danced through rainstorms and arrived somewhere drenched. Singing in the rain. Just like that first morning in the shower. That was one reason I loved her. She lived in her head, just like me.

And she didn't need other people. Didn't court their approval or allow herself to be swayed by their opinion. I saw the dynamics of that house at close quarters and she was Queen Bee, no doubt about that. She was the only one with a proper job, for a start. They all revolved around her. Claire was in awe of her, I think. Just a bit. Thrilled at her quick tongue and fearless embrace of everything life threw her way. Gemma was a practical realist, not a theorist like Claire. Gemma went out into the world and worked at it, cleaned it up. It was Gemma that would stem Claire's earnest book-fuelled philosophy babble with a simple blunt obstacle, a why, or a how, or prove it. Show me. Not aggressive, no edge of confrontation, just a genuine question. How does that apply to the real world of rent and work and people who don't give a fuck about the reasons why they do things? Claire loved that. I got the impression Claire came from a nice family with money and expectations. Everything fitted together like clockwork and ticked along nicely for Claire. She was Brett's friend from the University, didn't have any part in Gemma's world outside of the house and the people that visited. Brett, he got on with everyone. His enduring friendship with Eric attested to that. Eric took advantage of his gentle beatific fug, forever dipping his hand in Brett's dope tin or tapping him up for cash. But Brett hardly ever raised a protest. Brett got on with everyone, mainly by default of the fact that he hardly opened his mouth to speak and when he did it was usually some cryptic utterance steeped in THC. And everyone in the house loved Brett, in the same way you'd love a battered old sofa or an ancient snoozing dog. But Gemma was the matriarch. Eric, with his innate cunning, recognised this status and while he played everyone else in that house, used his practiced charm to abuse their time, goodwill and possessions, he waltzed a careful dance around Gemma. A well rehearsed waltz, as well. They had some sort of history. I sensed that. Not romantic. There was not an ounce of romance in Eric's soul, despite his flair for fiction.

Gemma's soul though. Softer than a field in summer. Flowers, yes. She was an orchid in a hand grenade, that girl, the quick tongue and sharp corners only there to defend the raw and naked new-born at her centre. She cushioned herself with music and wisecracks and clothes and early morning swimming and silly hats and keeping busy and a sudden downpour did not phase her. That was the main reason I loved Gemma. She fitted perfectly into her own self and moved the air around her.

She was also hilarious on a frequent basis. Whenever Brett and Claire started wandering too far down Philosophical Avenue she'd de-rail them with some choice interjection or anecdote. Like the night they were all debating the existence or otherwise of God. Claire getting all metaphysical, Brett with his ganja fuelled cod-Rasta platitudes and Eric's designated devil's advocate stance. Round and round the room they went, kicking the Almighty back and forth and wrapping themselves into ever-tighter knots of nonsense until Gemma piped up:

I went to church for six months.

You?

Yeah. When I was engaged to Alex. He wanted a church wedding ... well, his silly bitch of a mother did, anyway. So, yeah, we turned up every Sunday, six months on the trot.

And whit did ye reckon, eh?

Waste of a good lie in.

What sort of a church was it?

Big and draughty with a half naked bloke nailed to the wall.

No, was it like Catholic or Protestant or what?

No idea. Peace be upon you. That's what they'd say at the end of every session. They'd all start hugging each other. Freaked me out the first time we went. This old fella coming in for hugs. Peace be upon you. Aye, and you love, I said.

Did you not give him a cuddle?

Did I bollocks. And then they'd come round with the basket.

Basket?

Oh yeah, every week. On the tap. They'd all put money in these envelopes and drop them in the basket. Cheeky bastards. They were getting a grand for the fucking wedding. A thousand pounds for freezing your tits off for forty minutes and saying I do?

So you didnae contribute, no?

I did not. I said to the woman, I said, I'm sorry love, I've not got one of those envelopes. After the second week they stopped asking me.

Ha! I bet they all went home and prayed for you.

I put me foot right in it one week. There's this fella sat in the pew across the aisle and he's all bent double.

She slumps over to one side, head nodding, tongue lolling from her mouth.

Like that. Like he's about to pass out at any minute. I nudge Alex and I whisper, hey, look, this bloke's fallen asleep and he's about to topple over. So I'm looking behind me, trying to catch someone's eye. Psssst! I'm going. Psssst! Pointing at this fella. Hey! Give him a nudge, he's about to drop off! Whispering, yeah? But everyone's just looking at me like that – adopts an expression of frozen distaste – like I've took me knickers off and thrown them at the vicar. They're all making a big thing of ignoring me. So I poke the woman in front and she turns round and she's like, yes, what is it? All impatient and hushed. What is it, what do you want? And I points to this old fella and says, I think someone should prop him back up, he's about to fall into the aisle.

She pauses and takes a drag on her smoke, exhales. Taps ash.

Anyway, turns out he's fucking disabled innit.

No!

Ha ha ha!

You are joking!

Cerebral palsy, I think he had. They all knew him. That was his normal posture.

Oh Gemma! Oh my God! Claire's taken her glasses off and wiping tears of laughter.

Yeah, oh my God indeed. That was the last session I attended. I thought bollocks to that, I obviously ain't ever gonna part of that mob.

And you didn't even get married there, no?

Did I fuck. Split up with him two weeks later after I found out he'd been banging one of the sales bitches at work. Cancelled the lot. His mother was gutted.

Ha ha ha!

Never got the fucking deposit back, either. Robbing bastards.

I liked it when they were all together. The front room gatherings were the best. These would generally start round about Thursday tea-time and carry on and off until Sunday night, extended drinking and smoking sessions with various other people coming and going, the TV flickering in the corner with the sound turned down, the music on the decks just loud enough that they had to raise their voices. Claire was funny when she was stoned. She would espouse some newly studied theory or other and get picked up on some minor point thereof, usually by Eric, who had zero interest in philosophy but loved to wind people up. He was always the one to rev Claire up and watch her go. She'd get all earnest and intense, launch into some rambling convoluted explanation that exhaustively covered every minor point, there and back again. She never tippled that she was being wound up like a cheap watch. Eric's favourite trick was to counter each of her explanations with why? Yeah, but why? he'd go, why? Claire would frown and suck upon the spliff and attempt to respond with as much detail as she could muster, pulled along by her own train of thought and tying herself in increasingly tangled knots of words, only realizing that Eric was taking the piss after the sixth or seventh yeah but hang on, why? Then she'd throw a shoe or a cushion across the room and tell him to get to fuck as the room erupted with laughter.

I wanted to tell her, there's no point in asking why. It's like that song by Van Morrison, that song where he's saying it ain't why, why, why, it ain't why,

why, why, it just is. It just is. Claire didn't seem to want to entertain that idea. I loved that record. Gemma used to play Van Morrison on a Sunday morning when everyone else was still in bed. Summertime in England, at the tail end of the cold dark winter and the beginning of spring. I liked nearly all the music they played in that house. I think that was one of the other reasons I stayed at 37 Buckingham Street, especially after I got my hearing back – they played great music.

Music really helped me. I think I must have loved music before I was born. It hit me so hard. I mean, everything else was a revelation, especially all the natural sounds you hear – the wind, the birdsong, the movement of water over rocks, all of that has a pure beauty. Man-made sounds are good too. Train wheels and snooker balls and that warm crackle of vinyl just before the song starts. But music, my God, music made by mankind. It's got to be the best art form ever expressed. Better than any visual man-made creation, better than any book or film. Music moves the air. I listened to so much stuff in that house. Most of my haunts before that, the music was a side concern at best. I used to like the radio, which was what you heard in a lot of places, both public and private, but at 37 Buckingham the music wasn't just on the periphery, it was central to the house, it was the hub, it fixed everything else around itself; mainly because of the people, the people's personalities informing the length and shape of the sound waves, setting the tempo, calling the tune. A little piece of each of them floating through the house.

Eric, for as much as he was a total wanker, he had OK taste in music. He played a lot of punk and new wave stuff. I found myself tuning in, getting twinges of recognition. Before my time, but I knew a lot if it. He played Bowie and Iggy Pop and Roxy Music. I didn't always know what it was when I first heard it. Some things chimed more than others. It was all a part of the gradual unfolding of myself. Music teased the petals open more than most things. Like that Live Forever tune in the supermarket; I knew immediately what that was as soon as I heard it, the name of the song and the artist dropping into my brain as certain as a stone dropped into a well. Eric played other stuff that I liked; obscure sixties and seventies stuff that I never knew the name of until I saw the cover or picked up on some thread of conversation (Oh no, please, I can't handle any Captain bloody

Beefheart, I've had a right day of it ... put something on that I don't have to listen to. Sigur Ros, something like that ...) I liked Captain Beefheart. It was interesting, like a drunken werewolf stumbling about in a junk shop. I liked most of Eric's stuff, to be fair; Captain Beefheart, The Velvet Underground, Steely Dan. It was all new to me. More interesting than the stuff Brettski put on, which was mainly gangsta hip-hop and the noisier guitar stuff. All-American jock boys whining and screaming. I think Brett had a secret desire to live in America and serve egg creams at a soda bar before heading out to Venice Beach on his skateboard. Make a bong out of a pumpkin and call everyone dude. Some of it was alright, to be fair, but it was a bit relentlessly one-dimensional. Dumbo rock. Bang, bang, bang. Music to start fights with. It put my back up as soon as I heard it. I'd had enough of that before in the previous life.

Gemma had superb taste in music though. The best. She was dead eclectic, she'd skip from decade to decade, dipping in and out of genres, but always flowing. You could follow her train of thought. She'd start off with some sixties reggae, move onto jazz, classic disco and then cherry pick the best of the early eighties and nineties pop, stopping off by way of Philly Soul and the more melodic bits of house and garage. I liked it best when Gemma got on the decks. Everything she played was designed to lift the spirit. She liked all sorts of stuff, but she always came back to the jazz era, the old singers like Ella Fitzgerald, Dinah Washington, Nina Simone. Bessie Smith. Etta James. Strong female music. Viva the diva. And in her most transcendently happy moments the music Gemma played expressed everything that was joyously good about that woman. And God, could she sing, bud. What a voice!

That was when I loved being with her the most, those days when we had the house to herself and she would run the hoover around and play her records at top volume and sing along. Happy, she'd be, filling the dampest corners of the house with her warm sunshine blast of a singing voice – that loud strong voice, self assured, utterly in control, scoring a bulls eye on every note. Effortless. Rejoicing in her own ability, bud. She was good and she knew it, but there was no showing off in the way that she sang, the manner in which each melody was lazily caressed and bent into supple new shapes, the notes elongated and pulled out and stroked, like lazy cats stretching. No self-adoration in that beautiful singing; just a sheer love of the music as she swayed and sashayed around the house, pushing the hoover over the fag-burnt carpet, bumping the furniture out of the way, like a swaying cartoon hippo.

That house, with its music and late night madness. I peeked into every corner and saw them all in ways they'd never reveal to each other or anyone else. They gave me something to think about, something other than my own sorry self and my question mark of an existence.

Something I'd almost forgotten to worry myself about until a month or so later, when I got my first proper clue.

... FRAGMENTS RETURNING ...

... birds above ... chorus of crickets below ... crack and sparkle .... shock of light in dark sky ... not stars ... not the many stars studded up there ... light that has no natural place ... sudden light put there on purpose ... whizz and BANG and whistle ... purple edged mountains briefly electrified, vast and distant and strangely close with this sudden noise slamming back ... climbing light, climbing red tailed lights ...distant high pitched whine and scream ... red lights that flare into flower ... chorus of crickets below and birds high up in the trees .... a dog barking somewhere in the distance ... a dog lifting its head and howling upwards in reply ... fading darkness singed by rising orange then sudden blue sky banking hard and the deafening clatter of blades overhead ... seasick with the sudden lurching ... dull yellow spattered with scarlet and then blue again ... burst of static ... a tiny voice made huge with panic ... flashes of yellow against rolling clouds of white ... SMACK MY BITCH UP ... flashes of yellow and spitting black against rolling clouds of white ... ACK-ACK-ACK-ACK-ACK-ACK ... gold scattered on caked hard yellow ... black cracked into hard caked yellow ... ACK-ACK-ACK-ACK-ACK-ACK ... black spat from the side, leaping away, falling like tiny teardrops ACK-ACK-ACK-ACK ... crouched in yellow clouds, caked on grey and green ... black snouts pointing upwards into brightest blue ... radial exploding in discs of white light again ... sonic BOOM bouncing back off the mountainside ... London voices and Scottish voices and Lancashire voices and American voices .... static noise burning a hole ... shaking the ground beneath ... hands dipped and fumbling into yellow, shaking, spilling, the entire picture shaking and the heat rising and white rolling clouds kicked up, swirling ... this constant cloak of heat haze swimming ... red dot in a black circle ... SEND THESE CAVEMEN FUCKS BACK TO THE STONE AGE ... crack and boom and the mountain side shakes ... red and orange ball ... and the crackle of falling snow, grey snow falling ....

PART THREE

SEPARATION AND CARE UNIT
CELL 1/005
01.37 AM

I remember the sunshine that day. Blinding. It lit up the back kitchen and spilled across the kitchen table. After threatening to make an appearance for a good few weeks, the summertime had finally switched itself on.

It was Gemma's day off. She was gabbing on the phone. I could hear her sister on the other end of the line, a tiny voice leaking from the earpiece. I was only half tuned in, staring at the dancing specks of dust in the sunbeams slanting through the window. But my radar snapped to attention when I picked up the following exchange:

… and we've had another bloody letter from the school …

… what, Connor? What's he done now?

… he's not been bloody going, that's what …

… oh the little sod. What's Lee said?

… I've not told him. Don't want him fucking kicking off as well …

… oh bloody hell, Stace …

… and he's been winding Ryan up as well …

… who, Connor?

… yeah … winding him something chronic about dead bodies and ghosts. Giving him bloody nightmares. He's still going round there, I know he is. I've told him a million times about going round the back of those houses … think they'd been using one of them as a den, him and that Harrison …

… well you need to put a stop to that, Stacey. Rotting to bits, some of them houses. Stairways and floorboards giving way. Death traps. Overrun with bleeding rats as well …

Oh I know, I've told them about playing in there … anyway, I was more worried about the school thing. I showed him the letter. I told him, I said, if you don't go to school, Connor, it's me who ends up in the bloody jail …

... didn't school say he could have some time off though? Much time as he needed, didn't they say? ...

... yeah, but it's not an open bleeding invitation is it? Been months now ...

... must have been horrible for them though, Stace ... did they ever find out who it was?

... what, the body? Can't remember. Don't think it was even in the paper was it?

... yeah, there was something ... I think he was ...

... be a homeless won't it. Alkie ...

... yeah, that's what I think it said ...

... what gets me though, why do they sleep in bombed out houses? That's what I can never fathom. And in the middle of winter as well, Jesus. Must have been bleeding freezing. Why don't they just go to Henry Booth?

And that's how I found out that Connor was Stacey's boy. That phone call. I hadn't considered Stacey as being part of the picture. I'd forgotten all about her, to be honest. Didn't even realise she was Gemma's sister. I thought she was Eric's girl. No idea why, when I look back. Just an assumption, I suppose. Maybe he had an avuncular arm around her shoulder on that first night back from the pub. I bet he did, the sly bastard.

I'd not seen Stacey round the house since that very first evening. In fact, that phone call was the first time her and Gemma had spoken to each other for weeks. I cottoned on that they'd had some kind of fall out and Stacey was keeping her distance. That phone call was the first tentative olive branch. You know how it is with sisters. I reckon it must have been something to do with Beaumont. Stacey's fella. Her and Gemma had their little spats over this and that as family do, but Lee Beaumont was the major bone of contention between them. I'd heard of this Lee character before, just in passing from the odd occasion Gemma would mention him. I knew she didn't rate the guy, the way she spat his name out like a mouthful of bad medicine. I just assumed she was being overly protective. At that point, though, I didn't realise exactly how much of a thorough bred cunt he actually was.

Lee Beaumont. Rot in hell Beaumont, you scum sucking piece of excrement. No regrets there. Legitimate target, bud. Conscience clear, honour intact. But at this point in proceedings he was just another name batted around the house. There was a lot of names and information flying around. I had to learn to be selective. Lee Beaumont meant nothing to me at that point. But my ears pricked up at Connor.

I waited and waited for Stacey to show up at the house so I could follow her home. But she didn't appear. There was the odd phone conversation, but it was mainly courtesy calls. Stuff to do with their parents, usually. Very perfunctory. No loose-tongued chitchat. And no kids coming round. Relations were obviously still a bit strained. So eventually impatience got the better of me, and I decided to take matters into my own hands. A pre-emptive strike, if you will.

Henry Booth House. That was the only other bit of intelligence I had at my disposal. So I set off on a mission, and after following two homeless guys around for a couple of fruitless days, I eventually found the place.

Don't know if you've ever felt the rosy glow of hospitality that is Henry Booth House? Temporary home to indisposed gentlemen, the rootless and the transitional? And the occasional borderline psychopath, of course. Always a generous sprinkling of mental distress in the institutions. Those festering cooking pots of humanity. Like Martin, my old comrade of latter days. My best old drinking buddy who stood by me through the very worst the world could throw and then abandoned me at the bitter end. What a surprise, eh? After everything we went through.

If there's one thing my dealings with Martin impressed upon me it was man's endless capacity to forget. To blank out the things that hurt you. Unbelievable, really, how so much that was important can be obliterated. Momentous life-changing events washed away forever. Just add ten million gallons of toxic liquid and simmer on a low heat for eternity. All that effort swilled down the plughole. Sad. But that's the human race for you. They put their palms together and beg for enlightenment and then swarm towards the edge of darkness and hurl themselves into the abyss with gleeful abandon. Progress? Painfully slow, bud. Snail's pace. If my summertime with Martin taught me anything it was that mankind is a re-occurring mistake, condemned to repeat itself forever. Certain mistakes can't be forgotten or forgiven, though Burn them; burn them all on the bonfires of history.

So anyway, yeah, Henry Booth. Not a small place. Just over a hundred beds and about a dozen staff, I reckon. I got there bright and early and spent most of the morning flitting between the various quarters; the lounge, the dining room, the recreation room, the computer room with it's three ancient steam powered computers and a cosy little enclave at the back that I later learned was dubbed the reflection room, which seemed to be some kind of hippy crash pad complete with bean bags and subdued lighting and a pile of whale song CD's in the corner. There was also a small chapel tucked round the side with the agonized Christ nailed to the cross and the faces of the various saints staring balefully down. An upstairs faith room for the non-Christian among the clientele complete with prayer mats and wash rooms and scimitars and stars. I sailed around the building, plotting my mental map.

It was mostly empty, except for the staff. I don't know if you've ever had cause to live in a hostel, bud, but contrary to popular belief they're not just a state sponsored doss about. For one thing, you're encouraged to leave the building for much of the day. That first day, most of the residents were out and about on various manoeuvres. The men who remained were dotted around the communal gathering room, slumped on sofas looking at daytime TV. Nothing much stirred in there. Sporadic bits of low-key drama over petty nonsense, the occasional squabble over which channel to watch. But the mood was generally subdued. I stayed and watched TV and waited for some kind of signal.

Nothing happened all day. As dusk fell I considered sloping off back to the house, but then I noted a small band of merry men come swaying through the foyer and into the communal recreation room. I followed them through. They'd obviously all had a good drink. A couple of the staff hovered anxiously around them but they seemed well-mannered enough and there was no sign of any imminent upset, so they eventually melted into the background, back to their offices and cups of tea while the lads spread themselves around the room and played snooker and cards. They were a welcome intrusion, with their good-natured noise and laughter. I loved the sound of those snooker balls clicking together. One of the most satisfying noises in the modern leisure environment, don't you think? The dull thunk of the cue tip and then the click-click-click as the balls ricochet around the table. It sounds like secrets being unlocked. Like the inner mechanics of a safe falling into place. I watched them knock the balls around and deal each other hands of cards until one by one they all dropped away from the games and drifted off to their beds.

I did a quick tour of the living quarters. Most of the men were in bed with the lights off. Some had smuggled in bottles and cans, supping their booty away from the disapproving gaze of the staff, either on their own or crammed into bedrooms in small surreptitious groups of two or three. A few were zonked out on their beds fully clothed, bedside lights still blazing. Others were wanking away like fevered monkeys. It was all starting to get a bit dispiriting. I decided to go back to Buckingham Street and see what Gemma and the rest of the house were up to. I was moving through the bedrooms on the bottom corridor, a last token tour of the terrain before heading for the front reception and the way out. I'd stopped looking too closely, to be honest. I'd kind of got the idea by that point. Solitary men leading lost and desperate lives. I just wanted to get away.

So I wasn't paying too much attention when I sailed into Martin's quarters. He was just another guy sat staring out of another small window at the nothingness of the night, but as I passed behind him he glanced around, did a swift double take and almost fell out of his chair.

Jesus fucking Christ, he said. He lurched up onto to his feet and turned himself around to face me.

He was very drunk, I could see that. He could hardly stand up. But fear sharpened his senses double quick. Fear can do that. Brings you slap-bang back to earth. He backed himself into the windowsill, grabbed on for support and stared at me. Right at me, I mean. Where the eyes should be. Recognition, bang right there. It stopped me dead in my tracks. I think I was more shocked than him, actually. He could see me. He could fucking see me. He wasn't an irate dog or a giggling infant or anther lost and lonely spirit hanging about near a kid's playground, he was a human being. He was flesh and blood, he was alive and he could see me.

Martin. He was anywhere between thirty and sixty years old. It was hard to tell. His face looked like it had been sandblasted. Same as mine, I suppose. Same as a lot of us, bud. Some experiences just etch themselves into every inch of a person's bearing. I mean, you've not had an easy paper round, bud,

I can tell. Written all over your face. The hardness. Hard lines. No offence. Jesus, Martin, though, you could tell he'd taken some serious abuse. Those eyes. I can picture them now. The poor bastard. He had these eyes, these pale blue eyes that most of the time hung heavy with a kind of helpless desperation, but now they were the eyes of a cornered animal, tiny points of fear laser-locked onto mine. And he obviously didn't like what he saw, because his initial look of horror twisted into sudden sneering belligerence.

You, he says. You, yer bastard! Where's me fucking fiver? Eh?

His voice. I knew his voice. Northern. Yorkshire or Lancashire. Somewhere up there, somewhere that spoke of hills and rain-soaked viaducts and hardness and bleak ecky-thump horror. And there was something else there as well, something other than sound, something that invaded the space between us and saturated itself into my very essence. It was a *smell*. It was like a sudden rank awareness. I could smell him. Jesus, yes. He smelt of stale tobacco and sweat and harsh medicine and something else, something both familiar and frightening, some dreadful sourness that I couldn't quite place, but it enfolded me like the clammy, clinging arms of an old lover. It blasted on his breath and seeped from his every pore and hit me like a six-foot tidal wave, flooded me with a fresh and startling terror. Jesus Christ, that *stench*. What was it?

But I knew. I knew almost immediately what that stink was. It was everything I had been and everything he had been. Everything we still are, in fact. The both of us. Brothers in arms, Martin and me.

So anyway, yeah, we're stood staring at each other in disbelief and there's mutual acknowledgment flashing between us, an electric current so strong that it seems to push me backwards. Every single part of me is screaming RETREAT! RETREAT! but I'm too shocked to move. He must have sensed my disquiet and this seemed to embolden him.

He raises a trembling finger and aims it straight at my face.

What you doing in here? Eh? What you after? These is my private quarters. Private! And where's my money, cunt? Eh? *Eh!*

He launches himself at me, but of course the silly sausage sails clean through me and lands in a heap on his bed. He rolls himself around in the sheets and slides down onto the floor, scrambles to his feet and comes for me again. He goes crashing into the chair and bounces off the wall and this time he doesn't get up, just lays there looking up at me.

What yer after? Eh? What yer after Al? I ant got anything, he says. I've got fuck all.

Al. He called me by a name.

He grabs hold of the chair and pulls himself up, but his feet are all tangled up in the sheets from the bed and as soon as he tries to take a step he falls over again, like a felled oak, straight onto the small bedside table. One of the legs buckles and breaks and he goes sliding down the wall into a sad old heap again.

FUCK OFF! he roars, LEAVE US ALONE!

Banging on the wall from the next room. A voice raised in complaint. Shut that facking noise up, it says. Martin yells back. Insults are traded through the plasterboard partition. Effing and jeffing and various other pleasantries.

Then there was quiet. Martin in a heap on the floor. He stares up at me. I stare down at him, desperately trying to place him. Put his face somewhere I could recall. That horror show of a face. And that stink between us. Jesus.

Where yer been, Al? he asks me. Eh? Where yer been?"

He offers his hand up to me.

Help us up then, cunt.

I just look down on him, helpless.

Help us up, Al.

But I couldn't, of course. I could see him, I could hear him and I could certainly smell the bastard, but I couldn't help him up. All I could do was stand and stare in a new kind of shocked wonder.

Eventually he gets himself upright and leans against the wall for support, mumbling and cursing as he extracts his feet from the twisted puddle of sheets.

... not supposed to be in here ... private quarters ... been looking all over for yer, yer daft cunt ... five fucking quid ... they've got yer cheques in the office, Al ... where the fuck yer been? ...

He stands before me, swaying and glowering. The reek coming off him is unbelievable. I can feel it infesting the air between us, enveloping and immobilizing me with a sweet and sickly fug. I have to move. His window is open and I move across to where I can sense sweet fresh air hung outside, an alternative to this sickening hum in front of me. But he must have read that as an aggressive move, because my old pal Martin aims a wild swing at where he must have perceived my head to be. It was more of a weak ineffectual flail than a proper punch and the momentum sent him staggering across the room again. He spins back round and lunges again, starts launching swipes and kicks but he may as well have tried to harness a shadow to a bedpost. All he was doing was making a racket and wearing himself out. There was increased shouting and banging from the surrounding rooms and then I could hear the solid clump of approaching feet from the corridor outside. A rap-rap-rap on the door.

Martin? Martin, is there a problem?

FUCK OFF YER SET O' BASTARDS!

A click of a key turning and the door is opened. A young intense looking guy who smells of black coffee and digestive biscuits and newspapers. Christ, it's oppressive in that little cell of a room now, all sorts of smells rushing in, the entire melting pot of humanity with its lid lifted up just for me. It was too much. I couldn't breath. I was invaded. I could only inhale.

Martin ... come on .... What's the matter?

THIS IS *MY* ROOM! TELL HIM, ROB! TELL HIM!

Martin, calm down. Please. You're waking everybody up.

TELL *HIM* THEN! TELL *THAT* CUNT!

And Martin sends another haymaker sailing through thin air. The young guy takes a step backwards and raises his palms in appeal. The universal gesture of the professional pacifist.

Now come on, Martin. You're going to get yourself excluded again. C'mon, calm down, Martin ... just calm down, yeah?

WHERE'S ME FUCKIN FIVER?

I left them to it. I got out of there. Out through the wall and down the corridor and down the stairs and into the foyer. I could smell a thousand different odours as I passed through that building; tobacco, sweat, stale alcohol, fried food, boiled food, soap, un-flushed piss, shit, dregs of cold coffee, toothpaste spattered on mirrors, shaving foam in plugholes, stale deodorant on skin, stewed tea left standing in vats of polished metal, the dying static that clung to the television screen in the lounge, the long-snuffed scented candles in the chapel and overlaying all of this like a harsh chemical blanket the sharp and pungent stink of bleach, the floors and stairwells scrubbed clean but never quiet managing to mask the stench of communal life. Just like in here bud. You know that smell. It was the first thing I noticed when I sailed into this place, as soon as I passed through the gate and into the prison proper. The gamine smell of men and stale burn overlaid with bleach. All institutions smell like that. The secretions of the unchaste and the futile attempts to wipe clean the slate. Scrub away the stink of impending death. But they can't, can they bud? They can't scrub it away.

The scene outside was humming with fresh redolence as well, like the world was leaking its juices. I could detect petrol and rubber on the main road, the sap coming off the trees and the smell of rain on the breeze. I resisted the temptation to shortcut my way to Buckingham Street and took the scented scenic route. I floated past takeaways and restaurants and taxi ranks and chip shops and I slowed down, curious, to let it all soak in. Food, what was that? I'd noticed that people seemed to be permanently hungry at all times of day and night but I'd never took much notice, not sharing the same bodily desires myself. Eating was just another mundane task to observe without real comprehension, like falling asleep or getting a shower. But there's nothing like a suddenly keen sense of smell to awaken a culinary interest. I moved through a few late night take-away places and drank it all in; the turning spits of kebab meat and the heavy spices and trays of piquant salad, the rows of sweet multi-coloured sauces, the sudden tang of salt and vinegar and the vats of bubbling hot oil. The people on the street with their portable feasts, slobbering stains down their shirtfronts and spattering the pavements.

But then I came to a pub. A loud and banging hostelry, all light and raucous laughter and the pounding of music and I passed through the pale grey clouds of spent tobacco that hung over the loose gathering of smokers outside and, then, *fuck*, there it was again, that smell, that same powerful reek that had belted off Martin and knocked me for six, but cleaner now, fresher, more acute, the smell of hops and malt and yeast and distilled sugars and chemicals, grape and grain and *Jesus Christ*, that terror lit up within me once more and I couldn't get away from there quickly enough, bud, the vapour trail of booze chased me all the way down the street and drove me back to the sanctuary of my derelict bolt hole.

Alcohol.

That was the smell that had inflated the fear inside of me.

I needed to be on my own. Needed space to think. Two revelations in the space of one night. It was too much, bud, too much.

So I spent the next day wandering restlessly around my birthplace HQ, counting the cracks in the bedroom walls and the flowers by the fence in the garden. Stared into the empty drum of the washing machine. Smelt the rotting damp and decay in every room of the house and stood in the garden and smelt the weather on the wind. It smelt of something burning in the distance. Then when the night time came I stood and counted all the stars in the sky, and watched every cloud race across the moon and when the night finally faded to it's early morning orange, I took off for the busy part of town and lost myself in the flow of human traffic. Tried to distract myself with my newfound talent. The people going to work, their pores reeking of soap and shampoo and coffee. I stopped by the Internet café and eavesdropped on a few student lives. The place smelt of electricity and carpets and dust. I whisked myself back to Buckingham Street, but there was nobody in, not even Eric. I flew between several different locations, but wherever I planted myself and stared, looked, listened or inhaled, my mind refused to be diverted. It all kept coming back to Martin.

Martin. A real living person who knew me, knew my name, a definite connection to this world of skin and bones and solid walls and surfaces. I couldn't recall how I knew him, but I knew I had to go back to him and find out. Even though there was something about him that set me on edge and every nerve screamed DANGER! DANGER! RED ALERT! I had to go back. The adrenaline spurred me on, if anything. I couldn't resist the stinking bastard. So eventually, after flying around the city in ever decreasing circles, I headed back to Henry Booth house. Back to my old pal Martin, who I didn't even know.

His room was empty. I checked all the other rooms but there was no sign of him. What the hell to do? I waited until one of the other men left the building, a guy I recognized as being among the group Martin had returned to the hostel with on that first night, and I followed him to a small council playground nearby, set back from the main road behind a row of tall hedges. A group of men gathered on a bench at the perimeter, plastic bags full of cans at their feet and bingo, there was my main man among them, Martin himself, holding court with a tin in his hand.

I approached this little clan from the rear, wary of being spotted again. How many more of these fellows knew me in my previous state? I dunno, maybe I was completely visible to all chronic alcoholics. Maybe they had a lucidity born from years of dedicated abuse. I didn't want to just rock right up and cause mass hysterics in a public place. So I slid into a patch of bushes about twenty feet behind the bench and tuned in to the words.

Saw him plain as day, Martin was saying, plain as the nose on yer face. He wasn't getting much response from this motley crew though, most of them studiously ignoring his testimony, lost in their own inner space; more regard for the empty swings and roundabouts than tall tales of supernatural encounter. Martin was unperturbed though, he just chuntered on, re-enacting the previous night's battle with his invisible foe, to the mass indifference of the crowd.

I was a bit upset, I suppose at having to consider my past self as one of this lot. I mean, I knew the circumstances of my death meant that it was highly unlikely that I would have walked the earth as a noted member of society. A derelict house on a condemned street is hardly the resting place of an aristocrat is it? But still, I would have liked to think I would have spent my previous days doing something a tad more constructive than sitting in a kid's playground guzzling gut-rot cider and arguing the toss over imaginary insults like these fellas. I stayed undercover and maintained radio surveillance, but their conversations slurred and swayed and meandered all over the place and I soon became distracted by the olfactory aspects of my hiding place.

I could smell the dank greenery of the bush and the rich earthy soil beneath me, the subdued whiff of encrusted dog dirt and the sharp salty citric hit of a discarded crisp packet. I could also smell the cigarette smoke drifting over from the bench and the hoppy syrup of their popped open cans. Jesus, that stink. Another reason to keep my distance. There was another aroma mingled in with the smoke and the hops, a kind of sharp medical scent, like Germolene, like hand-wash or freshly scrubbed hospital floors.

All of this was so much distraction to me, the world now flooding in from three angles; the super high definition vision, the crystal-clear audio receiver and now this magical rush of smells and scents, this heady opening of the nostrils and the palette. Or where I was starting to sense such things could be. Yes, taste, that was jostling in there as well. I could almost swallow these smells.

Martin continued with his testimony but nobody was interested, and after a while my former comrade fell silent and morose, sat sucking on his can while the conversation shifted and wandered off around him. It was clear that the mashed up mind of Martin would offer me no further illumination so I slipped out of the other side of the bushes and made my way towards the city centre.

I ran through the tale I'd managed to spin together so far. What did I know? I knew I was homeless at some point during the last stage of my time on earth and that I had borrowed a fiver off Martin that he was rather keen to get back. And what was that other thing he had said about my cheques being in the office? I decided to head back for a nosey. But when I got there the cupboard was bare; by which I mean that none of the staff were in the office and there was nothing left out on the desks for me to scrutinize. If the key to my identity was in that room then it was locked safely away from prying eyes.

I went back at least twice a day for the next few days but found no joy whatsoever. I kept out of Martin's way completely and concentrated on the staff as they pored through paper work or typed up reports, but I couldn't see anything that remotely resembled a cheque, less still anything that featured the moniker Al or derivatives thereof. Either these mythical cheques had been sent back to the council or Martin was mistaken. Which, given his penchant for super-strength alcohol, was more than probable. The other men in his company weren't much help. I followed the odd traveller on their missions into the city centre but there was not much more in the way of information to be gleaned there, watching them sit stewing in pale blue offices or perched on benches and walls, usually with a can in their hand. I drifted in and around the area trying to pick up scraps of evidence but heard nothing of any note whatsoever. Nothing that could further my cause. It was deflating, bud, I don't mind telling you. I was starting to lose hope. I mean, I must admit, I was a tad disappointed to be a tramp, if that's what I was. But nobody is born a tramp are they bud? Very few, anyway. People become tramps by default. They just slide into that existence when their former life deserts them. Fall through the gaping holes blown into the fabric of society. Bad circumstances or bad luck or just plain bad decisions. I may have ended my days dossing down with drunkards, but I knew I must have been something else once.

I remember a quote Brett told Claire one night round at Buckingham Street. I don't know who coined it originally, some philosopher or poet type probably, but it always stuck with me. It was a quote about death. This guy had been asked what he thought about growing old and dying and he'd replied that he thought that it was such a strange thing to happen to a little boy. Always stayed with me, those words. I felt the same away about Martin. It's hard to imagine broken alcoholics as young lads playing out on a summer's evening. Kicking a football about before going back home to their Mums. But here they were. Little boys, grown up with broken minds and burnt out eyes.

I hung around Martin all of the summer, almost. For the most part it was a fruitless campaign. Martin was a man of narrow parameters. But I kept him in sight over the days and nights and weeks, circled him like a ravenous vulture. I was wary of getting too close in case he flipped out again, but it was frustrating to say the least. Boring even. Martin did not exactly lead a full and varied life, God bless him. His days and nights were primarily concerned with the pursuit and consumption of industrial strength alcohol, bouncing his merry self between the park, the benefit office, the TV room and the off-licence with the occasional trip to A&E to get patched up after one of his numerous meetings with pavement, wall or the fist of a fellow reveller. If he wasn't drunk he was sparked clean out and if he was neither of those he was asleep.

It made me wonder about my own past life. Is that what I did, spend my days in a stupor like Martin and his pals? Was that why I couldn't remember anything? Was I suffering an extended morning after the life before, the hangover to end all hangovers? No idea. Not at that point. But it was obvious that our meeting in his private quarters had had a massive impact on Martin. I could sense his unease. I was always on the edges of his vision and, I hoped, his mind. From my hiding place in the bushes on the edge of the playground I could hear him rattling on about Al this and Al that, but when he got no response he withdrew back into his self, confined his drinking club contributions to the occasional grunted acknowledgement.

So I was at a bit of an impasse. Frustration wasn't the word bud. I couldn't converse with the man and any close up contact just seemed to freak him out. I perfected the art of being out of eye's reach. He seemed to only sense me when I got to about ten foot or so away from him. I was like Haddock McTavish. You ever hear of him? You not got kids, bud? No? Haddock McTavish is this guy from one of Ryan's books. Haddock McTavish is shy, so he likes to blend in. He has suits made from the same patterns as brick walls and flowerbeds. Nobody ever notices him. I don't remember the rest of the story – something about being invited to the King's castle – but I remember the blending in part. He had a jacket that had book shelves pictured on the back. If anyone came into the library that he didn't want to talk to, he would just turn his back on them. Instantly disappear. I had to be Haddock McTavish when it came to haunting Martin. I just made sure I kept someway behind him. On his peripheries. It was like that game that little kids play in the playground – What Time Is It Mr Wolf? Creeping up on a predator from behind. I could angle in on him sometimes; get a bead on him without being picked up on his radar. I could properly observe him then. A sad and lost man, was Martin. Broke my heart, to be honest, bud.

He had nightmares. I used to watch him thrashing about in his bed in the dead of night. There was nothing I could do. I used to back myself right up against the wall and slip into his neighbour's room at the first glimpse of the whites of his eyes. The poor man was halfway to hell already; I didn't want him to wake up from one nightmare into another. Anyway, I had enough horrors of my own to contend with.

There were vague connections firing up. Those pesky troublesome daydreams again, bud, those snowstorm reveries, but this time it was the sunlight that set me off. If I kept to the shadows I was fine, skulking in the darker corners, slipping between the shade of tall buildings, no problem. It was patches of pure sunlight that messed me up. And it was a long hot summer wasn't it bud? Don't suppose you saw much sun banged up behind these concrete walls, but believe me, it was blinding out there. Literally blinding. Especially out on that airbase and some of the wider open spaces in the city. The parks, the rooftops, the empty back yards of the industrial outskirts. Anyplace where there was peace and quiet and pools of pure light collected. That's where I'd fall into daydreams. They say if you stare directly into the sun you can go blind. Well, I had the opposite problem. If I rested too long beneath the full glare of the mid-day sun I was flooded with enlightenment. And it was all too much bud, that unbearable lightness. All too much. I couldn't take it all in at once. It had to be revealed slowly, piece by piece, and not in my daydreams. It had to be in the real world there in front of me.

When the past all got a bit much I took refuge in my senses. My emerging sense of the here and now. The smell thing fascinated me. It was a chance to rediscover stuff again, to get a different angle on things. I went back to number 37 and inhaled the entire household there. Got to know them all over again. Gemma smelt of her workplace, all medical clean and chewing gum fresh. She smelt of fresh washing. Eric smelt of engine oil and second hand charity shirts suffocating beneath over-enthusiastic blasts of Lynx. Brett was a walking bag of marijuana mixed with the faintest hints of garlic and bollock sweat. Claire was all second-hand books and herbal tea and fruit shampoo. The house itself was full of the heavy stains of Eastern cooking and frying pans, ingrained smoke and damp on the walls and ceiling and the occasional blast of air freshener to hide the lingering green bouquet of weed.

And Eric's feet. Jesus Christ Almighty, Eric's feet. He slipped his shoes off one night when they were all gathered around the TV and it was like a dirty bomb going off. Sly and insidious at first, a vague cheesy hum that quickly blossomed into a full-on pong of offensive proportions, a poisonous mushroom cloud that rose rapidly and attacked every nostril in the room.

Fack's sake mate, go and give ya plates a scrub, yeah? Bleedin' liberty that is.

Oh. My. God. Is that your feet?

Bang out of order that, man...

Ach, Eric, that is fucking *rank!*

And Eric flexing his toes inside his rancid socks, chuckling away like a grubby little schoolboy, delighted at all the fuss and stink he'd kicked up.

Eric's feet aside, I liked the smells that permeated number 37. It was the closest I ever got to a home, so there was strong connection there. But I ended up fleeing out into the night one night after they'd had a major session on the record decks and the ganja, and they pulled the cork on a few bottles of red and a bottle of whiskey and a bottle of ouzo. Christ, that was the final straw for me. That whiskey. I stood it as long as I could but eventually it just got too much, like a veil of heavy hanging dread. The weed as well, good God, how could they pull that stuff into their lungs night after night? Like a sickly sweet fog, draping its claggy tendrils over every outward utterance. And tobacco. Christ, I never realised how much that house stank of tobacco. Never understood the appeal of that stuff. A slow and deliberate form of suicide.

So it was a quick exit stage left for me, back to the peace of the countryside under cover of night. I could almost see the stink recede as I left the streets, a luminous trail of bad effusions behind me; food, grime, petrol, every last spluttering cough and fart of the city. I wanted to take my time and relish all the new scents of the countryside so I didn't fast forward myself back to the airbase; I stuck to my tried and tested route and hugged the river bank, but even that made me gag with its reek of oil and rust and dead fish bones, so as soon as I lost the last traces of artificial light I stepped up the pace and pushed for the inland.

The air became cleaner the further I flew into the dark green edges. I pulled its sharp freshness into me all through the night, just glided blindly around over navy blue fields and pitch-black scrubland, until the sun came up and spread itself about again and all the flowers sprang open and smiled their sweetness at the brightening sky. That was gorgeous, bud, those flowers out there popping open. I could smell each and every one of them, the honey-centred yellows and dusky pinks and the deep reds, red like freshly splashed blood and the pale eggshell blues, so pale they were barely there, just the faintest brush on a petal. Blue that smells like a line of clean washing. Pink smells like a childhood sweetshop. And lavender, God yes, that lavender, one huge field of the stuff, like a freshly fallen purple snow. I moved through acres of fragrant colour and breathed it all in.

The airbase smelt of nothing but sharp shadows and grass carried on the wind. There were small bursts of flowers in and around the airstrips, occasional milky white sprays and the ubiquitous dandelions and daisies dotted around the furthest perimeters but nothing much among the buildings, just the Japanese knotweed that clung to the empty doorways and curled its way around the remains of the window frames. I stayed out there for a few days and tried to think about Martin. I couldn't remember where I knew him from. It was obvious that we'd spent time together. And I was fairly sure I'd lived in that place with him, that halfway house, although none of it looked even vaguely familiar to me. I wondered if he'd been with me in the house when I died. The house where I woke up. I even wondered if he'd killed me, and I constructed various lurid scenarios of how he may have carried out the foul act. Clubbing me to death with an empty bottle. Throttling the last breath out of me over an unpaid fiver.

But I knew somewhere deep inside that Martin was incapable of that. Not incapable of killing someone so much as killing me. I suppose I still thought of myself as something special back then. Delusions of adequacy. I stayed out there plotting and planning and dreaming up ever more dramatic scenes of my demise. But in the end I knew I had to go back and find out for sure.

At least I knew my name. I was Al. Two letters. One syllable. It was next to nothing, but it was all I had. It was a start. I decided I would have to adopt a more direct approach. All this skirting around the edges was getting me precisely nowhere. Haddock McTavish wasn't cutting it, bud. Those kind of tactics were OK in kid's books, but in the real world you have to face your enemy head on. The nights might have been long for Martin, but for me they were never ending. So I went back to Henry Booth House.

I waited until he was on his own in the park one day, everyone else drifted off. I glided out of the bushes and over to where he sat mumbling away to himself, head in hands. He looked up, alerted by, what, I don't know, some alcoholic's inkling, some street dweller spider sense for oncoming hassle, and his already ruddy countenance flared crimson with horror when he beheld me there in front of him. I wished I could see what he could see. I tried to zoom in on his pupils but all I saw was stark black fear. I know June had told me I was no oil painting but from the look on Martin's face you'd think he'd come face to face with Satan himself.

He swears out loud and launches himself from the bench, kicking over the collection of empty cans and bottles that surround his feet, dead soldiers in battle. He takes off across the park, half walking, half running, shaking his head in denial; no, no, no, he was saying, no, please, please leave me alone. Poor bastard must have thought he was going insane. I was relentless though. However fast his spaghetti legs trotted him, I was right there on his shoulder, speeding up effortlessly as he scurried out of the park and onto the road.

I keep him in my sights, locked onto his poor cowering shoulders like a heat seeking missile, him stealing the occasional terrified glance behind, causing passing citizens to scatter in his wake, a mother pulling a pushchair swiftly out of his way as he bounced between lampposts and pavement edge, almost falling in between two parked vehicles before he launches himself across the road, car horns cursing his crossing. He made his way back to Henry Booth, three steps forward and one step back, winding his way through the streets like a unhinged spinning top. I floated patiently behind him as he stabbed the buzzer at the front entrance. The door clicks open and he scrambles up the stairs and bounces down the corridor to his room, fumbling with his key in the lock, then wrenching the door open and slamming it shut behind him. I sail through the wood and take up sentry duty at the foot of his bed. The poor bastard actually climbed underneath the sheets and pulled them over his head, whimpering like a cornered dog.

Now I'm not a vindictive bloke, not really, but I couldn't afford my former comrade any mercy, not if I was to get any further with this. I needed answers and I was quite prepared to hang around like the ghost of alkie past until they were forthcoming. I had nothing but time. So I just stayed where I was and loomed over him like something out of a horror comic. Kept this shuddering bundle firmly in my sights. He stuck his head out once or twice, saw that I was still there and yelped with fear, stuck his head back under.

I became aware of a keen stench rising from the bed. The poor bastard had soiled himself. Oh, the humanity. But like I said, I was locked into selfish mode and the bowels of hell could have exploded and I still wouldn't have shifted from my spot. Eventually he emerges and regards me with those ruined tear-stained eyes.

What do yer want Al? What? What is it? It weren't my fault, he says. It weren't my fault. He keeps saying this over and over again. Trying to convince himself, I suppose. Then he slides out of the bed and drops to his knees, clenches his fists together and starts praying. He's whispering frantically to himself in between big gasping sobs for breath. I couldn't make out any of the words. After a while he realizes the Almighty is turning a deaf ear and abandons the praying but stays bowed down, clung to the edge of the bed, burying his head into the sheets. He's still crying. Then he sort of calms down and slides backwards until he's against the wall. There's runny brown liquid smeared around him, the poor bastard. He absolutely reeks. He looks up at me, beseeching.

What do yer want Al? he moans. What?

What I wanted was for him to tell me how I ended up dead in a derelict house, but obviously I had no way of telling him this. He sat there looking up at me with eyes of sunken red and face all shining wet. He didn't seem to notice he was sat in a puddle of his own shit. But then he started to speak, the words pushed out breathless gasps,

Al, I dint ... I dint know ... I dint know mate ... I thought you wa' just blitzed, like ... I thought you wa' ... I wa' gonna just let you sleep it off man, just sleep it off like normal, like all them ... I ... I prayed for yer man, I offered up a prayer, we all prayed for yer ... Al ... I thought the world o' yer, we all did man ... we all did ... why can't yer rest in peace, Al? ... Yer in a better place now Al, yer free of all this, yer soul should fly free mate ... we all prayed for yer, laid yer to rest give yer a good send off mate ... swear to God just go to sleep mate, its not my fault ... leave me alone, leave me alone fuck off go away go AWAY GO AWAY GO AWAY!

And he bursts into sobs again, starts properly screaming, starts punching himself on the side of his head as though he's trying to dislodge me from his vision.

An urgent rapping on the door.

Martin!

A woman's voice this time. Then the scrape of a key and she was in and over to him, a big blonde woman with flabby arms and a large heavy bosom. I'd seen her before. A senior member of staff. Maternal figure.

Come on Martin, come on now love, she said and she bent down and took a hold of his arm, halted his pummelling. Hey now come on love, she said. Martin, Martin, Martin, what's the matter love? What's the matter? He looked up and saw her, reached out and grabbed hold of her arm, clung on like a monkey. I could tell by the expression on her face that she'd registered the smell belting off of him but she was very professional, I'll give her that. She helped him to his feet with soothing words and all the while he's pointing at me, going he's there, oh fucking hell he's there, can't yer see him Sandy? Can't yer see him?

Who love she says? See who?

Al, he's there, he says.

There's nobody here but me and you Martin love, now come on, lets go and get you cleaned up. Come on now love, come on.

I was jealous of him, having someone to talk to him like that. To look after him and tell him it was all going to be alright.

I followed them out of the room and down the corridor, Martin still clinging onto this woman and shooting terrified glances behind him, but allowing himself to be led like a little boy towards the communal wash room where Sandy set the shower thundering into the bath, steam rising. Get them clothes off Martin and get yourself washed down. I'll get you some clean clothes out your room, don't you worry love, just get yourself sorted.

Don't leave me don't leave me, he begged.

I reckoned a tactical withdrawal was the best option at this point. I retreated out of the washroom and headed back to Martin's. After a few minutes Sandy appeared and surveyed the brown stain on the carpet, sighed and headed back down the stairs for a bucket of soap and water and some towels. I followed her down. The other young fella on duty emerged from the staff office.

Everything alright?

He's made a bit of a mess, I'll clean it up, don't worry.

Need a hand?

No, it's OK, Rob she said.

I'm going to have to write this up, said Rob, he's getting worse. It's agitating the other residents him coming in drunk all the time. He's breaking his contract.

No, she said, I don't think it's that, I think he's losing his way. He's having hallucinations.

What, dancing pink elephants?

No, she says he can see Al.

Al?

Yes.

Oh dear, says Rob. Do you want me to call his caseworker?

No, I'll see to him. Put the kettle on will you Rob?

Ok he nods I'll bring you both a brew up.

Thanks love.

A middle aged guy in a denim shirt and a seventies style feather cut wanders out of the TV room.

Is that Martin going mad again? he says. Is he alright?

He'll be fine Barry, says Sandy. Go back in there.

Is he seeing Al again?

Again? She looks at him sharply. Has he mentioned this to you?

Been going on about it all week, says Barry. Reckons he's come back to haunt him. Barry grins, lifts his hands and wiggles his fingers in front of his face.

Woooh! he says.

Alright Barry, says Sandy, that's enough, go on, get back to your film.

I pondered a few things as Sandy scrubbed the carpet in Martins room. If the other residents knew me and Sandy knew me, then I must have stayed there. But I'd received no signal of acknowledgment or empathy for the place, no pull of recognition. And why didn't the feather cut guy see me? What was it with this selective vision thing? Martin was the first flesh and blood punter to acknowledge my presence. Why? Was he my special buddy? What bond did we share? We were obviously close enough to crash out in a house together and from the state of the guy I could only assume we were drinking partners. Can't imagine we spent our evenings at whist drives or salsa dance class. Is that why the smell of drink gave me the fear? I didn't so much mind the stench of human waste or the rotting mounds of rubbish in the dustbins round the back of the shops or the fruity hum of unwashed feet in the communal doss houses, so why did the honk of alcohol repulse me? I was an alkie, must have been. Died through drink. That was the conclusion I was forming.

I decided to keep out of Martin's eye line for the time being. Proffering myself for inspection only served to terrify the poor bastard, render him to an incoherent mess. There was remorse there, sure, but for what? Leaving me to die? The frustrating thing was I wasn't out to wreak revenge. I just wanted answers. But how? I could see him, hear him, smell his personal scent, but I couldn't find a way of making him tell me what had happened. I reckoned the best thing to do was to get out of his face and hopefully he'd open up to his trusted Sandy, without me hovering about in his peripheries. Hopefully a warm and doughy maternal arm would loosen his tongue; but no, he just gibbered and trembled like a dog shitting razor blades, muttering breathless nonsense as she led him from the bathroom wrapped in a towel, me hanging back and out of the way and lingering outside his door until the old girl shushed-shushed him enough to tuck him into bed. I could hear him whimpering beneath the freshly changed covers as she pulled down the blind and exited the room.

Back in the office, Rob and Sandy debated whether or not to get the doctor out. He's going to get himself sectioned again said Rob. Again? I wondered if I'd ever been down that road. I didn't fancy popping up in the local loony bin and seeing if anyone there wanted to play ball. I could imagine my chances of a positive result there being less than zero. I considered floating back upstairs and seeing if Martin was still awake, but I reckoned another bout of haunting would tip the poor bastard over the edge and I didn't imagine I'd get much sense out of him if he was under heavy sedation in a room with rubber walls.

I gave it a few days and then one morning I was back round at Henry Booth bright and early. Martin had obviously made it back from the brink of insanity OK because he was in the queue for breakfast. He didn't look at all well, all drained and deathly white, flinching every time someone jostled him or brushed past. I'd terrified the life out of the poor fella. As fast he was refuelling, I was sucking the juice back out of him. Constant fear, bud. All senses on hyper-alert. Only problem for Martin, he was badly out of condition, no way could he deal with this level of combat. His senses were blasted red raw by years and years of loyal service to alcohol and tobacco and various other stimulants or depressants, plus bad diet and general institution-born disease. Living in a state of constant torment. A right jumpy bag of jitters, our brave little soldier. He took his plate of egg, beans and bread and went to sit with the rest of the lads, but he never tasted a morsel, just moved his food around the plate with his fork. He looked shattered, halfway to death already. I was looking forward to that. Sounds spiteful, but I reckoned he could at least be someone to talk to, maybe.

He was one of the last to leave the table and as he was scraping his congealed breakfast remains into the waste bin Rob came up and put his hand on his shoulder, led him away to the office. I'd been scoping the situation from the far end of the room, careful to keep myself out of Martin's direct line of vision. I didn't want a repeat of the other night's hysterics, for fear of the old liquid cosh and the long ride in a windowless van. He was no good to me in a prison or a madhouse. But I was loath to leave him fully alone. Had to have answers. Had to get a clue. Had to know. Mission must be accomplished, or else I'd go mad myself. So I kept a respectable distance and followed them both into the office, edged around the back wall and positioned myself behind the chair where Rob invited Martin to sit down.

The young lad probed him gently, didn't ridicule him. How are we feeling today, Martin, got any plans? But Martin wasn't being very forthcoming. He just sat there with his head bowed, all non-committal vagueness. Rob was trying to decide about the other night's antics. Red flag status, or could it be justifiably dismissed, filed away as a standard case of the horrors? I could tell Rob didn't want any drama, that he thought Martin was a harmless enough soul, to other people at least. But then again, there was the nagging issue of seeing ghosts. That surely had to be written down somewhere, yes? But the guy didn't seem to want to move for his pen. Just a gentle grilling. No definite action. I couldn't tell whether this was human altruism or laziness or moral cowardice, or some strange hybrid of all three. Liberals, bud. Weird bastards. Never could work them out.

I could tell that Martin was cracking up for a drink, though. That much was easy to deduce. I could almost taste the stale alcohol belting off him in heady waves of stink. Like it was being chased out of his flesh by silently screaming demons, their forked tongues hanging out like sandpaper. I'm sure matters of the supernatural must have been preying on his mind too, but by now it was dangerously close to mid-morning, and Martin just wanted out. I wanted him to tell Rob that he'd seen me though. I wanted him to describe me. Talk about me. I wanted both of them to talk about me.

But Martin knew the game; however wrecked he was, some deep-seated survival gene kept him out of the madhouse. He knew the care in the community system. He knew full well that him claiming to have seen his dead mate was a more than hazardous move, especially when you are constantly circled by nervy social workers, probation officers and amateur psychologists. They all love a good ghost story. Voices in the head, swatting imaginary flies, they love all of that. It keeps them in a job. You know that, bud. They can't do anything about it, but they like to watch.

So he just batted it off when Rob finally brought it up: You know Al is dead, Martin. You were there at the funeral.

Martin's eyes are on the floor, but he nods.

Do you want to talk about Al?

I'm thinking yes you bastard, c'mon, starting talking. Was I your friend, was I your enemy, what? Come on, man! Engage! Engage!

Not a word from Martin.

Rob asks him if he wants to go and remember Al in the chapel, light a candle for him, maybe. But Martin didn't want to do, that, no. The selfish bastard. He just kept tight lipped and contrite and shrugged everything off, like it was no big deal, just some minor episode. Eventually Rob sighs and pats him on the shoulder, tells him to get himself out and about, breathe in some fresh air. To not dwell on things. Martin's up like a shot, spins round and heads for the door and I had to pull a swift retreat back through the wall and out into the corridor before he could see me.

With hindsight, I should have played the long ball game with Martin. Should have some other way of coaxing the info out of him. But I was living on planet selfish, you understand. I was on a mission, one aim only, and that was to find my previous place in the world. I promise you, hand on heart; I never meant to dislodge Martin from his place in the world. But that's what happened. There was no let up, no tactical retreat and no redesigning the battle plan.

Full steam ahead, bud.

All guns blazing.

Call it collateral damage.

I made my move in the park where the other members of the Henry Booth Drinking Battalion were gathered with their little weapons of aluminium and glass and plastic, carrier bags weighed down with toxic hand grenades. Weapons of Self Destruction. Someone handed Martin a gold can and he was soon launched into outer space again, the previous nights fuel re-ignited.

I took my customary position in the bushes but there was no talk of ghosts or ghastly visitations, no piss taking or probing from his comrades. Nobody seemed interested in Martin's travails of the previous night and Martin didn't seem to be in much of a mood to revive his sorrows for public consumption. Well, there's only one thing worse than being talked about, and so after a few mind numbing minutes of petty trivia, nausea and the fifteenth whining complaint, I sprang myself from the greenery and I approached the bench, your honour. Martin saw me straight away but he didn't pull his usual stunt of throwing himself into a screaming foetal ball. He'd obviously dug deep and found a core of steel, decided to toughen it out. He shot me a quick tremulous look then stared fixedly ahead, refusing to acknowledge my non-existence. Funny, looking back. Like a pair of quarrelling lovers. Ask your mother to pass the salt, dear. I stood a few feet away, at the edge of the group gathered around the bench. I willed him to look, but every time I caught his eye he glanced away like a shy and drunken deer.

A pair of helmets wander up to the merry gathering. A pair of police constables, I mean, a man and a woman. They exchange a few brief pleasantries and then tell everyone they'll have to disperse for the day. There'd been a complaint from a concerned parent and Martin and the gang are making the place look untidy. I'd seen this happen a couple of times before. They generally all just sloped off to their various corners of the city before reconvening at some other local hot spot favoured by alfresco hedonists. They gathered up their mess under the gentle guidance of the constabulary and wandered off in groups of two or three to wherever would tolerate them next. Not Martin, though. He refuses offers of accompaniment or invitations to other destinations and strikes off on a solo mission towards the city centre. I fell in and floated alongside beside him, burning the side of his face with my gaze.

I was intrigued by his sudden calm demeanour. Uneasy as well. I'm not saying I knew what he was going to do for certain, but I can smell death a mile off, bud. I smelt it all over Martin that morning and it wasn't just the chemicals. I mean, he was pissed off his face, no two ways about it, but he wasn't staggering about and scaring the local citizens, nor was he reacting to me with his usual displays of terror and belligerence. We just ambled off side by side, like a pair of old pals out on an aimlessly happy saunter. It was almost like I wasn't there. I knew he could see me though. I could tell by the way his eyes watered and the set of his jaw. And that tang of death around him.

Then he starts whispering. Doesn't make eye contact, just starts mouthing words. A casual passer by would have just seen a down at heel drunk guy mouthing inanities to himself. But I know it's me he's addressing. He's whispering and his voice is shaking. I have to lean in to hear, right on his shoulder to tune in.

He told me he was sorry that I couldn't rest and he wished he could do something to help me find peace. Well, that was nice of him. But he'd been thinking about it and there really was nothing he could do. Oh shucks! He said he'd been praying to God for guidance and that God had listened to him and told him what he had to do. Then he started talking about someone else, some name or names that meant nothing to me. A woman's name, and other names, younger sounding, children I think. His, I suppose. As if I gave a flying fuck about *his* past life! Sounds harsh, I know, bud. But I was living on Planet Selfish by this point.

Martin keeps up this this meandering monologue as he walks to the central station and descends the steps down to the underground entrance. I can see him now. He tells me about Christmases and birthdays and how proud he is of his eldest and how worried he is about his youngest as he stands at the ticket machine and digs into his pocket for change, feeds it into the slot and takes his ticket and walks through the barrier, down the escalator into the glowing yellow and white lit tunnels with their smell of diesel and dirt and dust and bodies slathered in sweat and perfume and the food on people's breath, and mints and coffee and the beads of perspiration crawling down backs tired to breaking point. Then the harsh squeal of distant grinding gears and the oncoming rumble and the sudden swoop of yellow headlights curving around the corner and bearing towards us, me and Martin among the loose gathering of travellers, and mind the gap says the voice above us, mind the gap.

I remember when I was little, said Martin. I was never a big lad, he said.

I wish I had arms to hold him with. I felt it keenly more than ever, bud, right then, right at that precise moment, my useless fucking lack of physical presence; no arms to move, no hands to reach out and pull him back as Martin stepped off the platform and dropped, disappeared from view. The shuddering of the brakes and the smell of hot metal and the solitary cry of one woman, just one word screamed hard and quick, like NO! but too late, far too late to stop that silent drop and the grinding groan of metal on bones.

I melted back into the gathering throng as a few of them moved towards the edge of the platform. I don't know what they thought they were going to do. Most of the people stepped back, couldn't look. I slipped through all of them, backwards. I saw one man peer over down the side of the train and then reel away, his hand clamped over his mouth. I turned away myself and headed back to the escalator. I looked back down before I reached the top and saw Martin get up and stagger around in a wide weaving circle before stumbling away down the tunnel. Drunk, still. Dead drunk. I thought of going back, but then thought no, fuck it, forget it. Let him go.

Let him work it all out for himself.

... FRAGMENTS RETURNING ...

... cold mouthfuls of grateful cold gulping cold in hot gulps of air ... grain and crack and sizzle of cold .... sizzle of ice cold sliding down hot neck ... and the stink of hot meat ... burning meat and thick black smoke ... sweet and thick and cloying scent of pink flowers ...apricots and lemons and the nodding fields of pink ... dank vegetation ... dank dark green ... sweat and the tongue dabbed upwards the smell of salt on the soaking dark wet shirt ... human shit and cattle shit and goat shit and the sharp stink of fear ... copper smell ... iron smell ... brown blood stained like human shit ... life sprayed across hot metal .. and the taste of hot nothing in the mouth ... the taste of hard dry nothing ... bits of hot hard dry nothing waiting for cold ... and orange through a disc ...pale amber eyes ... fields of nodding pink ... pitch black sky pinpricked by white dots ... the same dots that follow red tailed shooting trails ... ACK ACK ACK ACK ACK ... diesel ... ACK ACK ACK ACK ACK ... the smell of diesel and burning rubber tyres ... fading darkness singed by rising orange then sudden blue sky banking this way and that and the deafening clatter of blades overhead ... a voice crackling in the inner ear ... deep purple velvet ... line of grey squares ... SMACK MY BITCH UP ... a line of slow moving grey squares in the distance framed in shimmering heat haze ... small at first, then growing larger, these grey squares ... pale amber eyes ... MISTER! MISTER! ... white teeth smiling ... ACK ACK ACK ACK ACK .... then not smiling ... huddled together ... damp bodies ... steam rising close together ... salt on skin the tongue dabbed upward ... red white and blue fluttering against pale blue ... halos of light ... antiseptic on salt skin ... medicine stink antiseptic stink on skin ... beams of light sweeping pink sky .... blue ink on fingers and necks ... a green cross locking ... SEND THESE CAVEMEN FUCKS BACK TO THE STONE AGE ...... red dot in a black circle ... sharp stink of terror in the guts ... crack and boom and the purple mountain side shaking ... black clouds rolling ... rising ash ... floating grey stars dying ... cordite cooling and the smell of grey snowflakes falling down ...

PART FOUR

SEPARATION AND CARE UNIT
CELL 1/005
02.43 AM

Dusk was falling between two and three minutes earlier every evening. A negligible difference perhaps, but when you're up twenty four seven you tend to develop a somewhat obsessive attention to detail. The days were still golden for the most part, but now I could smell the bonfires in the back gardens and the slight touch of frost in the morning, taste the creeping chill of night time. The sun and the moon both sharing the same sky. The lights popping on in the windows of the houses. The leaves all turning yellow and drifting down from the trees. I use to watch them for hours in that back garden, count each shred of amber as it spiralled to the ground. Fading heaps of brown gathered above the roots.

I'll be honest with you bud; I got a spell of the deep blue blues after Martin died. So much for spiritual detachment, eh? I should have gone and looked for his ghost, I suppose. Got a full and detailed de-briefing. But the picture I'd already assembled was bleak enough. I was an alcoholic who had been left to die in a condemned house in the middle of winter. What more did I need to know? And even if I were something more than that, what good would knowing it serve me anyway? I wasn't that person anymore. I was a fucking ghost. Whatever chance I had had been and gone. I mean, for instance, let's suppose I was a rich and powerful man who had fallen on hard times, a, I dunno, a deposed duke who had lost his marbles and wandered off into the wilderness, but still happened to have a stately home waiting for him out in the sticks with chests of family silver and a cellar full of fine wines? What then? What was I going to do, go back and reclaim my rightful estate? No. All I could do was press my nose up against the window and watch the gamekeeper service my ex-duchess by the roaring fireside.

I started to think of myself as a baby. A baby doesn't know why it's here, does it? And a baby doesn't care either. It just reaches out to the world that surrounds it, inflicts itself on the immediate environment. But of course I couldn't do that, could I? I couldn't throw my rattle out of the pram or scream the house down every time I was scared or lonely or hungry or messed my pants. I couldn't assert myself in any way, shape or form.

I couldn't even mess my pants.

The main thing I couldn't work out was why the hell I'd come back. If I'd fallen so low why was I being given another chance? If indeed it was a chance? Maybe it was some form of punishment? Someone's idea of a sick joke? I started to think that must be the case. I'd heard Brett talking about reincarnation. One of his favourite subjects. He had this theory that all fascists and bread heads and evil Babylon bastards would be spat back onto the earth as dumb and crawling animals. In retrospect, I think he was right. I was being punished by the universe for being such an affront to decent humanity. For causing death and misery and untold anguish. For falling so low that I lay down in a bombed out building and never got up again. This was my sentence dished out by the gods of armchair karma. To wander the earth unwanted and unloved and forever on the margins.

I got hit really bad by those blues, bud. Even though the world was revealing itself to me bit by bit, I still couldn't find a place for myself. If I wasn't moping around the birthplace I was drifting up and down the High Street like a lost soul. Literally. A wandering absence. I'd stop at the Oxfam window and examine every inch of glass for the faintest hint of my presence. Nothing. Just the street and its citizens marching behind me, no hint of myself at all. Not a flicker. I scoured the screens at the Internet café and a hundred different households, the smart phones everyone fiddled with on the buses and tubes and found no answers there or anywhere else.

I even asked God for guidance. Well, went to his house, anyway. I was out wandering one morning and I passed a church. People were pulling up and getting out of cars, black people, mainly, all dressed up in their Sunday best. At first I thought it was a wedding. Some of the women were in traditional African stuff. They looked amazing, like a flock of tropical birds had landed on the pavement, all wrapped in swathes of bright yellow and green and red, painted nails and headdresses piled up high. And the little kids buttoned up tight in collars and jackets and neatly ironed party dresses. I stopped and watched the Pastor greet everyone as they made their way into the church. He looked so delighted to see them all. Hello, hello, come in, how are you? Hello John, hello Cynthia, hello children. So glad to see you again. Welcome back, welcome back. As the last person passed through the door I slipped in behind them and positioned myself at the back.

I think it was a Baptist church. Or Pentecostal? I'm not really up on all the various denominations. But I stayed through it all, the singing and the swaying and the proclamations and the people being helped down the front for the touch of a healing hand on their forehead. I liked the hymns and the handclaps and the hope that was generated, the sweet and touching faith that saying someone's name over and over again could in some way nudge you that tiny bit closer to paradise. Oh Jesus, Oh Jesus, oh Jesus Christ my Lord, I love you, you love me, we love you Jesus. Together in heaven we shall be. Deliver us, deliver us. All that jazz. I liked it. I didn't know the guy myself, not even remotely, but I was glad that everyone there was such a fan. I felt rock solid certainty in that church. I felt joy as well. Neither of those commodities felt unwelcome to me at that point, bud, I have to say. Yeah, I lapped it up in that place. Felt insulated. I could have stayed there forever. I did stay there, as it happened, stayed there all that night, long after the people had departed. Staring at the coloured lights on the floor and the sad and gentle face of Jesus hung up on that cross.

I'll be straight with you bud; I'm as confused as the next man when it comes to The Almighty. My time as a ghost never afforded me any insights in that respect. Not for one solitary second. I'm more inclined to believe in the idea of many Gods. Like the Hindus, or the Transcendentalists. A God for each department. This universe is far too complex and confusing to be the work of one creator. I don't like the idea of it all being on Jesus's head. Or his Dad's, even. Too much responsibility. And I'm not sure about all that heaven and hell business either. Not as the far-off metaphysical promised lands they're painted as, at any rate. If heaven does exist it's down here, bud. It's in the sunset on the deserted winter beaches or the creased up old stick of a man kissing his wife on their diamond wedding night. It's in the laughter of dogs and children and birds and the hammering of rain on a caravan roof when you're all tucked up and cosy beneath a soft summer sky on the coast. You don't have to be good to go to heaven. You don't even have to look far beyond your front door. And the same goes for hell. You don't have to be an evil bastard to go to hell. You want fire and brimstone and wilful acts of agony? Sign on the dotted line, bud, and you can be unpacking your kit by dinnertime tomorrow.

One thing I am convinced of: asking God for answers is completely futile. Sorry to break it to you, bud, if you're a believer. But God will not help you. As far as I can tell he doesn't even know you exist. The bastard never answered my prayers, that's for sure. Maybe he just gave up on me. But there's nothing wrong in praising him, or her, or whatever you imagine God to be. If it feels good, do it. If it feels good, do it again. Do it every Sunday. Those people came out of that church glowing, bud. Lit up like Christmas Day, every single one of them. I watched the holy man, the pastor, the leader of the band, I watched him shake everyone's hand on the way out just like he did when he welcomed then in. Thank you for coming. Peace be with you brother. Peace be with you my sister. Yeah, and you, my child. And the lesson that day had been what? I don't know, bud. I don't know. I didn't want to question it. To be there was enough.

It ain't why, why, why, it just is.

It just is.

So after a couple of weeks rueful musing, I took refuge back at 37 Buckingham Street. I felt at home there. Felt safe. Safer than I did at the birthplace. I didn't want to be on my own in that fucked up house, despite the fact that I was alone everywhere I went. I just needed to be around people. And they were a tonic, that company. They cheered me up. Eric was essentially a duplicitous wanker, but I buzzed off the rest of them, little earnest Claire and big dopey Brett and his hippy dippy bullshit, but especially it was Gemma that pulled me back, Gemma and her exuberance and her optimism and her unquenchable lust for life. That voice. No better morning spent than following my stripe haired songstress around the hospital wards as she serenaded the blankets and bedpans to the soundtrack in her head. I thought as long as I stuck around her I'd be OK. I craved a bit of sweetness and light after all that down and out dinginess.

And in any case, I wanted to see where her sister lived. She was still my best connection to my last moments among the living. Well, her kids at any rate, those lovable little rascals who had had the misfortune of stumbling across my corpse. They were still my only hope of unravelling myself. It was through her that I'd found Martin and found out my name, at least. Al. Like the song. You can call me Al. And as Gemma and her music thawed out the deep cold blues and the pain of Martin and his passing faded, I found myself back and fully focused.

Back on fact-find patrol.

I waited and waited patiently and finally one afternoon Stacey came round to see Gemma and I waited again through their endless cups of tea and cigarettes and nattering before Stacey finally took her leave, leading me a merry dance around the local shops for bread and milk and beans before heading down to a local primary school gate where she picked up her boys; Connor, who I'd first seen at the house and his little brother Ryan.

Connor was a hard-faced little terror who babbled inanities at a million miles an hour and obviously had far too much energy for the primary school education system, hence his frequent self-imposed absences. He was a handful; I could see that from the minute I clapped eyes on him. There was just no off switch with the boy. He jabbered on relentlessly, jumping from one juvenile non sequitur to the next, Stacey's well-rehearsed briskness batting off his relentless questions and requests. Ryan, by contrast was a solemnly silent little fella who clung to his mother's side like a half drowned waif to a lifeboat. I followed them back home, to a small terraced house on the other side of the park.

As soon as we were over the front doorstep Connor dumped his bag and was straight out the back, slamming a football against the yard wall. Ryan sat at the kitchen table with a book and a beaker of juice. After a few near misses with plant pots and windows, Connor was instructed by his mother to get himself from under her feet. Go and see if Harrison's playing out, she said. I followed him four doors down to where his miniature partner in crime lived. Harrison was a slightly smaller and heftier version of Connor. Freckle faced little lump. The two of them booted the ball up and down the back alleyways that ran behind the houses. They kicked over bins and rattled garage doors and ran away from irate neighbours. They were best pals, Harrison and Connor. Did everything together. Pair of little bastards, they were.

But bastards aren't born, bud, they're made. We both know that, don't we? Bastards are a man-made phenomenon.

I'm living testament to that.

Some people find kids amusing, I know, but I find it all a bit tedious, all that yelling and shouting and jostling about. Lads especially. Grubby little goblins, most of them, grating on your nerves with their noise and nonsense. I know they have to go through all the usual rites of passage and processes before they get to fully formed human being status, but I'd much rather they did out of my sight and earshot. So yeah, I must admit, they got on my wick, those two. I had to stick with them though, the destructive duo, had to swoop behind them as they bombed around their little patch together, tuning in to every bit of their psycho-babble, in case they let something slip about yours truly. Surely finding a dead tramp in a burnt out house would make some kind of lasting impression? You'd have thought it would have been a frequent topic. But what I've learned is, for the most part, kids only exist in the here and now. Their lives are all constant stimulation and present tense mini-drama. When they did talk about me it was brutally casual:

Do you think we'll ever find another one?

What if his mates come looking for him?

They only die in the winter when it's cold.

And, best of all: Do you think his ghost haunts the house?

On two or three occasions, against all strict maternal instruction, they would sneak back to the derelict houses and my heart would make a hopeful leap. They went into every other building, but avoided my place. They never admitted as much to each other, but they were scared. I know what fear looks like, and I could see it pulsing off them. Adrenaline, bud. Everyone gets scared; it's what you do with that energy that counts. Fight or flight. These two were firmly in the latter camp. Their bravado slipped away the nearer they ventured to my back door.

My Dad said you had to watch out for needles, if you stand on one and it stabs your foot you can die from drugs.

They got rats in there, giant rats with rabies.

You can get AIDS off blood on the floor.

Other times they were talking about me and I didn't even know it. Not at the time, anyway.

I want to be Kingdom!

No way, you were Kingdom last time!

That was the first time I heard my name. I didn't realize it was my name at the time. I thought it was just some game they played. Kingdom. They would play it around the back gardens of the derelict houses. They both took it in turns to be Kingdom. Like being "It". The Kingdom game mainly involved running around and shooting guns at each other. Harrison had a toy machine gun that propelled plastic-tipped foam darts. They would chase each other up and down the back alleys and gardens. One of them would get a head start of fifty and then the other would set off in mad pursuit, pink bullets bouncing off walls and fences and broken windows. They were playing war, but they called it Kingdom. I didn't really think anything about it. It was just another war game.

I thought they were defending their Kingdom.

I forgot all about tracking down the ghost of Martin or buzzing off the boys and girls of Buckingham Street and I devoted all my energies to these two lads. I was there at every school playtime when they got together and every early evening game of football or soldiers or Star Wars or the endless Call Of Duty computer game sessions they spent, mostly round at Harrison's house, the pair of them glued to the exploding screen with it's flames and bombs and smart-arse American dialogue and endless rat-a-tat-tat, arguing and shouting and snatching the controls from each other until an irate adult tired of their noise and sent them packing. And when they went their separate ways after coming in from the park or the back alleys or the bombed out houses, when they were finally called in by their mothers for their bath times or evening meals, I'd split my evening stake-out time between the homes, alternating between the two. Sit and watch the family dynamics.

Harrison had a big noisy family with two other boys and one teenage girl. I couldn't hear myself think in there; TV constantly blaring, music banging behind bedroom doors, all manner of rowdy activity. And a dog, a big white muscle bound Staffie who would tolerate me most of the time but erupted into furious fits of barking if he caught my eye one too many times. I did my best to stay out of the kitchen, which was where he usually hung out, curled beneath the radiator in his basket. It was a happy place, though, despite the bedlam and the constant coming and going of bodies. There was more laughter than harshness in that house.

Connor's house, though, that was different. Not such a happy household there. Not with that scumbag Beaumont sucking up the oxygen.

I don't know whether you had the misfortune to come across Lee Beaumont? He did the last part of his sentence here, I believe. In this very prison. Six years for a Section 18. The story was that he'd battered a nonce. A pervert who preyed on young girls. His oft-repeated tale was that some innocent damsel in distress had sought his help, one of his mate's younger cousins, and like a knight in a Stone Island sweater he'd leapt valiantly to her defence and put the guy in hospital. Intensive care job. I never knew for certain, but I strongly suspect that this was bullshit. A load of nonsense spun around his fan base to justify his psycho behaviour. More than likely the guy just had the misfortune to have been in the same pub as Beaumont on one of his off days.

I moved into Stacey's house just after he'd been released and had inveigled his way back into the family home. Well, not his family, strictly speaking. The kids weren't his. I never did find out who their dad was or what had happened to him. Stacey had a photo but she kept it in her bedside drawer. I saw her take it out and look at it a couple of times, but never in sight of Beaumont. Beaumont didn't allow images of false idols. He was God in that house. The centre of all attention. He'd been out of prison about two weeks when I moved in. The honeymoon period. He was still in full-on homecoming party mode. Giddy with his newfound freedom. I must admit, I thought he was alright at first. Well, tolerable I suppose. I could see why Stacey had fallen for him. He was a good-looking bastard, I must admit. Clean-cut film star looks. All that flash designer clobber. And he had an undeniable charm when he chose to turn it on. He had stories and jokes and a deep well of confidence. He had money too. That helped the job along.

New clothes for Stacey, a fridge full of food and booze and piles of presents for the kids; a new Xbox to share and a scooter each and replica football tops and afternoons out to the cinema with ice-creams and popcorn and Happy Meals at Maccy D's. Connor lapped it up. You could tell he worshipped the bastard. He was forever bigging him up to Harrison – my Dad this and my Dad that. I think he knew Beaumont wasn't actually his Dad, but he was more than happy to bestow the title upon him. Every little lad needs a Dad, eh bud?

Yeah, right.

Ryan, he was a little more reserved. He never remembered Beaumont from before he went away. He was too young, I think. He'd have been little more than a toddler when Beaumont got locked up. Ryan was polite, said please and thank you, but he kept his distance, in the main. I think Beaumont's rough exuberance unnerved Ryan, sensitive little soul that he was. He learnt to call him Dad, but the name never sat easily on his lips.

The first few nights I witnessed round there were one long extended jolly up. Chinese takeaways and lager and vodka and endless rounds of visitors. Beaumont cracking everyone up with his hilarious anecdotes of jailhouse japery that always cast him as the star of the show, overcoming authority and slow witted adversaries with his superior strength and cunning. He'd hold court to a captive audience of like-minded idiots attracted by his freshly found exuberance. The king was in his castle and everyone had to bow down. They'd play music and chop lines of cocaine out after the kids had gone to bed and stay up till the early hours snorting and drinking and entertaining. I think Stacey was just as excited as him at first. He was a novelty again. Money, bud. Money and influence and that heady rush of power. It knocks a lot of the rough corners off.

I knew Gemma wasn't impressed though. She had Beaumont's card marked from the very beginning. This had been the cause of her and Stacey's little fall out. She'd been getting on Stacey's case about her letting him back in the house, but Beaumont had given Stacey the puppy dog eyes and the big emotional speech about how prison had changed him and he knew how lucky he was, and how she meant the world to him and blah blah fucking blah. He put the onus all on her. The classic tactic of the polished manipulator. Achingly sincere. Don't set me up to fail Stace. Those were his words. Don't set me up to fail, babe. It's you and me Stace. Fresh start. Nobody has ever given me a chance apart from you. You're the only one, babe. I owe you big time, Stace. Never going back. It's all about you and me now. You, me and the boys. I can't do this without you, babe.

But the thing is, Mr Listener, I can smell bullshit from a hundred paces. I can get in close and personal and see the pupils widen, smell the sweat trickle down the temples, hear the heart start beating just that little bit faster with the rhythm of deceit. And Beaumont was nothing but an actor. He was good; I'll give him that. He'd had plenty of practice. He almost convinced himself, I think. But he had no intention of settling back into the straight life. He was the type of bloke who needed constant stimulation. A child, really. An overgrown kid who had to be the permanent centre of attention. And, sure enough, as the visitors gradually tailed off and the euphoria of his new found freedom started to fade, the harsh reality kicked in. Boredom, bud. Mundane routine. I could tell it didn't sit well with him. After the party wound down, that's when the problems began. That's when the bastard's true and dirty soul shone through.

He started snorting coke on the quiet. Stacey wasn't averse to a tickle on the weekend, but she had a level head on her when it came down to the reality of day-to-day living. A mother's common sense. Calm it down now, Lee. Those were her words. Reel it in babe. But Beaumont had no intention of reeling it in. Barely a day went by without him topping up the toxic cocktail that kept his belligerence burning. He snuck his little white bags into the house and started round about mid-afternoon, bolting himself into the toilet every couple of hours. And he drank every night and all day and night on Fridays and Saturdays, forever reaching into the fridge to pop another can of Stella. That's when he started to irritate me. Pop, fizz, gulp, gulp, gulp. Swaying on his feet. Evening meals left uneaten. That fucking smell again.

At first I had no idea what he got up to when he left the house because I never followed him. I was glad to be rid of him. Besides, I was still focused on the kids. Still waiting for another clue. But after a week or so I had a nosey and drifted off after him on his evening manoeuvres.

He was basically a fourth division villain. Strictly amateur league stuff. Low level wheeling and dealing and mooching about the clubs on a weekend. Fancied himself as a hard man. What he was, in fact, was a fucking bully. His partners in crime were mostly sycophantic saps and petty thief louts with fewer brains than a bag of cabbages. One of them in particular, a dead-eyed dolt who grew marijuana in his back bedroom. Three or four others. They'd sit round each other's houses and blow a lot of hot air up each other's arses; all the top jobs they were going to pull off and all the adversaries that were going to get ironed out. Little boys trying to big themselves up. I stuck it out on a few occasions and then stopped following him on his escapades out of the house. Drugs, deals, money, this man, that man. This job, that job. Talk of earners and payback and let's have it right, bruv. The big one always round the corner. Constant hanging air of aggression. Like one of Brett's bad movies. It would have been funny if it weren't so depressing.

His domestic input was, to put it generously, non-existent. After the initial ostentatious displays of gift giving, he took zero interest in the kids, only acknowledging their presence with snaps and snarls when their noise intruded on his hangover. Connor's non-stop yapping wound him up like a cheap wristwatch and the boy soon started giving him a wide berth, scooting upstairs or out the back and round to Harrison's as soon as he heard the first rumblings of discontent. Ryan just used to fade away to his room with his books and his Lego. He never went to Harrison's house. Connor would never let him tag along, never entertained his presence at all.

Stacey could see it all unravelling. Whenever she pulled Beaumont up on his parental duties he took great delight in reminding her that they were her flesh and blood, not his. Despite his claim on the paternal title, he never acted like no father figure. His mood swings became more frequent and more severe. Any attempt to engage him in anything approaching civil conversation would be met with growls of indifference at best, outright barking aggression at worst. The bickering and the sniping would escalate and explode into full-on confrontation. Stacey stood up to him, to give the girl her due; she was no doormat. But it wore her down, this constant battery of verbal violence and selfish pig ignorance and eventually they just co-existed in a state of mutual antagonism. Honeymoon period over.

He started staying out all night, usually at the weekends. Personally, I was delighted. But I could see the strain in every line on Stacey's face; hear the crack in her voice as she chatted to her sister on the phone, pretending everything was normal. Saving face. Gemma would never come round to the house whenever Beaumont was there. She'd wait until she knew he was out and then come round for a quick cup of tea or to take the kids out. If their paths did cross they barely exchanged a word that wasn't dripping in sarcasm. But Gemma wasn't phased by the bastard, just gave him the same sweet blank-faced smile. Didn't rise to any of his digs or snide asides. Her indifference to his pseudo friendly sneers drove him demented. Gemma had the measure of that bastard.

He's dead now, Lee Beaumont. I killed him. Murdered him, in fact. Out of all the people I've killed, he's the only one I don't regret. If I hadn't have taken him out he'd have done some real damage. No doubt about it. Even without all the stuff with Ryan, his behaviour in general was going rapidly downhill. Intervention required, bud. Exercise in damage limitation. The arguments were getting worse, the pair of them tearing strips off each other behind slammed shut doors, furious eruptions in the background as Connor's thumb pressed the volume UP button on the TV remote and Ryan would bury his head deeper into his book. His book of facts. Ryan loved that book. He loved reading. That beautiful little boy. Whenever I got worn out by Stacey and Beaumont's fighting, or Connor and Harrison's juvenile bullshit, I'd settle next to Ryan and his Bumper Book of Amazing Facts.

He couldn't read too well. I think he just liked the pictures. He was trying though. He liked the outer space facts best. The planets and the constellations. There was a double spread drawing of the moon, a huge silver globe hung up in a sky full of stars. Ryan would run his finger along the page and mouth the words. I had to move in close to hear him:

... some ... pee-pull ... be-lieve ... that ... ma-ny – years – a-go - the - Moon – was - a - part - of - the – Earth ...

Fascinated him that did. He learned, re-learned and repeated this fact to Beaumont one Friday evening when Beaumont was sat sniffing and seething in front of the TV, can of beer in hand.

Dad, he said, the moon used to be part of the Earth.

Beaumont had just snorted a big fat line of cocaine in the bathroom and at this particular point in time his brain could not handle thoughts of this magnitude. He told Ryan not to be so fucking stupid and Ryan retreated, embarrassed and confused.

Ryan was always getting dismissed by the bigger people in his life, and not just the ones who took cocaine. His Mum was too preoccupied with the giant adult child in the house to notice her last born blinking up at her. And his brother didn't pay him any attention or time at all; acted like he was a nuisance at best. Connor ran too fast for Ryan's little legs to catch up. I'm not sure how much younger Ryan was – a couple of years I think. Maybe more. From the books that he kept piled up by his bedside I would say he was no more than seven. Maybe younger. Small for his age. Like a miniature old man, all frown-browed and serious. He would ignore the domestic storms around him by retreating into spaceships and monsters and superheroes, living between the pages of comics and books.

One night, during a particularly vicious slanging match, I swept up the stairs to find Ryan with his head buried beneath his pillows, trying to block out the noise. The commotion below and the noise of his own sobbing. Broke my heart, that did. That's another thing, bud. Human suffering was getting to me like never before. Starting to properly affect me. Personally, I mean. I was rawer than an open wound. It seemed like the more I could grasp of the world, the more of its sounds and smells and sights that rushed in, the worse it would pain me. I noticed it happening. The yearning. My non-existent heart. My non-existent arms.

When I was in my infancy, when I was just a witness, I would see stuff and not bat an eyelid, not feel much about it one way or another. Triumph or tragedy, it was all the same to me. Just moving pictures acted out before me. I remember watching four lads kick an old man into a bloody heap one night round the back of a pub. Kicked him and stamped on him and robbed him. Went through his pockets, pulled the watch off his wrist. I just stood and observed. His face like a lump of pulverized meat. It didn't seem real to me, same as the families at the train station who embraced and wept with joy at seeing each other again, or the many couples whose homes I crept into, watching them coupled up together on sofas and tangled up later in bedrooms. Love and pain and intense configurations; it was all just scenery unfolding before me. But the more I sensed of people and their unguarded moments the more my insides would churn. Empathy, Mr Listener. That's the word for the disease I was catching. Empathy. They try and teach you that in here, don't they? Put you on courses and stuff. Victim awareness. Empathy. Look it up in the library. A very human illness. Guard against it, bud. Stay immune.

At first I thought it was just the domestic drama at Ryan's house that was getting me down but no, I'd feel the symptoms creeping up on me more and more, stealing into my off-duty hours, those odd occasions when I allowed myself a wander around the neighbourhood. I'd see things and the hollow at my centre would just howl with anguish. A drunken father coming in from the pub to an empty house and sobbing over photographs of his children. A dog kicked out into a backyard and tied to a fence, hunched and shivering beneath the battering rain. An old lady being helped off a commode, the bruised dignity shimmering in her eyes as the home help wiped her arse and helped her back into her nightgown, chatting away, oblivious.

And this little lad shuddering and sobbing beneath his Ben Ten duvet, frightened at the shouting and banging downstairs. It killed me, bud. Absolutely slaughtered me. And it was happening two, three times a week at least. I'd stand by his bed with my useless invisible arms and try and radiate some kind of comfort while the drunken arguments raged downstairs.

Yeah, I'm glad I killed Beaumont. He repulsed me. He radiated evil, that bastard. It came belting off him in waves. Most of the time the arguments stopped short of the outright physical but I knew it was only a matter of time. He'd been paying sneaky little visits to a crack house on a nearby estate. Sucking on the glass dick. His behaviour was getting worse. I could feel him tightening like a steel cable. The warning signs were there. You could feel the tension rising in Stacey as well. The set of his jaw when the door slammed behind him. Scraping uneaten meals off plates into the bin.

Then one night they both lost the plot and properly went for each other.

It had been brewing since early evening. The usual snide banter going backwards and forwards. I wasn't taking much notice. I'd become deaf to it by then. I was watching the TV. There was some programme on about Africa.

Used to fascinate me, those programmes. Wildlife and foreign landscapes. I suppose in hindsight there would have been nothing to stop me getting on a plane and flying to Africa if I'd have so desired. Or America or China or Lapland or anywhere, come to that. I could have seen the world, bud. I could have gone wherever I wished. But I had enough trouble getting to grips with the world right there in front of me.

But anyway, yes, this evening there was a documentary about Africa on the box. Jungles and deserts and vast endless plains. A big watering hole where the animals gathered. A herd of gazelles dipping their noses into this communal pond, skittery, spindly little fellas, and these crocodiles are submerged in the muddy depths, evil slits of eyes and snouts just visible, patrolling the edges of this watering hole in search of an unsuspecting dinner. And they'd inch nearer and nearer to those tawny heads lowered and lapping and then launch themselves, come flying out of the water and clamp their jaws around those poor gazelle's necks and try and drag them back into their watery lair, thrashing and churning and sending the rest of the herd scattering like a flock of four legged birds. Sometimes the gazelles would pull themselves free, raw fear acting as the spur, a newfound strength through terror. Crocodiles, bud. They don't bite you in half you know. They don't chew you up. They just clamp on tight and roll you around, round and round and round, fast, like a washing machine on maximum spin, till you come apart into easily digestible chunks. Amazing fact number three hundred and four: crocodiles have got two eyelids, one of them transparent so they can see underwater. Sneaky bastards. Very difficult opponents.

Anyway, I was enjoying all this exotic information and action, trying to ignore the relentless sniping coming from the sofa when I heard:

... and that fat fucking slag of a sister of yours ...

And that was it; Stacey just sprang up from the chair and launched herself at him. He grabs hold of her wrists and pulls her down onto the couch and the next second they're rolling around on the floor, grappling like a couple of alley cats. The coffee table goes over with his can of beer and the ashtray, dumping its contents all over the carpet. She's trying to claw his eyes, trying to get her fingers in his face and Stacey's not a small girl, but he's a strong, wiry bastard and he soon has her on her back, arms pinned above her head, roaring all the cunts and bastards into her face, her bucking and snarling beneath him.

And I just had to stand there, bud. Stand there and watch all of this.

They only stop when they realize Ryan is in the room. He's heard the commotion and come trailing down the stairs. He stands in the doorway looking at them, still fuzzy with sleep. You woke me up he says. What you doing? His Mum rolls her eyes back in her head to look at him from her position on the floor. Ryan, she says. What you doing? Go to bed sweetheart, she says.

The boy just looks at them.

Ryan, said Beaumont. We're ... just ... playing. His words came between hard pants for breath. We're ... playing ... crocodiles. Go to bed.

Ryan, still groggy with sleep. Rubs his eyes.

Ryan, says Beaumont, go to bed.

Can I have a drink of water, please, says Ryan.

GO - TO - FUCKING - BED!

Ryan flinches like he's been slapped, bursts into tears and Beaumont leaps up from the floor and grabs him by the arm, just yanks the poor little bastard off his feet and drags him out of the room.

Instant chaos.

Ryan's screaming, Stacey's screaming. She scrambles to her feet and runs after them. I'm right behind her, right on the bastard's tail as he drags Ryan up the stairs and throws him onto his bed like a bag of washing and slams the door shut, turns and shoves Stacey out the way, runs back downstairs and straight through me and out the front door.

I flew after him and stayed on his shoulder, through the streets and the park and all the way to the boozer into which the cunt calmly saunters and carries on his drinking, stood there among a group of stupid grinning docile looking bastards, throwing lager down his neck and laughing and joking like he hadn't just left behind a traumatised child and a screaming woman, both of them terrified out of their wits.

I think I felt raw and utter hatred for the first time then, bud. I mean proper fucking hatred. Really felt the heat of it in my gut. And it was all the worse for it's impotence. I got right into his face in that pub, stood in the middle of that circle of dickheads and stared right into his nasty little yellowing eyeballs, breathed in that chemical stink that seeped from his horrible clammy skin and willed the cunt to see me, feel, taste me, touch me, know I was there. But he just laughed his empty sneering laugh at the inane soundtrack of drunken conversation, at the sound of his own jokes. Poured more lager down his throat, slotted coins into the bandit, smashed pool balls around a table and sloped off to the toilets at forty minute intervals to snort more cocaine, with me forever on his back trying to provoke the cunt into combat by psychic will alone.

But nothing. No impact. I was less than a faint breeze behind him.

I went back to the house and stood guard.

Stacey's initial reaction was encouraging. I am not having that bastard touch my kids. Those were her words when Gemma came round to visit. He's crossed a line, Gem, she said. Nobody lays a finger on my children. Nobody. If he comes to this doorstep again I'm calling the police. She was adamant, and I was delighted because like the naïve idiot I was, I believed her.

But, as sure as night follows day, her resolve was gradually eroded during a series of grovelling phone calls and a tense and tearful meeting in a local pub where Beaumont gripped her arm and gazed into her eyes and swore his deep and self-flagellating sorrow and after four more days and endless phone calls he finally came back and made a big show of apologizing to everyone. He bought a peace making present for Ryan, a Nintendo DS. I'm sorry about the other night mate, he told him. Ryan just stared at the floor. Connor wanted to know where his present was. Stacey told him not to be so bloody rude but Beaumont just laughed and reached into his wallet and pulled out a twenty-pound note. Here you go big man, he said and Connor was out the door with a triumphant whoop. Beaumont proffered his hand to Ryan. Still mates, yeah? And the poor little fella had no option but to take that big meaty shovel and flap at it weakly while his mother looked on with anxious eyes. Good boy Ryan, she said. Good lad, said Beaumont. Best mates, me and you, yeah? Best buddies!

The phony bastard.

I watched him like a hawk after that. I'm no dummy, bud. I know a false flag when I see one. And that was a mere warm up. Reconnaissance mission. I knew there'd be something else. I just fucking knew. That horrible, hateful bastard. Evil was hard-wired within him.

And it wasn't too long before I was proved right.

It was a Saturday. Beaumont was in the bathroom spitting a mouthful of toothpaste into the basin when Ryan ran in.

I need a wee, he says. I'm desperate.

He stands over the bowl and pulls the front of his pyjamas down and starts to urinate. Beaumont is looking at him in the mirror. I could see his fucking eyes narrow. Read his mind, almost. He wipes his mouth on a towel, rubs his hands on his jeans, walks over to the toilet and nudges Ryan to one side with his leg. Takes his cock out and points it at the bowl. He's holding it right next to the boy's cheek. Ryan's mortified but there's nowhere for him to move. He's penned in a corner. And he's still in the middle of his wee.

Hey Ryan, says Beaumont, do you ever do this?

What?

This. Look.

Ryan looks. Beaumont waggles his penis up and down.

Do you ever do that?

Ryan looks quickly away.

No, he says.

Ryan's cheeks were burning red. He couldn't stop pissing. It was an endless waterfall of nerves. I could tell that all he wanted to do, more than anything in the world, was to finish his business and get out of there.

Don't you? says Beaumont. Why not?

I don't know.

I do it. All the time.

He waggles it again. And again. Gross fucking slug bouncing about in the air, inches from the lad's face.

Ryan, look, he says.

Ryan doesn't look.

Finally, finally, finally, his urine trickles to a halt. He shakes himself once, twice, and flips his pyjama bottoms back up.

You lying little get, says Beaumont, you just did it!

Ryan doesn't reply, just spins around and makes a move for the door but Beaumont has a hand clamped on the boys shoulder.

Hey! What are we forgetting?

Ryan doesn't look or move or speak, just stands still and waits for the next thing.

Ryan!

What?

Hands!

He pushes the lad towards the basin and Ryan runs his hands under a quick squirt of the tap.

Properly, says Beaumont. With soap!

Ryan finds the soap and washes his hands. Beaumont regards him over his shoulder, seeks him out in the bathroom mirror. Ryan keeps his eyes on his hands. He looks absolutely petrified.

What's up with your face?

Nothing.

Beaumont's withering look of disdain as he turns away and starts to piss a heavy swathe. It smells of alcohol and chemicals. The water turning dirty yellow in the bowl.

Don't be such a pussy hole, he says. It's only a fucking laugh.

Dirty bastard pissed all over the rim of the toilet bowl. Got some on the floor as well. And he never washed his hands.

I maintained constant surveillance after that. Whenever that filthy animal was in the house at the same time as Ryan, I was there, my three working senses pulled tighter than piano wire. Anytime he ventured anywhere the lad. Christ knows what I thought I could do, but I was there. And about as much use as tits on a butterfly.

There's nothing worse than feeling powerless, bud.

But then I found my voice, which was a small leap forward. At least it stopped me feeling utterly alone. Helped the job along, I can tell you.

At first I was just whispering. Sotto voice, I believe it's called. But although our thespian brothers and sisters do it for dramatic effect, with me it was borne out of necessity. A whisper was all I could muster. If I was able, I'd have set avalanches loose down mountainsides right from the word go.

But when it happened it was a revelation.

It was just after bedtime and Ryan was sat up in bed with his Bumper Book Of Amazing Facts. I couldn't stand to be downstairs with those two pecking bits out of each other, so I read Ryan's book with him. He was checking out the Wildlife section: The Amazing Animal Kingdom! He mouthed the words, tentative and unsure:

The-croc-oh-dile-has-been-a-round-since-the-time-of-di-no-saurs- ...

He was a good reader. I followed the sentences with him. If he came to a word he didn't recognize he would take several run ups at it before mastering and moving on. He didn't get flustered, just ploughed ahead with a quiet determination.

There-are-twen-ty-three –diff-er-ent-spe –spe- spe –spe ....

Species. He had a couple of goes before settling on "speckies" and moving on:

... speck-ees - they-are-be-ing-tay-ken-oh-ver-by-hu-man-ki... ki ... ki ...

The word was "civilization" but he was pronouncing it with a hard k sound rather than the soft c:

ki-ki-kivi-kivi-livi-kivi...

His needle was stuck. Like Cookie drifting off on the couch at Buckingham Street after a gallon of red wine:

kiv-kiv-kiv...

Siv, I whispered.

Siv, he said. His eyes lifted from the page and he turned his face towards me.

I'd said it without thinking. Or, no, I'd said it *with* thinking. I'd thought the word and then there it was. It was more a breath than anything, the slightest gossamer sigh. I'd heard louder flowers unfolding. But it was there, bud. It was there and it was outside of me, and Ryan had heard it. I was elated. A tiny thrill ran right through me like a tiny blue crackle of electricity. I tried it again:

Siv.

Ryan bent his head back over the book.

Siv ... he repeated.

And waited.

Ill, I said.

... ill ...

eye

... eye...

zay ...

... zay ...

shun...

... shun ...

Siv – ill ...

... Siv – ill ...

eye – zay ...

... eye – zay ...

shun.

... shun.

Siv-ill-eye-zay-shun.

... Siv-ill-eye-zay-shun.

Good boy, I said. Good boy.

He smiled, his eyes still on the page.

Well that was it, Mr Listener. I'd found my voice.

I whispered to Ryan whenever I could after that. I read his book with him. Helped him with the tricky words. I followed him to school and breathed the answers into his ear. He blossomed, I'm pleased to report. From being a shy and withdrawn pupil he gathered the confidence to respond in a group setting. That was a big thing for him, because he was such a timid little fella. But once he started getting the answers right he was flushed with a newly found vigour. Question time found him with his hand up at every opportunity. At the end of that first school week of whispering he got ten out of ten in his Friday spelling test and Stacey stuck his gold starred paper up on the fridge door.

Educational purists may have considered this cheating. The way I looked at it, the way the system was set up, you had to use every advantage you could get hold of. There were far too many kids in the classes at that school, and Ryan's class had more than its fair share of raucous little boys and girls who took up most of the teacher's attention and energy with their noise and distraction. I was just lending a helping hand. An invisible teacher's aide, if you will.

Just think, bud, if all those psychic medium types on the TV were actually really psychic, they could save the Minister for Education a fortune. Instead of wasting their time conversing with dead Apache shamans or Victorian Kings and Queens they could just hire the finest dead minds of the past generations to put a shift in at each and every school throughout the land. Of course you'd probably get the top public schools creaming off the best ghostly brainboxes for their pupils, but surely there's enough dead academics to go round all the struggling state schools. A personal ghost for every pupil. You could even have one for every subject. A mere pipe dream, I suppose, but it would be nice wouldn't it?

Anyway, Ryan's teachers were pleased with him and his self-belief soared. As did mine. The more I conversed, the stronger I got. I went from tentative whispers to a vaguely urgent murmur. But that was as loud as I could get. Try as I may, I could not raise my voice to anything above the slightest susurration. Ryan never seemed to notice me unless I spoke to him, never acknowledged my presence unless I zoomed right in and whispered close to his ear. I started talking to Ryan more and more. At first I wasn't sure whether he was receiving me or not, because he was such a silent, solemn little lad anyway, but on odd occasions I'd see his head tilt and that would alert me to action stations: radio contact, possible message incoming, do you receive, over?

After a couple of weeks or so Ryan started to talk back. Sometimes I'd be in the kitchen watching Stacey make a cup of tea and I'd be aware that Ryan was upstairs in his room yapping merrily away to nobody. He'd prattle on about what he was doing at school, what he had for his dinner or the latest TV programme he was watching. Then he started asking me questions. What did I look like? Where did I come from? What's it like being invisible? I'd whisk myself straight upstairs and answer.

His Mum popped her head round the door one day – Ryan, who on earth are you talking to?

Al, he said.

Who's Al?

Al's my pal, he said.

That's what I'd told him. Al's your pal. I didn't tell him about waking up dead or wandering the earth looking for answers or any of the existential claptrap that I had to deal with on a daily, hourly, minute by bloody minute basis. Didn't want to burden the poor boy with any of that nonsense. I didn't even mention the 'G' word. I just talked to him like a normal friend would, a casual playmate who had popped by for a natter.

I talked to myself as well, usually in the wee small hours when everyone in the house was fast asleep. Strange, hearing my own voice. As opposed to hearing my own thoughts. I didn't sound how I thought I would. Being able to think doesn't mean you're alive, but hearing your own voice outside of yourself suggests some outward expulsion, surely, some breath, some life. A sign of life stirring within.

But I still couldn't tell where my inside met the outside. Spire: to breath, as in respire, breath again. Amazing fact number two hundred and eighty four - the word breathe comes from the Latin word spirare. But spirare itself comes from the Latin root word for spirit, which is spiritus. So to breathe, or to respire, literally means to bring spirit into ourselves, again and again. The fellas in the Bible were inspired to write their stories after God spoke to them, or breathed his word into them. Inspire means to breathe from within. And when you breathe your last you're dead. No more spirit.

So that's what I was doing, bud. I was breathing from within.

I was inspired.

I tried getting into Connor and Harrison but I may as well have talked to the traffic in the street. No response whatsoever. Harrison, well I think he was just a bit dense to be honest. Not a lot going on upstairs. Or maybe there was too much racket at his house. Connor, forget him, he never shut up long enough to hear a real person, let alone a whispering spirit.

His tongue did let something slip, though, finally. They were round at Harrison's playing their computer game. Mowing people down in hails of gunfire. Ear splitting volume:

ACK ACK ACK ACK! KER-BOOM! KER-BOOM!

Helicopter blades and screaming. The noise was insane and relentless. It drove the Staffie out into the backyard. I stood behind them and watched.

BANG BANG BANG! KER-BOOM! KER-BOOM!

Pointless. Mind numbing.

Eventually Connor throws the controller down.

This is just gay, he says. We need the new one.

I know, says Harrison. Seen the trailer? Sick.

We need to get it.

How though?

We could use his cards, says Connor.

Harrison aims an RPG at an oncoming tank, hits a button and the screen explodes in a ball of red and orange.

It's too easy, now, this, he says.

I know. Let's use his cards.

Yeah but if you don't know the number the machine just swallows it. You've already lost one of them.

Fuck off. It wasn't me who lost it was you. Loser.

You're the loser.

Connor switches the machine off and the screen shrivels to black.

Hey, says Harrison.

Come on, says Connor, let's go and get his cards.

What for? We don't know the number.

We can sell them.

They might not even be there still.

They will. Come on.

How we going to sell them though? Nobody knows the number.

Jermaine says his cousin knows how to copy them. He knows how to get the number.

Jermaine at Deansbrook? How?

I don't know, do I?

How much would he give us?

How much is the new Call Of Duty?

Thirty four ninety nine. But Gears Of War is out as well. That's sick.

We'll ask him for forty quid, then.

Think he'll give us forty quid?

Yeah. They're worth hundreds those cards. Thousands.

They're not worth thousands.

How do you know, dickhead?

Fuck off. You're the dickhead.

Connor jumps to his feet.

Come on, let's go and get the cards.

They run out to the back yard and pick up their bikes and bomb round to the house. I'm there a good few minutes before them. They skid to a halt in the back alleyway when they see the two men in hard hats and clipboards standing in the back garden. One of the men is pointing up at the guttering and the roof and the other is making notes. The two boys watch until one of the men glances round and notices them, then they pedal off as fast as they can.

Me, I stuck around. I got up close and listened to these two fellas. Council workers. They were spouting a lot of technical jargon but one word leapt out: demolition.

They were going to tear the street down.

I had to work fast, bud. The next day Connor and Harrison were round at Stacey's. They were on the Xbox. Beaumont was out. Stacey was upstairs on her computer, looking at Facebook. She'd already shouted down various warnings about the noise. It was supposed to be for both of the brothers to share, that Xbox, but Ryan never got a look in. He was in the kitchen reading his comic. I got up close and whispered in his ear:

Ryan. Ryan, it's Al. Ask Connor if you can play Kingdom.

He frowned and shook his head, pretended he didn't hear. But I kept on and on at him until he finally folded his comic shut and went through into the front room.

Connor, he said, can we play Kingdom?

No answer. They were playing football. Spurs v Arsenal. Spurs were winning ten goals to six. A pixelated man in a white shirt swivelled on the edge of the area and bent a beauty into the top left corner. Eleven six to Spurs. The crowd went wild.

Yes, said Connor. Epic skills!

Ask him again, I said. Tell him the men will be gone by now.

Ryan repeated the words.

Connor twisted his head from the screen and glared at his little brother. What men, he said. You been following us, you little dickhead?

No, said Ryan.

What men, then?

I don't know, said Ryan. Al told me to say it.

Connor snorted and turned back to the screen, his thumbs jabbing away like pistons.

Who's Al? asked Harrison.

His invisible friend, said Connor. He's mental. He's a sad mental case.

No I'm not, said Ryan. His bottom lip started to wobble and his eyes were getting wet. I could tell he just wanted to go back into the kitchen, back to his comic.

Another goal from Spurs. Oh pick that one out, said the commentator.

YESSSSSS!!!! shouted Connor.

He turned and looked at Ryan again.

What you looking at, dickhead?

I tell you bud, if I had a working pair of hands I would have cuffed the little bastard until his head rang. Bullies. Can't abide them. And it was all learnt behaviour, I could tell. I'd observed the change in both of those boys since Beaumont had got his feet back under the table. Ryan withdrawing ever more into his own personal world, Connor doing his best to inflate himself to fill the world around him. He was getting bigger, and throwing his weight around. I couldn't stand it. And I should have left well alone, bud, because I had no place in their world or anyone else's, but I couldn't help myself. I thought for a second. Then I leaned into Ryan's ear again.

Tell him you can do magic, I whispered.

Ryan's face creased in a frown. He shook his head and turned away to slip back into the kitchen, back to his comic, but I was incensed and whispered again, more urgent:

Tell them. I'll show you how to do it, bud. I'll give you magic powers, Ryan. Super powers!

I can do magic, he said.

No response. Two unturned heads and two sets of thumbs battering buttons and the roar of the artificial crowd.

Say, "I'll bet you a pound I can do magic."

Ryan repeated the words.

Harrison looked round at him.

You ain't got a pound, he said.

I've got ten pounds sixty three pence in my moneybox, said Ryan.

Don't take any notice of him, said Connor. He's mental.

But Harrison was interested now.

Go on, then, he said. Do a magic trick.

Tell him you'll go into the kitchen, I said, and he has to touch something in the room. Then he has to call you back in and you'll tell him what he's touched.

I could tell Ryan was dubious but the boy trusted me, bud. I was his special secret invisible friend. That's what hurts me now, knowing that he trusted me and I abused that trust. I caused him all that pain. But like a good little boy he does as he's told, he repeats my instructions and trots out to the kitchen. Harrison jumps up and touches the TV screen and sits back down. Calls Ryan back through.

The TV screen, I tell Ryan.

The TV screen, he says.

Fuck off, says Connor. That was obvious.

Tell him you'll do it again, I whisper.

And he does. He pulls the trick another three times. Harrison touches the lamp, a coffee mug and the underside of the chair and Ryan gets it right every time. By this point, the football match has been abandoned and Connor is taking an interest.

Bet you can't do it to me, he says.

So Ryan dutifully disappears to the kitchen and Connor touches the window. When Ryan comes back through and gets it right, his brother gets him in a headlock.

How do you do it, he says.

Connor, says Ryan, you're hurting me.

Tell me how you do it then.

He tells me how to do it.

Who?

Al.

How?

He just tells me.

Like fuck. Weirdo!

He was really clamping Ryan tight. The little lad was gurgling and gasping and his face was getting redder and redder. Even Harrison looked concerned. Connor, he said, leave it, lets just go out.

He shouldn't tell lies, said Connor.

See how it goes, bud? Learned behaviour off his elder and so called better. Casual use of brutality. An accepted form of conduct. Conscience clear, honour intact.

Training, bud. Kicks in every time.

Ryan's really crying now and Stacey comes running down the stairs. Connor let go of him just as she flew into the room and I flew out.

I couldn't stand it. Child abuse, bud. That's what it was. All down to me and my useless attempts to establish myself. To slot myself into the world. A world that wasn't built for me, or my kind.

And it was the next day, the Monday, one bright and brilliant October Monday when the sun was low in the sky and the leaves had mushed up golden on the grass verges and the sides of the roads. That was the day when I finally found out my name. My full name I mean. The name I was born with.

It was on the lunchtime. I followed Connor and Harrison on their bikes out of the school gates and down to the newsagent where they met another boy on a bike, an older boy, maybe, twelve or thirteen. I followed the three of them to my street and into the back garden of another derelict house, three doors down from mine. They dumped their bikes and ran inside and up the stairs to the front bedroom. Connor prised open a floorboard and pulled out the treasure.

A wallet. A wallet stolen from the pocket of a dead man.

The older boy snatched it from Connor as soon as it was offered and pulled out the small rectangles of plastic one by one, a cursory glance at each, dropping them to the ground until he held up one and then another.

Yes, nice one, he said.

Told you, didn't we, said Harrison.

The lad slipped the cards into the pockets of his jeans and threw the wallet underhand, sent it skimming into the corner of the room. He turned to leave and Connor caught hold of his arm.

Hey, Jermaine, he said, you have to give us some money now. You said you'd give us -

The lad turned and backhanded Connor across the face, who erupted into instant howling tears. Then he pushed Harrison hard in the chest, dumped him flat onto his arse.

Pussies, he said. Then he left the house, laughing.

I zoomed out after him, fastened onto his shoulder and followed him as far as the end of the street before I realized the futility of the thing. I stood and watched him pedal away.

HEY!

He skidded to a halt and looked back. He must have expected to see a man standing there, a grown up. But all he saw was the empty street.

I went back to the house. The other two bikes were gone from the garden. I went back inside and upstairs. They'd left the wallet where it had fallen on the floor, alongside the cards. There were three: an Organ Donor card, two membership cards, one for a casino and one for a nightclub, laying face up.

A. KINGDOM on the first two and ALISTAIR KINGDOM on the third.

So that was it, bud. Now I knew my name.

Now I could broadcast it far and wide.

And I did. For the next few days and nights, I flew around the city, whispering those two words into people's ears. At every quiet table in every empty lunchtime pub. In and out of houses where the TV was turned off and only the ticking of the clock on the mantelpiece punctuated the silence. The single dwellers and solitary souls. The loners. The cold unheated kitchens that smelt of fried food and un-emptied bins and condensation. My kind of people.

Not a peep, though, bud. Not a dickie bird. The city was the problem. It's impossible. Or, rather, not the city, the people in the city. Too much static in their heads. Too much background noise. No one can hear you in the city, not adults, anyway. I tried the children, and one or two of them responded but they were either frightened or nonplussed. None of them offered any insight. Why would the children know me? And what insight could they offer if they did? And anyway, I'd already caused too much trouble among the children.

I gave up on strangers. I shot back to 37 Buckingham. Claire was the only one home. She was up in her room on her laptop talking to her sister in Glasgow. Video call. What's it called, Skype? A Skype call. They were talking about people from their old school. She finished the call and started looking people up on Facebook. I tried whispering it into her ear: Alistair Kingdom, Alistair Kingdom, Alistair Kingdom. But I couldn't connect. She just kept on looking for her Duncans and Isobels and Stuarts. I hung around until the rest of them wandered home. Brett dumped his books and got straight on the bong. Some serial killer nonsense on the TV. No joy there, then. The house could have collapsed around his ears and it wouldn't have registered.

Gemma and Eric turned up a while later with Chinese food and bottles of wine. They were laughing together over some little secret. I could smell the pub on them. They ate their food in the kitchen, at the table and on plates rather than on their laps in front of the TV, which was their usual wont. Something was going on, I could tell. Eric even helped with the washing up. After they'd eaten they went through to the front room and skinned up. Claire came downstairs and they played music and talked around the two TV's with the sound off. Standard procedure. I couldn't take any joy from them though. There was something wrong.

Gemma and Eric. The balance had been altered while I'd been away. I could sense it in the giggling and the whispered asides and the touching knees on the settee. Eric and his stupid fucking grin. The smell of the wine was getting to me, but I wanted to see what was going. Wanted to be wrong, bud.

Claire was the first to slope off. She had a lecture in the morning. Brett had fallen asleep in the battered old chair in the corner, the drooling fool. Same old song. The needle stuck at the end of the record. Click, bump, click bump, click bump. Gemma nudged him awake and helped him to his feet. He grabbed his bag of greenery and stumbled up the wooden hill to Bedfordshire. That left love's young dream huddled together on the settee.

I had to see it for myself. I didn't want to see it, but I had to be sure. My worst fears confirmed.

And, sure enough, up they went together, hand in hand, all stifled laughter and frantic shushing, knees bumping off the bannister rail, barely held excitement. And the pair of them tip-toed into Gemma's room and ever so quietly clicked the door shut behind them.

I slipped inside after them but soon slipped straight back out again. I won't tell you what I saw bud. I'm sure your vivid imagination will serve you well enough.

My stripe-haired sweetheart and that slimy old con artist. That bastard. I couldn't believe it.

I couldn't handle it, actually. I could feel it all welling up, the heat of my anger. I left the house and I flew around the city at a hundred miles an hour. Ended up in some scummy student night at a club near the river. Stood in the middle of the dance floor and flooded my senses with their noise and sweat and vodka and Red Bull breath. I wanted to shut it all off. Then the lights came up and they all cleared the club and poured themselves into their cabs and their night buses, back to their shared houses and bedsits and halls of residence to smoke and drink some more and wrap themselves tightly around each other until the sun rose on another day in paradise.

I just trailed around the streets like a sad little spectre. I just felt like nothing, bud, a massive black hole of shell shocked nothing. I wanted to die.

But how do you die when you're not even alive?

When the daytime swung into action and the people and the traffic started to trickle back onto the streets I went back to my place of birth. I'd had it with you lot. Human beings, I mean. I could see you, hear you, smell you, almost taste you, even. But the only one who knew I existed was a frightened little boy with no friends of his own and no way of talking back.

I hatched a plan that day. I was going to find Martin and face up to facts. I got it into my head that we could go and haunt the airbase together. Excommunicate ourselves from the whole sorry set-up. Comrades again. Brothers in arms. Me and him. That was my plan. If I was a broken down bum during life, I may as well continue the show into the afterlife. I didn't know whether or not he would be up for it, but I decided to go and find him anyway. I didn't want to be on my own anymore. I mean, June had seen me, right? And a few other ghosts I'd seen drifting around, they could see me, even if none of the bastards would talk to me. But anyway, I didn't want the burden of a stranger. Martin may have left me to die, but he was the nearest thing I had to a friend.

I spent most of the morning at the house then I went back to the Internet Café. I knew that Facebook would be the best bet for me in regards to finding Alistair Kingdom. It seemed every living breathing soul had their details recorded on that thing. Like they had two lives, one in the real world and one on a computer screen. I remembered Brett telling Eric that everything people put on the Internet stayed there forever, even after they died. Surely whatever life I had left behind would be on there somewhere.

I went from machine to machine whispering my name at every ear. Nothing. Not a flicker. They were all engrossed in their own cyber reflections. I stayed there for a while and then decided to give up the ghost and go and find Martin. But first I wanted to go and say goodbye to Ryan. Just to tell him that I was sorry for getting him into trouble and that I wouldn't be bothering him no more. I thought it was the least I could do.

And when I got there Beaumont had the front room set up like a boxing ring. All the furniture pushed back to the wall. Him on his knees facing Ryan, both of them with cushions as boxing gloves, Beaumont holding them up to his face in classic scrapper stance. Ryan looked petrified, big patchwork pancakes hung heavy at the end of those little pipe cleaner arms. He looked like he was about to burst into tears. Beaumont was oblivious, rocking back and forth on his knees, bobbing his big stupid head up and down, snorting, slipping out playful jabs to the chest and taps to the side of the head. Trying to cajole the boy to box. To fight.

Come on Ryan, he said, put your hands up. Get em up. Come on, he'll knock you about every day if you don't learn to look after yourself, bruv. That means putting your hands up. Come on!

Tap tap jab.

But there's not an ounce of fight in the little fella, not a single spark of aggression. He lifts the cushions and places them in front of his face, flinching, hiding.

Come on, don't be a pussy! What's wrong with ya? Do you wanna be bullied? Course not. So get em up.

Jab jab tap.

Ryan, you're not even trying.

I don't want to fight.

Well you're gonna have to ain't ya? Anyway, it ain't fighting it's defending yourself. Come on!

Beaumont drops his cushions and pulls Ryan's arms away from his face, adjusts them into a defensive guard shape. The two cushions raised, tentative, but no real desire to join in.

Good boy, says Beaumont. Now ...

He picks up the cushions again.

Jab jab tap tap jab.

Come on Ryan, fucks sake ...

Tap tap jab jab tap. The cushions swinging harder now. Beaumont snorting hard through his nose with every jab. I can smell the bastard's sweat. Smell his excitement.

TAP!

Ow! Dad!

Oh fuck off, that didn't hurt!

But Ryan's hands have dropped and his eyes are swimming up.

Don't tell me that hurt! Fucks sake!

Beaumont's got this glazed look in his eyes. He swings again: JAB! TAP! TAP, and Ryan moves his head back on the second right hook and Beaumont's cushioned fist catches his nose and there is a sudden spout of red.

A second where everything stands still and then Ryan sees the blood drip to the carpet and screams. And I mean really screams, like a scream that almost rips the room in two.

Beaumont drops the cushion and swings an open handed slap to the side of the boy's head, knocks him clean off his feet. A proper dig, bud, a proper slap from a hairy arsed fifteen stone man. Do you know what I mean? Like, bang, have that. Bounces him off the settee and drops him onto the floor. And Ryan's not even big for a seven year old. Jesus, man, he just batted the poor little bastard off his feet.

That cunt. That stupid dumb fucking animal. I can still see that boy's head snap to the side. Jesus. He could have given that kid brain damage.

Beaumont swears and gets up off his knees, slings the cushions away and storms off into the kitchen. Ryan's laid out on the floor. He's not making a noise and for one horrible fucking moment I think he's knocked him clean out, but he gets to his feet in a pocket of shocked silence and then the screaming and the wailing starts.

The hurt, bud. Not the physical hurt - well, yeah, obviously physical, of course; you could see the red handprint blooming on one entire side of his face - but that screaming was nothing but pure fear. Ever heard that noise, bud? It's not the pain of the body that gives birth to that noise. It's terror, bud. Raw and undiluted terror. When pure and proper fear comes to visit you and grips you firmly by the bollocks it's beyond fight or flight. It's beyond any training. A line had been crossed and that little lad knew it. He wasn't safe any more. Jesus, that crying, man. The depths of those sobs wrenched up from that tiny little chest. He tried to dab at his nose to stop the blood, wincing, making his hands all wet with smeared crimson and tears. I could smell the dampness of his hair as I crouched down next to him and tried to wrap him up safe and warm with whispered words. Don't be scared Ryan, don't be frightened mate, I told him. He's just a bully, I said. He's a coward. I'll sort this cowardly bastard out for you Ryan, don't you worry. I won't let him hurt you any more. Tell your Mum, though, Ryan, I said. You have to tell your Mum.

Beaumont eventually came back with a can of beer and a roll of kitchen towels. The sick bastard acted like nothing had happened. He stood the boy up straight and wiped the blood from his hands and his face, sighing and tutting like the lad had fallen off his fucking bike and was being a big baby about it all.

Ryan's nose hadn't bled too heavily for too long and as far as I could see it wasn't broken. Apart from a few spots on the carpet, most of it was down the front of his T Shirt. Beaumont whipped it off him and took it outside, slung it in the dustbin. Sly bastard never put it in the wash. Then he brought a bowl of hot water from the kitchen and made a half-hearted attempt to clean the blood out of the carpet. Ryan managed to jolt himself out of his trance and escaped, ran upstairs to his room. I followed him up there and kept talking to him, kept surrounding him with soft words of kindness. Eventually he stopped crying and managed to quiet himself down, only the occasional shuddering sob. He got in bed and wrapped Ben Ten around himself, clamped his eyes shut tight and lay there trembling.

Eventually Beaumont comes up the stairs and into Ryan's room. He lifts the boy's chin up and inspects his face. There's an angry red mark, but it's fading. Ryan's eyes are still clamped shut, he's shaking and his teeth are chattering. He's gone into shock, the poor little bastard. Beaumont ruffles his hair, like he's a benevolent fucking scoutmaster handing out a prize.

Good lad, said Beaumont. You did well, son. Proud of you.

I wish my sensory powers extended to reading minds, bud, because I'd love to know what perverted sense of logic brought him to that conclusion. What actually went through what was left of his bombed out brain? Some fractured form of self-hypnosis? Did this piece of pond life really think he was doling out vital life lessons? And son. Calling him son. That really boiled my piss. Not right, bud. No right at all.

And do you know what, Ryan never did tell his Mum, despite my pleading and cajoling and stern voiced instructions. I tried everything to make him tell. But he didn't open his mouth. He just got smaller and quieter, shrunk himself to the corners of the house and kept away from everyone; his Mum, his brother, Beaumont. Especially Beaumont. He even winced when I tried to talk to him. Shook his head and buried it deeper into his books and comics. I had to accept that I was no longer a help or a comfort to him.

I was just another torment.

I thought I'd better get off. I couldn't take it, bud. Couldn't stand to see whatever happened next and not be able to step in and help him. Guilty bystander. It was just unbearable. Fucking unbearable. I headed back to 37, but then I remembered Gemma, her being with that prick. My narrow little world had imploded, bud. It had all come on top.

So I got on a train. I went down to the station and got on the first train I saw. People kissing each other and hugging each other and waving each other goodbye and none of them knew of dead tramps and frightened little boys and the name Alistair Kingdom meant less than nothing to them and to me neither. I stood on the train as it rolled out of the station and picked up speed, past the sidings and the marshalling yards and the stacks of pallets and tyres and rusting hulks of piled up junk and the graffiti tagged walls and signal boxes and picking up speed as it rattled through the sparse suburban stations and the backs of houses, and fewer and fewer houses and then into the countryside, the two lines of bodies sat side by side staring at screens and newspapers and magazines and rain smudged glass out at green and brown fields filled with nothing.

I was raging after he hit that boy. The impotent fury was eating me up inside. But what could I do? Zero. Anything I did do only ended up making everything worse for Ryan. I was best off the scene. So once again, unencumbered by the burdens of others, I was back to square one. Me, myself and I. And even though I had the name, I still had no idea how to go about finding Alistair Kingdom. I was starting to think he didn't exist. So I tried to escape the essential nature of my non-being. Make myself utterly rootless, utterly transitory. No more 37, no more other people's kids, no more airbases and self-absorbed pondering. I thought I might as well lose myself in the world. Getting on and off trains at random, back and forth from the city to the country, two days and nights of endless motion where I tried to empty myself of everything. Every doubt and fear and daydream and every nagging fragment of humanity that I had managed to burden myself with. Every last scrap of human remains.

After three days and nights I was just blank. Nullified. Worse than that, I was starting to build up new reservoirs of animosity. There are only so many spread-sheets and games of Candy Crush you can absorb before you start wishing damnation on the collective soul of humanity. Only so long before the harsh detergent stink of the toilet and the soft aroma of the coffee machine starts to choke you.

So I decided to play Russian Roulette with cars. I went through my hitchhiking phase, if you can call it that. Jumping a cab, technically, I suppose. I'd just get into people's cars and go wherever they were going. Or get out if they stopped anywhere interesting along the journey. I took rides in stranger's cars. No idea where I wanted to go. Nothing I could think of to do. No grand purpose or mission, just abandoning myself to the universe. In a way, a constant change of scenery is just the same as staring at an endless blank wall. Everything merges into one. I suppose I was daring myself, in a way. Giving up any attempt at steering. You're given this vehicle and you have to drive it as best you can until it crashes. Or you crash it. That's what I was doing. Look Ma, no hands.

And it was all out of my hands. I ended up with this guy. I've no idea where he had come from, or where he was going. I only got into his car because he was playing music. He picked out some music. That's why I chose him. He came out of a newsagents and got into his car. I wouldn't have taken much notice, except he didn't just drive straight off. He started looking through a booklet of CD's. Picking the right soundtrack for his ride. I think he was about the same age as me. June had said late twenties, maybe older. This guy was round about there. He spent an age going through these CD's. It was important to him. Had to have the right music. I liked that. He considered each one then selected a disc and slid it into the slot. That was what piqued my interest. I wanted to hear what he'd chosen. I slipped into the car beside him and off we went.

It was music that I'd never heard before; this deep hypnotic instrumental thing, slow and heavy, powerful, but not the electronic stuff that Brett sometimes played, this was organic instruments, something like an orchestral hymn, the scrape of fingers on metal and wood, the hum and crackle of electricity and these choral parts, human voices lifted in harmony and strings and bursts of harmonica floating above. All anchored to this steady bass-heavy beat. And he had it on loud. As loud as a person could stand it, I suppose, looking back now. But it was good; it suited my mood. Music for tuning out to, a soundtrack for looking out at the city slipping by with all it's noise turned off and it's colour turned up, the buildings and signs smudging into one long streak of abstract scenery, until you hit the outskirts, the sparse industrial parts with the newer buildings and fewer people, and then hardly any buildings and no people at all. And then you're out onto the motorway, part of a moving line of dots on a grey ribbon cut into green.

I tell you, the funniest thing, bud, about having no long-term memory - or the most serious thing, should I say - if something bad happens to you, there's no escape. No place to hide in your mind. You can't cast yourself into the future because, having no sense of self, you can't imagine how it could turn out for the better, how you'd adapt yourself to fit into the picture. And you can't take retreat in rosy memories from way back when. You're left to dwell in the moment. Music was always the one thing that allowed me to escape the present. And the music in this car was transcendental. Everything outside was a blur and everything inside was standing still.

It starts to rain outside. I'm just staring out of the passenger window, letting the passing landscape wipe clean my tapes.

This guy driving, he's doing nothing to distract me. Nothing in his manner or bearing to suggest the danger looming in the distance. If I'd have been doing my usual people watching instead of immersing myself in the music, I would have noted the state he was in. I remember catching a glimpse of red-eyed fatigue in the rear view mirror, but then just looking away. I had no desire to engage, the mood I was in. I'd seen enough weeping to last me several lifetimes. It was starting to weigh heavily on me, the life of the unwilling witness. The notion did start to suggest itself to me, there and then, actually - abandon the quest. I knew, though, I knew deep down, that if I did do that, if I forgot my name and number and lived as a blank piece of paper blowing in the wind, then I would never know peace. Ever. I'd be like those tormented spooks round the back of the bombed out houses, those drifting shadows locked in the arms of eternal torment.

So, check this, bud. We're turning off a dual carriageway onto a long stretch of road. Country road. There are fields either side. I have no idea where we are. We're hurtling along. Then we slow right down. And I seem to feel the car slow down, the momentum of the car and the weight of myself within my surroundings. I feel ever so briefly that I am being pinned into my seat. Velocity, bud. This is a new one for me. Music has probed me in many ways that went beyond flesh and bone, but I could never feel the trains slowing down, or any other cars, for that matter. I just used to get out whenever I wanted. Step on and off speeding vehicles, in the same way that I would walk through a door or a wall or the middle of a bonfire. Useful trick. Anyway, the movement pulls me out of my reverie and I look up there's a silver car about twenty metres in front of us. And in front of the silver car there's a tractor trundling along. We're being forced to slow down. But it's OK. The music is lulling now, a meandering pattern of cymbals and bass drum, a pulse, fragmentary piano notes scattering over the top and the faint swell of strings, or voices maybe, voices raised in chorus. I was trying to work out the words. I couldn't understand them. I don't think they were even in English. I remember thinking that maybe I could learn a new language and go and live somewhere else in the world. Fly first class, why not. It made no difference to me.

Winking orange light on the corner of the silver car in front of us. It swings out and overtakes the tractor. The fella sat next to me decides to follow suit. Except he's a good way behind this silver car and what this guy hasn't realized is, this is no longer a dual carriage way. This is not one-way traffic. The road is curving away in front of us, and we build up speed up, draw level with the silver car and as it slips in front of the tractor to the left I can see a line of traffic in front of us, getting bigger in the windscreen.

Coming head-on towards us.

We're on the wrong side of the road and we can't get out of the way.

I can literally feel the guy seize up in his seat next to me. Feel the lightning bolt of pure and utter fear that jolts his bones. And this is fucking electrifying for me too, Mr Listener. And remember, I was a man who had no fear of the physical world. I passed through every obstacle uncontested. This truck could smash clean through me now and I would emerge without a scratch. I know this without thinking.

But now I feel fear. Physical dread. It leaps from him to me, a cold blue spark that strikes me hot and cold at once. This guy, he knows he's staring death right in the face.

Empathy, you son of a bitch.

Fight or flight.

Split second choice: if we slam the brakes on and try to get back into line, we'll probably flip the car. We're going too fast and there's no way of knowing what's going to happen behind us. So we gun the engine and we go for it, and I swear I can feel every particle of that vehicle tremble and moan with fear, every scrap of metal and steel and rubber and glass shudder with the knowledge of it's own delicacy.

We're speeding straight into the arms of oncoming death. Half a ton of machinery reduced to the strength of a snowflake.

A lorry looming huge in the windscreen now. I can read the name above the cab: WYNDSOR, written in slanting block green capitals. It's right in front of us. I can see the face of the driver, sat up high in his cab, higher than us, higher than God. A face split open with sudden shock. The face of man who doesn't know whether he's going to be alive or dead in the next ten seconds.

We need to get in front of the silver car.

We put our foot down and the engine screams and I'm thrown back into the seat as the rubber burns beneath us.

And we do it, but only just, only fucking just, the horn of the lorry blaring as we arrow into the smallest of gaps, silver flashing one side of us, the weight of the lorry hurtling past on the other. I spin round and see the silver car perform a quick wobble, sashaying across the road, once, twice, but then righting itself. Open-mouthed shock of the driver behind, shrinking rapidly behind us to a tiny silver dot.

We are still going insanely fast. Nothing in front of us but empty road.

The fella beside me starts shouting.

OH CHRIST! he goes. OH *JESUS FUCKING CHRIST!*

And then: YOU *CUNT!* YOU STUPID FUCKING THOUGHTLESS *CUNT!* OH HELEN! COURTNEY! OH COURTNEY! I'M SORRY BABY! FUCK! *FUCK!*

Then he starts crying. Or what sounds like crying. Like the shriek of an animal. Shock, that's what it was. I don't look. He's crying and banging on the steering wheel. I look out of the window on my side, at the fields flashing by. Gradually, he stops crying and he slows right down, pulls over in a lay-by behind two big lorries and he gets out of the car, lights a cigarette. His hands are trembling. Leans against the car and double drags his cigarette to the nub then fumbles another from the packet, blazes up again. He stands and smokes. Gradually he calms down. He calms down and he gets back into the car and he sits there on the hard shoulder and waits for the adrenaline to subside.

Courtney, he's saying. Oh my baby. I'm sorry. I am so sorry.

Eventually, he gathers what's left of his frazzled nerves back together and pulls back out into the traffic. Heads for home to the loving arms of his wife and children and his comfy warm slippers by the fireside.

At least I presume that's what he does. I'm long gone by then. I'm in the cab of a truck on the other side of the road, heading back to the city, listening to a Danish lorry driver singing along to a 1980's power ballad on the radio.

Thing is, I felt it, bud That glorious and terrifying rush of adrenaline that can only come with being alive. I felt it as sure as I felt the music in my chest or the slow down lurch of the car. The seat beneath me. Me, sat down. The sensation of being sat down. Seated. Tied to something. You've no idea how that felt. It was only a flash-frame, a snatched moment of sensation, but it was there. I knew for certain that it was. As real as the bars on that window.

I noticed it again when I got back to the city and started to move along the street. I started to feel the hint of something firm beneath me. The princess and the pea. Ever read that one? That was me, bud. A newly sensitive soul, the act of propulsion somewhere beneath me. A sense of landscape. Terrain. Not surefooted, no, not solid at first, but a definite awareness of forward momentum. Pushing forward. A sense of occupying a space and moving through it. No longer that hollow at the centre, but something more, something vaguely substantial, spreading all ways outward. I came to a decision, there and then, I think.

I decided that I didn't want to be a ghost any more.

... FRAGMENTS RETURNING ...

... and panting hard the breaths going in and out like knives and the throat ragged and hard and bits of nothing stinging ... weight behind and weight above sagging bones of exhaustion ... heft of hard metal on bone, the weight of the world on your shoulder ... burst of static ... brown blood stained like human shit ... life sprayed across hot metal .. and the taste of hot nothing in the mouth ... the taste of hard dry nothing ... bits of hot hard dry nothing waiting for cold ... heat burning up one side ... crackle of voice tiny ... burst of static ... ACK ACK ACK ACK ACK ACK ACK ..... tiny black teardrops scattered on hard caked yellow ... feet hot in boots dragging over endless caked yellow ... ... birds above ... chorus of crickets below ... crack and sparkle .... shock of light in dark sky ... not stars ... not the many stars studded up there ... light that has no natural place ... sudden light put there on purpose ... whizz and BANG and whistle ... purple edged mountains briefly electrified ... water on cracked dry lips and water spread on sand ... hot touch of metal beneath flesh ... heavy cloth stuck to skin ... heavy with sweat and the stiffness of salt ... SMACK MY BITCH UP ....apricots and lemons and the nodding fields of pink .. dank vegetation ... dank dark green ... sweat and the tongue dabbed upwards the smell of salt on the soaking dark wet shirt ... human shit and cattle shit and goat shit and the sharp stink of fear ...SEND THESE CAVEMEN FUCKS BACK TO THE STONE AGE ... and Yorkshire voices and London voices, American voices .... single squeeze of a finger on metal .... and the sudden blinding flash and boom and a red ball of fire and the black cloud billowing upwards and out and filling the sky above and then the gentle flutter of warm grey snow descending ... warm grey snow and pale green eyes ... mister, mister ... mister, mister ... ... square block of dull yellow now a ball of red and orange ... heat firing up one side ... sweat crawling down your back and black clouds rolling ... rising ash ... floating grey stars dying ... spiralling upwards ... and the stars are dead ... all the stars have died by the time the light hits your eyes ... by the time the light hits the back of your eyes, all the stars are dead ...

PART FIVE

SEPARATION AND CARE UNIT
CELL 1/005
04.11 AM

Love the tattoo, by the way. They're very popular on the neck, aren't they? Especially in here, I've noticed. Same designs over and over again, though. Stars and initials and dates of birth. Names of wives and girlfriends and children. And that one you've got there: Only God Can Judge Me, that's a favourite isn't it? Writ large in Biblical scroll where everyone can see it. Suitably defiant, eh, bud? A bold renouncement of all responsibility. And guilt as well, I suppose. Who inspired you to engrave that on yourself? Because it's hardly an original epitaph, is it? Tupac Shakur, I presume? The Mohammed of the thug population. Brett used to play Tupac a lot. He liked the salty vernacular, I think - bitch, pussy, ho, motherfucker. Another nice middle-class lad living out his daydreams of violence in a second-hand gangster paradise. I'm assuming it is Tupac you're channelling, and not Tony Blair? Because that was one of his lines as well, wasn't it? God will be my judge. Or some such nonsense. Well, as much as I can understand the need for such a sentiment amongst common or garden criminals, personally, I can't fully concur.

You see, bud, I don't want God to judge me. For two reasons, really; one, my own personal powers of judgment leave me in no doubt about the nature of my crimes, and two, if God is as benevolent and forgiving as they say he is, then I can safely assume whatever he has in store for me will fall far short of the fate I deserve. No, bud, God cannot judge me. Besides, he's already been beaten to it; once by the general public, and again, by my own self. I'll be the judge of me, and nobody else. Not you, not him, not the seven hundred and fifty two friends I've got on Facebook. Anyway, like I told you, I'm not even sure there is a God. Or a devil, or a heaven, or a hell. All I know is this. This is all there is. There is nothing, and then there's this. And after this, there's another big portion of nothing. I dearly hope so, anyway.

So where were we? Touch. Yes. The missing piece of the puzzle.

That narrow escape on the road had heightened my senses and brought the physical world a little bit closer. I stood in the garden a few mornings later and felt the wind on my face. Or maybe it was the memory of the wind on my face. Either way, there was definitely something there. I moved around and felt something beneath me. Some resistance between myself and the space around me. Where I ended and the world began. And something else had changed: I couldn't just think myself into a physical space any more. I had to walk everywhere, bud. A ponderous pedestrian, just like you. The scenes had to be joined up by interludes. No more disappearing in a puff of smoke. I was glad in a way. It was a marked progression from the previous trans-migratory nonsense. But I wasn't the finished article just yet. The borders were only just beginning to be established. I was still a good way from full engagement.

It was Beaumont who inspired the final push.

I killed Lee Beaumont on November the fifth. Bonfire night. There was a firework display in the park. We were all there – me, Gemma, Eric, Claire, Brett, Cookie, Stacey, the kids, Cookie's kids and some other little girl, a mate of Cookie's daughter, I think. A proper family outing. Gemma and Stacey and Cookie took the kids for tea in a local bar and met up with the rest of us later. We were on the side of the hill at the far end of the park. Beaumont wasn't with us. Him and Stacey had had an almighty bust up a few nights before. She'd gone through the washing and found a crack pipe in his jeans pocket. Little glass dick emblazoned with I LOVE LONDON. It all kicked off royal style. He tried to front it, but Stacey was wired and got him on the back foot. Much shouting and threatening from both parties. He ended up punching a cupboard door off its hinges and slamming his way out of the house. Hadn't been home since. I was praying he would never come back. So much more peaceful without him. Gemma had made Stacey swear on their mother's lives that she wouldn't have him back.

I never heard any reference to the thing with Ryan. There was no way she could have known. Ryan had been cowed into silence; that much was obvious. He wouldn't even speak to me when I came back, the first few times. I reckoned I'd better leave him alone for a while until he regained the confidence that bastard had walloped out of him. I just hung back and watched and waited. He spent a lot of time with his Auntie Gemma. They were a tight little unit again without that cunt Beaumont looming in the background.

There was a good crowd in the park, a couple of hundred at least. I'd never seen it so full. I lost all physical sense of myself in crowds. All the vague suggestions of terra firma and external ebb and flow seem to diminish with the presence of other bodies. Almost like the existence of others detracted from my own. And this was a big crowd, the biggest I'd been a part of. I just melted among them.

The main bonfire was on the crest of the hill, where the ground flattened out and stretched to the big town houses at the edges. It was a fierce and mighty sight, a huge red and orange monster licking its yellow tongues upwards, cracking and banging. There was a wooden totem pole planted behind it, a giant column of painted faces; birds and animals and grotesque monsters. This is where they were letting the fireworks off at 8pm. The main display. There were smaller bonfires lit here and there, and the occasional rocket fizzed upwards; angry snakes with tails of white and yellow. Whizz-bang crack, an occasional shower of stars that drew gasps of delight from the crowd, but there was a sense that it was premature, all too quick. The excitement was being reigned in, in anticipation of the main event. It was tangible. Kids conducting invisible orchestras with fizzing batons, leaving tiny trails of sparks in the dark. There were floodlights around the main footpath, but the patches of grass between the bonfires were solid darkness. Passing people were looming shadows and faces lit by firelight. I could almost feel the heat from the flames as we passed by. I thought I could, anyway. Almost. A definite flicker.

Then I saw him. Beaumont. He was a good way off, stood talking to a loose collection of other miscreants about ten feet from a moderate sized bonfire. Hard-faced men in hoods and jeans and trainers. Men in their thirties dressed as teenage boys. I could tell by his stance and general bearing that he was completely smashed. The feet planted apart. The Neanderthal head rolling on the thick bull neck. An obligatory joint glowing in cupped hand. I scooted over and checked his eyes. Tiny black dots of dullness. Like staring into the eyes of some sub-aquatic bottom level feeder fish. He reeked of alcohol and crack and industrial strength marijuana. A rapid stream of bullshit leaving his spittle-flecked mouth.

I glanced back at Ryan. He'd spotted him too, and I could see he was getting agitated. I zipped back over and tried to console him. It's OK mate, I whispered, it's OK. Don't be frightened. He clung onto his mother, who patted and rubbed his head, mistaking his nerves for starry eyed excitement, blithely chatting away to Cookie about the firework display she used to go to before they lived round here, the one on the other side of town. Not as good as this one, apparently. This one was special. People came from all over the city to see this display. And it was nearly upon us, the main event. Nearly time to light the main touch paper. People were getting impatient; you could feel it, the collective tension.

Then the rockets shooting into the sky started to multiply, one single streak of light following another, then two close together, then three, then four. Zip –zip - zip - zip. All heads tilted upwards. Soon they were whizzing and banging every two or three seconds, falling stars replaced by fresh showers of light. All the colours, but mainly white, and other colours that you could have mistaken for yellow, but were really a dirty phosphorous white. They started to shoot up thick and fast, but this was a mere warm up, a bit of snack crackle and pop to tickle the blood before the real show. Despite my unease at the presence of Beaumont, I was excited. The way they'd been bigging it up, I was expecting Apocalypse Now choreographed by Walt Disney.

They were very good though, I must admit. I was impressed. In fact, when I think about it, it was the fireworks that fired me up. And believe me, bud, I've seen proper pyrotechnics. I've seen the heavens open and spew forth hell. This display on the park was nothing like that, obviously. But it was the nearest I'd been to it in this lifetime. This emerging lifetime, should I say. Maybe that was why I ended up taking him out. He was the victim of a blast from the past. Because the past was letting off the fireworks in my head.

It all started getting rather serious. The crowd were craning their heads back as it all unfolded above them. Sudden balls of colour that burst out of nowhere with a CRACK and hung suddenly huge in the sky - blue, white, purple, red planets that existed for a second or so then shrunk to dots of nothing. Squeals from the crowd. Genuine shrieks of pleasure. Then your eyes became accustomed to the pitch black of the sky and you started to spot the sources of light, started to pick out the missiles and the rockets: the phut-phut-phut-phut-phut like a jet propelled fountain spitting up tiny bars of gold; these barely discernible climbing dots and that elegant soaring whistle, then SHREIK BANG CRACK, instant globes of electric colour and whiplash lariats of gold and fading haloes and showers of molten lava, and the longer I look and the harder I stare, I start to see shapes and forms in all these false stars spread above me.

I see everything, bud; leering monkey faces and grinning cats and kings and queens and rainbows and diamonds and birds and spaceships and the severed head of Shakespeare served up on a plate. I see a rocking horse and an orchestra and a tidal wave of treasure; gold and silver coins, diamonds, chains and cups and medals and trophies spilled across the sky, overflowing from a golden horn of plenty. Screams and whistles coming thick and fast now, explosions that paint a thousand rapid-fire pictures and machine gun bursts of titanium snowflakes, soaring birds that spread their wings and then suddenly detonate, flowers rapidly bursting into electric blooms of blue, red, green, yellow, white, purple, orange, and each of them brushing the other with their beauty. A bouquet that never stops unfolding. And the heat, bud. I could feel the heat above me, and the flames leaping from the bonfires.

I was glowing inside and out.

Then it kicked up a gear: oblong blocks of searchlights stabbing upwards and freeze-framing the treetops and the buildings in the distance, the two hundred or so up-tilted faces freeze-framed by more and more clouds of stars, like swipes from a wet paintbrush gradually drying and crumbling and flaking away, scraps of light falling from the black wall of the sky and the crowd going WOOH and WOAH and Stacey saying to herself how do they even do that and Brettski starting to explain how they do that and Gemma telling him to shut the fuck up. And little Ryan with his head snapped back and his eyes shining with flames and falling stars.

Then the climax, a battery of heavy duty artillery that floods everything above in blanket upon blanket of starburst, a cacophonous riot of colour, then an almighty BANG and a rapidly expanding death star fills the sky, draws a huge collective gasp and whistles and cheers and applause as it swells enormous and grows spikes of gold, then a lions mane of bright yellow exploding into a halo of impossibly white and blinding light. Like that same flash of white that signalled my birth and everything illuminated, bud, the sky and the stars and the massed ranks below, everything caught and enraptured. Then a final flurry of neon arrows and the sky fading and the smoke hanging heavy and the stink of rotten eggs clinging to the air and right there bud, right there in that tiny pocket of silence I sucked in my first breath and felt the sharp tug of Planet Earth somewhere deep within me as the crowd held its collective breath for one long moment and then cheered as one, a sudden deafening roar of approval and applause that made Brett raise his fingers to his mouth and whistle and Ryan clamp his hands over his ears.

The crowd started to move away. We turned and moved with them, headed back down the hill. The waves of people thinned out the further we walked. And yeah, I was walking, bud. I was treading the damp and heavy earth. I could feel it sucking at my feet beneath me.

And then he was there, right in front of us. He was on his own, walking back to the main bonfire. He saw Gemma first, stopped dead in his tracks, then his eyes found Stacey and that dull light of savagery ignited. Game on. He came with sneers and swagger and Stacey clutched the kids to her, cowed, but Gemma was straight on the front foot. The men, Cookie and Eric and Brett ... well, forget Brett, I don't think he even registered what was happening, stars in his eyes still, but the rest of the unit, the men among the group, they bottled it totally. Never said a word. Frightened. Gemma was the only one with any balls.

She strode forward and planted herself in front of her sister and nephews and grabbed a handful of Beaumont's jacket as he tried to get round her.

Just fuck off, Lee, she says. Get the fuck away from them and stay away.

I was right next to her, shoulder to shoulder. I was fired up by light and explosions. I thought for a second that Beaumont was going to kick off but there were yellow-vested stewards circling the edges of the crowd, attracted by the raised voices. They carried enough official presence to quell Mr Beaumont's ardour. He was hopelessly pissed and juiced up, snarling like a tiger, but he was also, as Gemma reminded him, on licence.

You'll go straight back inside, Lee, she told him. One phone call. That's all it takes.

She held his eyes and never wavered. You can tell when someone is serious. When they really fucking mean it. That core of steel at the centre.

Beaumont hesitated for that vital moment and the rest of them made their move. Gemma kept a tight hold of his jacket as Stacey and the kids and the rest of them filed silently past. Then she turned and pushed him up the hill. Launched him towards the flames. Now you go that way and we'll go the other, she said. He stumbled backwards, nearly fell over. Keep walking, she said. He hurled a load of foul-mouthed rubbish at her – fucking fat slag, ugly fucking dyke bitch etc. etc. She just laughed and turned her back on him. Walked away. He stood clenching and unclenching his fists, burning a hole in her back with his eyes and for a second I thought he was going to launch himself at her, but instead he spat at her, the dirty animal, launched a mouthful of filthy gob through the air and spattered the back of her jacket. A couple of the yellow vests were closing in and he turned and headed up the hill.

Something snapped inside of me bud. Or, rather, something connected. Yeah, that's the one. Something clicked. Slotted together like the parts of a rifle. I followed him up the hill. I was fucking burning inside bud, but a *cold* burning, a cold blue flame of absolute focused fury. Training kicked in. He was in my sights. The bastard was in my cross hairs. I sped up until I was right on his shoulder. Beaumont, you piece of shit, I whispered.

And he heard me. The dirty fucking animal pricked his ears up and heard me. Stopped dead in his tracks and looked round and saw no one. Everyone was walking around him, moving in the opposite direction, back down the hill. Nobody meeting his bleary-eyed gaze of belligerence.

It's me, you piece of shit, I told him. Alistair Kingdom. I am Alistair Kingdom. Remember that name, cunt, because you're gonna take it down to hell with you.

He shook his head and started up again. But he was rattled, I could tell.

Fear had made him unsteady. I could smell it leaking from every part of him. I just kept whispering my mantra into his ear, my promise of everlasting damnation. I swung around in front of him, walking backwards and chewing his face off. You're going to hell, I told him. You're going straight to hell you fucking piece of scum sucking shit.

He sped up. Broke into a rapid stumble, barging through the oncoming crowd, bodies bouncing off of him. Raised voices. Hands reaching out to snatch. Two yellow vests closing in behind us.

We break free of the crowd and head for the light.

So now we're up against the main bonfire. Huge and raging pyramid of flames. I can feel the heat on one side of myself. I can feel it, bud, it's there. I'm there. I'm half lit up. I follow him round the edges, Beaumont, this lurching animal. That's what he is to me now. I tell him that he's an animal, a sick diseased beast that needs to be put down as I pursue him around the rear of the pyre. And I can hear hard breathing and I realise it's me. The sound of myself. There are two shadows spilling across the grass, two long black shadows. Him and me. There's hardly anybody else, the people are all streaming down the hill on the other side. Just a few yellow vests, still circling. Beaumont stops and fumbles about in his pockets, pulls out a packet of cigarettes and puts one in his mouth. Stands swaying, flame cupped, but his hands are trembling and he can't get a light.

Beaumont!

I call him by his name. He looks up, startled, cigarette still unlit, and he sees me. He fucking sees me, bud. His eyes widen and I make my move, I rush at the bastard and send him flying. Full contact bud, flesh and blood and bone colliding. Direct hit. Oh, Christ, nothing so joyous, bud! Nothing so sweet and true and fucking righteous! I smash into him and he flies backwards and hits the ground. I can't believe it. All those months of absence and here I am, at long, long last. The world no longer beyond my reach.

I can feel every sinew sing.

But there's no time to start feeling triumphant about myself because he's straight back up again, all jelly-legged and arms flailing. I don't even think about it, no internal debate, no jousting for position, just pure response. Hard instinctive action. It ain't why, why, why; it just is. I grab him by the scruff of the neck and spin him around, arm jammed up behind his back, and I frog march the bastard towards the pyre, right to the edge of the flames, the heat roaring around us, and I send him straight to hell. Throw him into the fire with every ounce of my newfound strength. He goes stumbling forward and the burning wood collapses and crashes around him and he's engulfed.

He put up a decent fight, though; I'll give the bastard that. Three times he struggled back to his feet and came thrashing back out of the inferno and three times I kicked him back in. Smashed him back into a collapsing avalanche of wood and flame. The final time he crawled out, his clothes on fire, his hair on fire, the flesh sloughing off his hands and face, I just stood back and watched him foam and bubble at my feet. The smell of him and myself in the cold night air. That sweet and awful stink. Burning flesh. I knew that smell, bud. I knew it like a baby knows it's own mother.

The yellow vests started swarming around his blackened body, beating at him with jackets and blankets. They managed to put him out, but by that point he didn't resemble anything much like a human being. He was a piece of purple meat, a giant pepperoni with a burnt black match for a head. They covered him up and kept the few straggling onlookers away until the ambulance arrived and then he was surrounded by paramedics who got him onto a stretcher and raced him away with an accompanying chorus of shrieking blue lights.

I went along for the ride. I wanted to make sure he was dead. I sat next to him in the ambulance. Nobody seemed to notice me, or if they did they didn't seem to care. All their attention was focussed on the barely breathing Beaumont. Christ, he stunk. I was almost gagging in that ambulance. We sped through the streets like a screaming blue rocket. Hold on son, this paramedic guy kept saying. Hold on, son.

But I knew he was fucked.

They got him into intensive care and went through the frenzied routines of life-saving, assaulting him with dressings and drips and oxygen masks, but it was no good. A waste of public resources if you ask me. He was burnt to the bone. I could see bits of him glistening beneath the operating lights. At six am he finally gave up the ghost and they pulled their gloves off, switched off the machines and walked away. Went and had a much needed coffee and waited for the next hopeless case.

I was elated. Not so much with Beaumont and the manner of his passing, but with my new found powers of touch. This is where it all kicked off, bud. It all started to slot into place after that. Touch. That was the one. The most underrated of the five senses, I reckon. You see, after touch came feeling. I could start to feel the planet exerting its pull on me. I found out who I was by touch. Not by killing Beaumont, although that was part of it. That was easy, killing Beaumont. Utterly straightforward. Morally, I mean. I could square that one, no danger. Conscience clear, honour intact. I felt bad for Connor, because for better or worse he did look up to his adopted Dad. But I saw that as misdirected affection. He was better off without him. Growing up and calling that Dad? No. No, no, no. Not good. We'd have just ended up with another Beaumont on our hands. The way I saw it, I'd done the world a favour.

Mission accomplished.

I was still anonymous, though. I realised that after I left the hospital. I'd ridden back in the ambulance and stood over the operating theatre and it wasn't until I wandered back out blinking under the early morning street lights that I realised nobody had questioned my presence. I was still buzzing from his passing, so at first it didn't register. I remember telling everybody in the hospital that I was a friend, a concerned friend, but nobody had paid me any notice. I presumed they were all too intent on doing their job, saving his worthless life. But the fact of the matter was I was still invisible. For all my new-found connection I was still a fucking ghost to the everyday citizen.

So, like every other one of your human emotions, elation didn't last. I traipsed through the early morning commuters and not an eye met mine. Even the lost and lonely souls from the other side of the veil seemed to be giving me a wider berth than usual. All the ghosts skulking in the doorways and hovering on the corners, all those fellow spectres, even they seemed to shrink away from my gaze. I looked down at myself and there was still nothing there, no arms, no legs, still that absence, still hidden from my own self.

I could reach out and touch the world but I still had no discernible place there.

I think it was at that point that I knew who I was, if I'm being truthful. What I'd done. The real and unchangeable essence of my nature. I felt the weather closing in on me, the damp coldness of early winter sinking into my bones and I knew, bud. I knew what I was. The fragments were falling upon me thick and fast and starting to weigh me down.

Beaumont, I didn't give two shits about him. And Martin, well, that was inevitable, really. That would have happened with or without my help. It was all the others I couldn't cope with. The women and the children, mainly. And, yeah the men, if I'm being truthful. Even those who I could class as the enemy, those I could justify under the terms of engagement. But the children. The fucking children, bud, in the schools and the hospitals and the playgrounds.

I couldn't bear to think about it.

I walked all the way out of the city and back to the airbase. It was cold out there, colder than the city with all its constant hum of cars and bodies and buildings. I didn't care though. I needed the space and the time to think, and the cold was a welcome distraction. I walked around the abandoned shells of the prefabs and put my hands all over the concrete walls, felt the cracks and the peeling paint. Scuffed my feet on the concrete and walked to the end of the runway, stood at the edge of the field and watched the skyline. A vee of geese honking overhead, on their way to warmer climes. Amazing fact number two hundred and forty eight: birds who fly in formation over long distances take it in turns to fly at the head. When the leader gets tired he drops behind and has a rest, glides along on the wind generated by the beating of the wings in front. That way, they get to cover long distances without wearing everybody out at once. Teamwork, bud. Pretty cool, yeah? I stood there and watched them fly away towards that big pale sun and I wished I were a goose.

Something caught my eye closer to the ground. The grass moving. Rabbits darting about in the field. Two of them flashed close by, about ten feet or so way and before I knew what I was doing, I'd took off after them. One of them peeled away and disappeared down a hole but the other veered off in the other direction and raced away at top speed, ears back, legs flying behind him. I ran and ran and ran as fast as I could, tried to keep him in sight, ran until I thought I would burst wide open and at one point I was nearly on him bud, nearly on top of him, but the little bastard kicked up another gear and left me sprawling and gasping in the damp dewed grass. I lay there for a good long while and listened to the thump of my heart on the earth.

I was alive, bud.

It was happening.

I stuck around the airbase for a while until the sun climbed to ten o'clock then I wandered through the fields and straightened up along the riverbank, walked back into the city. Kept looking down to see if my feet would show themselves. Feet don't fail me now. But it wasn't happening. Still a big no-show on the physical front.

When I go to the first main road I decided to do the Pepsi challenge. There wasn't much traffic about, just the occasional passing car, but they were doing a fair old speed. I waited for a gap and walked out into the middle of the tarmac. A small dot appeared on the horizon and got bigger and bigger and bigger. A black VW Golf. I could see the badge on the grill taking shape and the bonnet above it, the face behind the wheel. A woman with dark hair tied back off her face and large square glasses. Her face registered nothing as she thundered towards me. And then I did something I never thought I could do, something that I'd never attempted to pull off before, something that I had never even occurred to me, now I come to think about it, but at that precise moment I did it without even thinking.

I closed my eyes.

As the car roared towards me I closed my eyes and waited for the impact. Goodbye, cruel world. Then I felt the weight of the wind blast straight through me and I was lifted onto the balls of my feet and then set down again as gently as a baby being lowered into its cot. Lovingly, almost. It was like being on a rollercoaster, bud. That plunging thrill of danger, and the proximity of death.

But I wasn't dead.

By the time I got back onto my home patch it was midday. Time to pull back the curtain and face the mirror. I knew where to go. I'd seen the routine.

Everybody who was anybody in this world had two lives; one in the real world and one on a computer screen. Next stop, the Internet café.

I hung about until it was nearly closing time. I had to summon the courage, bud. I was about to unwrap the Christmas present. When the last straggler student picked his bag up and vacated the premises I slipped into his seat and put my fingers to the keyboard. People often took off and left a bit of credit in the bank. I had five minutes left.

I'd seen Claire do it a thousand times before. Watched her summon up people at will. I got onto Facebook and typed my name and the city into the search box.

And there I was. Hair cut short and clean-shaven my square face and heavy brow and those small dark eyes set back. Che Guevara my arse. Simian. That's what I looked like. A brutal scowling monkey in a uniform. My face, and the purple and black banner behind me; the medal and the two silhouettes, carrying their fallen friend on a stretcher.

Help for Heroes.

Faces and words in the boxes below. I sat and stared at the screen as the clock ticked away the remaining seconds in the top right hand corner.

About.

Timeline.

Photos.

Friends.

God bless you mate.

We'll never forget you, Al.

Love from Sapper Keith and all the lads.

Billy likes this.

This one's for you, Al.

Men with metal limbs giving the thumbs up.

Sign up here for 10K Charity Run.

It's National Hug Day.

Always In Our Hearts, Al.

Love and Respect, mate x

I clicked and clicked and clicked, leapt from one box to the next, but I didn't recognise any of the faces.

Two minutes or so left.

I put my name into Google and found a newspaper article.

The body of Alistair Kingdom had been found dead in a derelict house on the morning of January the twelfth 2013. Mr Kingdom, a former paratrooper in Her Majesty's 2nd Battalion Parachute Regiment had struggled to adapt to civilian life after his time in service. Friends had reported that Mr Kingdom had become increasingly depressed since his return from Afghanistan and had struggled with a drink problem. There were concerns that Mr Kingdom was suffering from Post Traumatic Stress Disorder. He had lost touch with former colleagues and friends in the months leading up to his death. Cause of death was reported as coronary arrest brought about by acute intoxication and prolonged exposure to the elements.

There was more, but that was the essence of it.

I Googled Alistair Kingdom, Afghanistan.

Another article. Seventeen Afghani children had died when Coalition Forces aimed a rocket-propelled grenade at a religious school in an attack against the Taliban in the Zarghun Shah District of Paktika Province. An army spokesmen said several al-Qa'eda insurgents were killed and one captured in the attack. It came hours after a suicide bomber killed 28 people in Kabul, the largest single loss of life in a Taliban attack since 2001. US-led coalition forces accepted responsibility for the Paktika raid, but accused the Taliban of using the children as human shields. "We are saddened and outraged by the innocent lives that were lost as a result of extremist militants' cowardice," said Lieutenant Colonel Adam Dawson.

2Para Alistair Kingdom had been awarded the Operational Service Medal following the raid, serving with distinction in armed combat.

I remember a few things now. From earlier, I mean. Not just my time out there. Not many. Just fragments, really. I can see snatches of scenes, but it's like it's not me, like it's a film starring someone else. A little boy marching up and down in front of a pebbledash wall with a sweeping brush propped over his shoulder. Left right, left right. That same little boy pushing a toy truck along a cold kitchen floor. Dappled light on the lino and voices above me. Bigger people. Grown-ups. A big house with other small children. A row of beds. Green fields and the sound of the sea somewhere. Salt spray on my face. There's no Mum or Dad in the memory bank. Nothing on

Facebook either. You'd have thought there would be, wouldn't you, bud? A loving message from a mother. And Dads usually cast a long shadow, don't they, absent or not? Maybe I never had parents to begin with. Or maybe they were both dead before me? But there's no reference anywhere. My Facebook friends are mainly from the forces. I liked music, I know that. There's videos dedicated to me, soundtrack to my life, it seems – Kings Of Leon, Stereophonics, Oasis. Songs I've never heard of. But that song was up there, that Live Forever. I knew that one. This one's for you, Al. That's what it said underneath. You and I are gonna Live Forever. From a stern faced fella called Jimmy with a maroon beret and a full black beard. There's a picture of him with a small girl cradled in his arms. He's holding her up to his face and kissing her. Christ knows who he is.

I've got seven hundred and fifty two friends on Facebook and I don't know a single fucking one of them.

The time ran out and I took my leave. I trudged along the High Street. Everything looked utterly foreign to me. This place that had become so familiar, and it was like I'd been away for months and months. Years. Stranger in a strange land.

I decided to head for home.

I pass the swimming pool. There's a small dog tied up outside. A Jack Russell, little lemon-white thing with half a patched brown face. He catches sight of me and he starts yelping and barking. He's rearing up and pulling tight his lead, front legs pedaling the air. I go over to him and hunker down, ruffle his ears and stroke under his chops. I can feel his skull beneath the fur. The dome of his head and the narrow bony jaw. He's licking my hand. I can feel his little sandpaper tongue where my hand should be. He's the first living thing that seems pleased to see me. Delighted, in fact. He rolls over onto his back and shows me his pale pink underneath. I tickle him up and down; rub my hands all over his belly and throat. I can feel his engine running beneath that warm downy skin. His heart and lungs and liver. Amazing fact about the Jack Russell: the gene that gives their coat its distinctive white colouring is the same gene that makes them prone to deafness. I snap my fingers next to his ear and his head jerks and he springs up onto his feet. There's a silver disc hung from his collar: Denny. I unclip the lead from his harness and walk away, clapping my thigh. Come on Denny, I say. Come on boy. He trots after me, follows me down the main road and through the side streets, past GAS OFF and DO NOT ENTER - DANGER OF DEATH and KITTEN LOST, BLACK AND WHITE CALL 07968043568 and JASON = NONCE. and BIRCHY OV OPE and FAGGOT AND BRINGHAM - SHIT ROOF BUYERS. Follows me back to the place of birth.

I'm still not sure why I did that. Why I kidnapped him, I mean. Impulsive act. Stupid, really; burdening myself down with an extra body when I was on a mission. But he was great, that little dog. I played with him in the back garden for while, throwing a stick for him to fetch. He brought it back every time, dropped it at my feet and looked up at me, panting, ears cocked, tail wagging like a furious clockwork toy, all excited and expectant.

He was my first proper friend.

I kept throwing the stick and he never got tired of the game. He knew tricks as well. He knew sit and lay down and give me your paw and roll over. It was fantastic, bud. He followed every order. I held the stick up and he leaped up to grab it, snapping and falling, snapping and falling, up and down like a jumping jack.

We played for a while, until the sky began to darken and then I started to feel guilty about his owner. I knew he'd be worried about him. I led him back to the swimming baths, but the lead was gone. I told him to stay and wait but he wasn't having any of it. I turned and walked quick march away, but he just came scampering after me, barking his barmy little head off. Friend for life, bud.

So then I had a bright idea. I decided I'd give him to Ryan. Two birds with one stone. I'd been putting it off, to be truthful. I knew I'd have to go and face him at some point. Explain what I'd done. Beaumont, I mean. I did consider just leaving it, but I reckoned I owed him an explanation at least. I didn't want those grown ups filling his head with lies. Besides, I wanted to say goodbye to the lad. He was a good kid. He deserved something in the way of a proper farewell, I thought, after everything I'd put him through. And I didn't want him to think I'd just abandoned him, just faded away into the background. Wanted him to grow up knowing that I was real.

I went straight through the front door, leaving Denny barking away outside. Ryan was sat at the kitchen table reading his comic. He looked up as soon as I walked into the room.

Hello, he said.

That took me aback a touch. He could see me, bud.

My Mum's upstairs, he said.

I said, it's me, Ryan. Its Al. Al's your pal, remember?

He nods and sort of smiles, but he's looking a little bit pensive as well. A touch fearful.

Don't worry, I say to him, it's OK, mate. It's alright.

I sat opposite him.

I've come to say goodbye, I told him.

Where you going, he asked.

I've got to go away, I said.

He bit his lip and looked down at his comic. Poor little geezer. Must have felt like everyone that ever came into his life ended up doing a swift exit stage left.

Do you know what happened to your Dad? I asked him.

He shrugged and kept his eyes on his comic. Mum said he's not allowed back in the house, he said.

That's right, I told him. Because I made him go away. Listen to me, Ryan, I said.

He didn't look up, but he was listening. I could tell he was listening by the way he tilted his head.

Ryan, I said, I'm sorry I couldn't stop him hurting you. I'm sorry, mate. But I promise you this, buddy – he will never hurt you again. Not ever. Are you listening?

He nodded slowly, yes. I don't know whether he believed me or not, but I felt better for saying it. And at least I knew it was true.

Denny was barking his head off outside. I thought he'd get bored after a while and take off, but he was relentless.

Footsteps thumping down the stairs. Stacey.

That *bloody dog*, she says. She opens the front door and Denny's straight in, squirming between her legs, galloping down the hallway and through to the kitchen. Stacey swears and comes running after him.

Ryan! she yells, Ryan, get up on that chair! Stand on the chair!

He's alright, I tell Ryan, he won't hurt you, buddy. He's a nice dog. He's friendly. I brought him for you.

I stand up and move to the back door and Denny follows me. I squat down and he rolls onto his back and wriggles with delight.

Ryan slips down from his chair and comes over.

Ryan! says his mum, Ryan, don't you go near him!

It's alright mum, he says. He's friendly. We both rub the dog's belly.

He's called Denny, I tell him.

Hello Denny, says Ryan. He's smiling. Good boy, Denny, he says. Good boy.

Stacey's doubtful but she comes over to look. You know this dog, Ryan?

He's my dog, he tells her.

Stacey tells him not to be so silly. She gets down on her haunches and takes hold of Denny's collar, looks at the disc.

How did you know his name?

Al told me, says Ryan. Al brought him for me.

Stacey looks at Ryan, gives him a look like she's exasperated and ready to say something stern, but then her eyes change and she looks so sad. So very sad, bud. Like she's about to start crying.

Oh Ryan, she says. What we gonna do with you, eh?

She pets Denny. He's in his element, writhing on his back and grinning, little white needle teeth bared.

It's not our dog, Ryan, Stacey says. We'll have to ring up the people and get them to come and take him back.

He's mine though, Mum, says Ryan. Al gave him to me.

Ryan, she says, and she starts to say something else, but there's a knock on the door and we all stand up together, me, Ryan, Stacey and the dog.

I can see the silhouettes through the frosted glass. A male and a female. They've took their caps off, but it's obvious who they are. Stacey can see too.

Oh for Christ's sake, she says. What now.

I don't want to witness this. I'm down the hallway in front of her and past the pair of them before she opens the door.

I hope she doesn't blame herself over Beaumont. If it hadn't have been me it would have been somebody else. I certainly didn't feel bad about it.

My conscience is clear, bud, my honour intact. And Ryan is young enough to forget about him. In five years time he'll just be a vague memory. Like me, I suppose. I hope he forgets all about that fucking monster. And me as well.

I hope he forgets all about Alistair Kingdom.

Anyway, I couldn't afford to dwell too long on such matters. I was a man on a mission. Next stop Buckingham Street. Say goodbye.

I'm halfway across the park before I realise Denny has slipped through Stacey's front door and is trotting along below me. I try shooing him away, but he's not having it. I throw sticks and stones for him to chase, hurl them as far as I can in the opposite direction, but he's not playing. Every time I stop he stops, looks up at me with these big baleful brown eyes. What next, he's saying. What happens next? Those eyes. They put a quiet kind of desperation in me, bud. I didn't want to be anyone's leader. I could hardly navigate my own self. After several unsuccessful attempts to sever all ties, I just gave up and carried on. Me and my shadow. I thought it best to ignore him. He seemed content enough to just tag along.

As I exited out onto the road I saw a guy sat on a bench near the bus stop with a can of beer in his hand. I stand and look at him and then I change direction and head the other way.

The light was fading but it was still the afternoon, not yet four o'clock even. If Gemma were working then she wouldn't even be home by now. 37 Buckingham could wait. I needed to make a quick detour. One more score to settle.

I decided to go and find Martin.

He wasn't hard to locate. I found him in the grass enclosure near the playground, stood watching his former drinking pals. The old Henry Booth squad. I was up beside him before he realised I was there. He didn't look surprised to see me.

Martin, I said.

He just looked at me then looked away. No expression in his eyes. No trace of anger.

I'm sorry, Martin, I said.

He didn't say anything. I wondered if he was drunk, still. He spent most of his living days intoxicated, so I presumed he'd be the same as a ghost.

Preserved in alcohol for all eternity. But he didn't seem drunk. Not really. Just kind of sad and hollowed out. Death had sobered him up, it would seem.

I said his name again. He looked at me.

What yer want, Al? he said.

I want to know what happened, I told him.

Yer know what happened, he said. Yer chased me under a fucking train.

No, to me, I said. What happened to me. I can remember bits of it, fragments of shapes and colours, voices and certain smells even, but I can't get beyond that. What happened to me?

He shook his head.

I dunno, he said. We wa' having a session. It wa' cold. I woke up and you din't.

In the house, I said. In that boarded up house.

That deri aye, he said. It wa' early in morning. I tried to wake you up, but you wa' just laid there. I tried everything. I wa' kicking yer. Booting yer in't ribs, but yer wa' out the game. Yer wa' gone, Al.

He looked away again, back at the drinkers who were grumbling up some minor row.

Did you know who I was? I asked him.

How d'yer mean?

Did you know I was in the forces?

He didn't speak. He seemed to be thinking.

I think I remember someone saying summat about it int' 'ostel. When papers come aht.

He looked at me.

You wa' a ero, wannit? Afghanistan?

I wasn't a hero, Martin, I told him.

You wa' summat, though, he said.

We spoke for a while. Or rather, I spoke. I told him about what had happened to me, from waking up in the house and seeing everything for the first time and the garage and the magazines and the photo of Kate Middleton. All the wandering around the streets and the city, the pubs and the nightclubs, spying on people in their houses. I told him about Gemma and the swimming pool and the house full of laughter. About June and flying out to the countryside, the fields of flowers and the airbase. Waking up to the bird song and the rumble of the dustbin carts and the stink of alcohol and getting myself back together, piece by piece. I told him about the fireworks and the car rides and the kids.

I didn't tell him about Beaumont.

I talked and talked until I ran out of things to say. I don't even know if he was listening, really. Even Denny got bored. He went off to play with the drunks. One or two of them were making a fuss of him. He was enjoying himself, rolling around and barking. He kept shooting glances up at me, but when he was satisfied I wasn't going anywhere anytime soon, he carried on capering around the lads on the bench.

I tried to tell Martin that it was going to be alright. How he would find someone who could sense him and see him and accept him for what he was. I told him about Ryan and how he'd listen to me. How he taught me to speak. Eventually Martin started to open up. Little bits at first. About his old life up in Rotherham. How he lost his job at the steelworks and drank his redundancy. About the floods and how he never had any insurance. The stress and the arguments and more drinking. I kept listening, rapt, hung on his every word. He mentioned a house and another place, a holiday somewhere, I think, some place where they had all gone together, him and these other people, his family, I presume and then a long fragmented chain of memories, snapshots of happier times and notable occasions. He said some other things as well, some personal stuff, which I won't repeat to you here. Just stuff about how he came to be who he was and the slow and bewildering decline from family man to solitary drunk, who got moved on from parks and public places and slept in derelict houses with whoever he happened to be sharing a bottle with that day or night. The days and nights blurring together.

He told me about his wife and the two daughters that he hadn't seen since he didn't know when. She'd be about eight years old by now, he reckoned. He was worried about his youngest, he said. I told him to go back up there and find her. I thought of June, her grandchild and how she'd helped me. I told him about how I learnt to speak through Ryan. Don't just drift around, I told him. Gather yourself together, man. That's what I told him.

Then something occurred to me.

Can you see yourself, Martin? I asked him.

How d'yer mean lahk?

Can you see your own body? I mean, could you see your hand if you put it up in front of your face?

He frowned and shook his head, but I didn't take that as a negative. I think the thought of looking at himself had just never occurred to him. Can't say I blamed him, really. He wasn't missing much, to be perfectly honest. He still looked like death warmed up.

I got the impression he still hadn't grasped the fact that he was a ghost. I changed the subject. I told him about my plans, what I was going to do. I didn't tell him about the past. The real past, I mean. About what I'd done.

Denny came over and sat down in front of us, looked up, expectant.

Do you want this dog, Martin? I asked him. I can't take it with me where I'm going. Give him a stroke, Martin. Go on, bud, I said. Give him a tickle round the lugs.

Martin looked down at the dog. What's his name? he said.

Denny. He's no bother, bud.

Dunno if I can be arsed looking after a dog, he said.

Give it a go, I said.

It was getting dark. The streetlights had popped on around the edges of the playground.

So long, Martin, I said. I hope you find some peace, bud.

He didn't answer and he didn't look at me. Just stared into space, all morose. He'd gone off-air again. Resumed radio silence.

I walked away from him. When I got to the gap in the hedge that led back out to the road I turned round for one last look. Martin was stood with his back to me, Denny curled up at his feet.

As soon as I slid through the front window of 37 the sickly sweet stench hit me like a green brick wall – Brettski in the house. Brett and Cookie, to be exact, the pair of them slumped on the settee taking it in turns on The Death Star, Brett's flagship bong. The hubble-bubble toil and trouble top of the range mega mong out machine. This was obviously a serious session if Brett had launched The Death Star. I had a quick scoot round the gaff and there was nobody else present, so I settled myself down in the armchair opposite and joined in with them. Well, when I say joined in, all I did initially was listen with increasingly incredulous amusement at their inane banter. Meandering bullshit inflated with delusions of profundity by regular blasts of hot sticky air.

... yeah man, cos it's like, in Aus, yeah, the Abos have got like a totally different head on 'em when it comes to their turf, yeah? Like when those first white European heads went out there and they were trying to like divide up all the territory, yeah, they said to the wise man, the elder of the village, like, you tell us which bits are holy land yeah, and we'll keep those bits safe for ya squire, yeah? Keep those bits spare and sacred. D'youknowwhatImean? Like, token facking gesture of appeasement, yeah?

... innit though ...

... and the wise man looks at him like that yeah, and he's like, what ya saying bruv? No comprendo, ya get me? And these Euro's were like, just tell us which bits are sacred and the Abo looks at him and says it's all sacred man ... it's all facking sacred innit ....

... damn right ...

Pink Floyd revolving on the turntable; that song, breathe, breathe in the air, pulsing out, the warm buttery crackle of vinyl and the room hanging blue with second hand smoke. Breathe in the air. And that's exactly what I was doing. Brett's monotone voice droning on and on and Cookie's occasional slack-jawed interjection and before I knew what was happening it was like they were both an extra instrument in murmuring harmony with the music. I thought of birds in flight across a clear blue sky. I thought of pale yellow houses. I thought of nodding fields of pink and shimmering sand that swam away into the horizon forever.

I was stoned, bud. My head as heavy as a watermelon. Sunk deep down into that battered old armchair. The springs sagging below me and my feet planted firmly on the carpet. It felt fucking beautiful. So peaceful. Every molecule of myself gently vibrating. I inhaled and exhaled and I felt myself sing from the inside out. Breathe, bud. Breathe in the air. I was breathing. The music filled the room like a living thing and I breathed it in and out.

Inspired.

If Claire hadn't have come through the front door I think I would have fallen asleep in that room full of bass heavy murmurs. Her bag of books dropped to the floor and her feet running up the stairs snapped me wide-awake. Back in the land of the living. It took a massive effort of will to haul myself up out of the depths of that armchair and trek up after her.

By the time I got to her room she'd flipped open the laptop on and fired up a Skype session. Some pal of hers, a strawberry blond Scottish girl smoking in a student bedroom, a Kurt Cobain poster pinned to the wall behind her. I stood near the door and watched. They chatted about nothing in particular; mutual friends, plans for Christmas, an upcoming night out in some restaurant somewhere. I wasn't playing much attention. I was trying to clear my head from the Death Star fumes. I figured I was better hanging out with sweet and sensible Claire than Cheech and Chong downstairs.

Claire told her pal to hold on the now, she needed a tinkle. Two minutes, she said. She jumped up from her desk and vacated the room. I wandered over to the window and had a nosey outside. I was waiting for Gemma to come home. But there was nothing happening out there, just the occasional passing car. I turned away from the window and passed in front of the laptop. I glanced at the screen. The strawberry blond girl was biting her fingernails, staring absently at something off camera. Then her eyes flickered back and met mine.

She dipped her head and peered hard from the screen. Raised her eyebrows, gave half a smile. Lifted a hand and waved.

Hi, she said.

We stood looking at each other in dumb bemusement for a couple of frozen seconds. Then I stepped smartly out of her line of vision. I lifted my hands up in front of my face. Nothing. Just the desk and the bookshelf and the photographs on the wall. No hint of my own self. Not even a shadow.

Claire came back into the room and walked right past me, sat herself back down, started to roll a smoke.

Tell ye what, ahm pure pissed off with ma course the now, ah've goat ...

Who's the guy? asked her friend.

Whit guy?

Yon guy there.

Where?

Dinnae take the piss Claire! That guy that wis in ya room!

Whit the fuck ya on aboot?

There was a guy stood there, right there.

Claire swivelled her chair around, did a swift three sixty scope of her surroundings and swung back to the screen.

Ya fucking tripping or whit, Lisa?

I did a swift exit stage left, bud. Slunk my way back downstairs and waited in the kitchen. I felt sick and nervous, and it wasn't just the ganja smoke. Exposed, bud, that's how I felt. My cover was being blown. Bit by bit, I was being revealed.

After a few minutes Claire came downstairs. I could hear her talking to Brett and Cookie. Swear that crazy bitch is losing the plot, she said. Seeing fucking ghosties, she is.

Seeing ghosties.

I could hear the blood banging in my head.

I stayed in the kitchen until Gemma came home and filled the house with the smell of cooking and the sound of her singing. She sang along to Nina Simone and made a huge pan of spaghetti bolognese for everybody. I watched her busy herself between the oven and the fridge. I stared at her back and willed her to turn around and look. Look at me, look at me. The only person in the world I wanted to see me, and I may as well have been dead to her.

Then fucking lover boy came home, Eric, and they all sat and played music and took turns on the Death Star. I sat in the corner of the room sulking, fragments of conversation floating above my head:

... she's always bin a strange lassie, though, Lisa ... used tae catch her muttering tae herself all the time ... chatting away tae herself like a senile auld biddy ...

... Eric talks in his sleep ...

.. do I bollocks ...

... yes you do ... the other night you told me you'd won the lottery ...

... when? ...

... the other night ... I've got the bonus ball, you were saying ...

... probably just trying to tap a tenner off you ...

... ha ha ha ...

... I don't talk in my sleep ...

... how do you know if you're asleep? ...

... yeah, but all ghosts are, right, is like residue energy ...

... oh here we fucking go ... Derek bleedin' Acorah here ...

... nah, it ain't nothing to do with the so-called supernatural, it's more like ...

... know what gets me about geezers like that, all these Psychic Sues and that ...

... nah, listen ...

... what gets me is how they always get in touch with bleeding Red Indians and Aztec Kings and that ...

... hang on a minute, I did buy a Lottery ticket the other day ...

... why don't they ever have a spirit guide who's, like, a plumber from Crawley, or a bin man from Glasgow? Why they always make contact with exotic fuckers from ancient civilisations ...

... cos supernatural just means like nature that we ain't tapped into yet, the part of nature that our senses ain't developed enough to comprehend ...

... where did I put that ticket? ...

... like *super* and then *natural*, yeah? ...

... I wish she hadnae said that though, put the bloody creeps up me ...

... I've sometimes felt something strange in this house, though ...

... fuck off Cookie, dinnae you start ...

... no, honest, some nights when I've kipped on this couch, I've sorta felt like a weird presence ...

... that's Eric socks ....

... residue energy, that's all it is ...

... oh shut up you soppy tart and get that bong loaded ...

And so on and so forth until Cookie staggered home and the rest of them all gradually peeled off to bed, until there was just me, me myself and I, Alistair Kingdom, slumped halfway down the armchair, half stoned and morose and ignored, like the ghost of Christmas past.

I stayed down there in the darkness until the house had fallen completely silent save for the ticking of the clock on the mantelpiece and the occasional swish of traffic outside. I sat in that armchair and saw all it slot together in front of me. Watched it all play out in my clamouring head like a horror film in slow motion. The shouting and the screaming above the battering of gunfire and the sand stinging my face and the heft of the metal on my shoulder. The cold sheet of sweat on my back and the hot ball of terror in the pit of my stomach. My finger on the trigger and that pale yellow building exploding in a ball of red and orange flame and that black billowing smoke rolling up into the sky and the ash drifting down and falling like dark grey snowflakes.

Blow those cavemen fuckers back into the Stone Age.

I knew what I was going to do, bud. And I knew it was my last night there, in that house, among my adopted family. But I wasn't leaving without saying goodbye to Gemma.

The only light in her room came from the green digital glow of the bedside clock. I could just about make her out in the gloom. I used to have infa-red night vision bud, but the closer I got to becoming a human the harder it was to see in the dark. I stood over her bed, their bed, and waited until my eyes became accustomed.

All I wanted to do was kiss her goodbye, bud. I swear. Whatever else I am, I'm not a pervert. Like I said, I didn't have any base instincts at all. Still don't really. Not in that direction. It was love, bud, pure love. I loved that girl. Loved her with all of what's left of my useless fucking burnt out heart.

She was laid on her side facing Eric. The bulk of her beneath the blankets. I could see the blond stripe of her fringe falling across her face on the pillow. I lowered my head and listened to her steady breathing. I could feel the warmth of her breath as it moved in and out of her. Could smell the sweetness of the soap she used on her neck. I planted my lips upon her cheek, one soft and solitary kiss, and whispered goodbye and told her that I loved her.

Love you, Gemma, I whispered. Never forget you.

She sat bolt upright, gasping, as if she'd had scalding water flung over her. I stood back, panicked. Then Eric woke up.

Gem? Gem!? Whassamatta babe ...

Fucking Gem. Her name's Gemma. Prick. He pulled himself upright and fumbled for the bedside lamp switch, throwing the room into sudden stark light. Gemma had her face in her hands.

Oh my God, she said. Oh my God, oh my God, oh my God ...

I took off, bud. I sailed straight down those stairs and out the front door and I ran as fast as my non-existent legs would carry me.

So, all last night I roamed the freezing cold streets until dawn's first light found me stood in front of Oxfam's window. And there I was, fading in and out of focus. It was the same face on the Facebook page except with longer hair and a five-day growth of beard, but the same deep-set eyes and the same sullen mouth and the same furrowed monkey brow. I got close up to the window and saw my breath mist on the glass.

Inhale, exhale ... inhale, exhale ... inhale ...

I could see myself filling out with every breath. Expanding. Blowing myself up into 3D like a man-sized balloon. I held my breath and faded again, visibly melted away till there was nothing in the window except this weeks dress and second hand paperbacks.

It was happening quickly now. I could hear the blood pounding in my head.

I knew where the prison was. I'd passed it plenty of times on my way to Henry Booth house. I tried going through the wall, but the toes of my boots stopped dead and my hands stayed flat against the brickwork. Access denied. No more tradesman entrance for me, bud. So I hung around outside until I saw a couple of uniforms going in and then I just followed them inside. Nobody questioned me or stopped me or asked me what I was doing. Still invisible, it seemed. My timing was immaculate, for once. Or maybe I've just got one of those auras bud. Got being easily ignored down to a fine art.

Haddock McTavish, that's me.

I followed the uniforms through the gates and doors and corridors until I spotted the line of lads making their way into the library. I just tagged on the end and sat myself down among the bookshelves. I knew it wouldn't be long. I could see my hands forming on the arm of the chair and my shoes planted on the carpet.

I knew I'd arrived when the librarian caught my eye. I knew I was fully revealed then. And then along came the screw with the clipboard, and we had our little dance and the rest I'm sure you've heard about on the jungle drums. I definitely felt my newly found flesh sing when they twisted me up and carried me down here. It was a relief, in a way, to be confined by something as reassuringly solid as a twelve by twelve concrete and steel box.

I felt at home straight away.

So here I am. Alistair Kingdom of The Second Battalion Parachute Regiment, 16th Air Assault Brigade, Her Majesty's Armed Forces, now residing at Her Majesty's Pleasure in her specialist resting home for discarded servicemen. Alistair Kingdom, child killer, reporting for justice, sir. No, hang on, scrap that; not child killer, that sounds too gruesome, makes me sound like a wrong un. How about "killer of children." That's got a ring to it, hasn't it? Noble, almost. Like it's a proper job title. Alistair Kingdom, killer of children by Royal appointment. How many likes would that get on Facebook?

War kills everybody, bud. Everybody involved. It kills those on the end of the bullet or the bomb and those who pull the trigger.

I remember Ryan once asking me - does everyone get a chance of life? I didn't know what he meant. It's up to you how you live your life, I told him. The main thing is not to waste it. Life is precious, bud, I told him. No, Al, he said, I don't mean that, I mean, does everyone get their turn? I don't know what you mean Ryan, I said. And he got his book of Amazing Facts and showed me Amazing Fact Number two hundred and ninety three – the sun is getting closer to the Earth every day and in approximately six billion years time our planet will be consumed by fire and everything will cease to exist. He reads this out to me. I said don't worry mate, we'll both be long gone by then. It won't affect you or me. Six billion years is a very long time. So long you can't even begin to imagine it. I know, he said, but what about the people who are born ten seconds before it happens? Will there be babies who only get ten seconds of life?

I don't think that will happen, I told him.

But how do you know, he said. How do you know for certain, Al?

Think about that, bud. All those unborn babies. In six billion years that big ball of fire in the sky is going to explode and take us and everything we know to kingdom come. And there's a queue of souls all lined up, waiting for their crack of the whip. So start living. Get a move on.

Alright. That's enough. Go on, Mr Listener, go. Get some sleep before it gets light.

Me, I'm staying awake. I can't go to sleep. Starting to recall more and more. It's like snow piling up on a roof, a dead white weight above me. And I can't bear it, bud. I can't bear to remember any more.

No more.

Anyway, it's getting near dawn. Look, the light is leaking through the window. The shadows of the bars on the floor. Go on, bud, get yourself back to your bed and get some sleep. Thanks for listening.

I don't know.

You people.

You don't know you're born.

HER MAJESTY'S PRISON, 7.20 AM.

The officer moves along the landing, flicking open observation panels and unlocking doors, the clack of metal soled boots on concrete and the jangle of keys stirring those that hover on the cusp between fitful sleep and wide awake, and also those that have not yet slept; the occasional call of brusque encouragement to those still dozing beneath thin grey blankets. One by one the doors swing open and men emerge onto the landings; yawning, gaping, stretching, scratching bellies and digging hands down the front of shorts, some of them foamy mouthed with toothbrush scrubbing or waist-wrapped in towels, flips-flops slapping down the stairs towards the hiss of the shower room or leaning over railings to trade various items upwards or down; newspapers, shampoo, shower gel, bits of burn and razors. The sundry essentials of trade that grease the wheels of commerce inside.

The listener remains in his cell, excused from work that day due to his night-long stint on duty. He did not return to the wing until just gone half past five in the morning and is exhausted. He pulls the covers over his head at the noise on the landing outside and wills his shattered mind towards the welcome blackness of sleep.

Meanwhile, in the Separation And Care Unit, Her Majesty's Prison Officer 174 holds his key like a gun at cell 005, flips open the flap and looks inside. He sees the kneeling figure framed in the slim rectangle brick of glass, sees the tightly wound blanket holding the dead weight of the body taut as it sways, leaning forward as if in prayer but for the arms hanging limp, useless, the swollen tongue lolling from the grey-blue face that is bowed.

The officer stands for one impossible howling second before he punches the button and the morning explodes in clamouring bells, a stampede of boots and a riot of raised voices.

ACKNOWLEDGEMENTS

Huge thanks are extended to Shane Rhodes and Wrecking Ball Press, Jon Elek, Georgina Gordon-Smith and Yasmin McDonald at United Agents, Jenn Ashworth and Niall Griffiths for the words, Graham Scott for the image, Bob The Artist for the paintings, Astrid Williamson for the music, Jon Robson for the moving pictures, Simon Bristow for the years, Irene Garret and everyone at English Pen, Jill Penny and everyone at Arvon, the lads and staff of HMP Humber and my Mam and Dad for having me.

And to Ruth, Josie and Sonny for everything else.

Love conquers all.

Russ Litten
Kingston Upon Hull, 2015.
x